A WISH
AFTER MIDNIGHT

A WISH
AFTER MIDNIGHT

ZETTA ELLIOTT

PUBLISHED BY

PRODUCED BY

 MELCHER
MEDIA

Text copyright © 2008, 2010 Zetta Elliott
All rights reserved.
Printed in the United States of America

10 11 12 13 14 15 16 / 10 9 8 7 6 5 4 3 2 1

Published by AmazonEncore
P.O. Box 400818
Las Vegas, NV 89140

Produced by Melcher Media, Inc.
124 West 13th Street
New York, NY 10011
www.melcher.com

Library of Congress Control Number:

2009913664

ISBN-13: 978-0-98255-505-7
ISBN-10: 0-9825550-5-9

This novel was originally published, in a slightly different form, by Booksurge in 2009.

Cover design by Laura Klynstra
Interior design by Jessi Rymill
Front cover photographs: (top) © Andy & Michelle Kerry/Trevillion Images;
(bottom) © Design Pics/Jupiter Images/Getty Images; (left inset) © Hypestock/Shutterstock;
(right inset) courtesy of the Library of Congress.
Back cover illustration courtesy of the Library of Congress.
Author photo: © Zetta Elliott.

for Mellissa

IN MEMORIAM

Preface

This book is a work of fiction. It's important to keep that in mind as you read about Genna, Judah, and their journey back in time. I have always loved history, but I am not a trained historian—I am a writer with a vivid imagination and a mission to move our stories from the margins to the center. This novel is an example of "speculative fiction," so it has elements of both fantasy *and* reality; I looked at the present and the past, and then I imagined a different set of possibilities. There is evidence that the New York City Draft Riots of 1863 spilled over into Brooklyn. The racial tensions that rocked Manhattan that summer were also building in the city of Brooklyn—in August of 1862, an Irish mob numbering in the thousands trapped twenty black men, women, and children in the tobacco factory where they worked and attempted to set the place on fire. No lives were lost then, but the white immigrants made it clear that they would not tolerate blacks competing for jobs in Brooklyn. During the draft riots of 1863, African Americans were targeted and brutally murdered by raging mobs, but there were also many white victims and other courageous whites who helped blacks to escape. History is complicated, and I wanted my novel to reflect that complexity. My hope is that readers will become intrigued by the past and start to investigate and speculate even more.

History is written by people who interpret the past, and those interpretations often vary. The most important fact is that *everyone* has a story to tell, so if your story hasn't yet made it into a book, it might be time to start writing …

I would like to thank the Crown Street girls who participated in our book and garden club back in 2001. Their intelligence, resilience, and creativity inspired me to write this novel; I hope at least some of those pennies we tossed in the fountain have become wishes fulfilled.

I am grateful to the educators at the Brooklyn Historical Society and the New-York Historical Society for generously sharing their resources on black life in the antebellum period with my middle-grade students and me ten years ago. I would also like to thank the staff of the Weeksville Heritage Center for keeping this vital Brooklyn community alive and relevant. I am indebted to the many librarians at the Central Branch of the Brooklyn Public Library—one of my favorite destinations and an incredible resource for anyone who wants to learn about the past, present, or future. Lastly, I thank the small army of workers who protect and maintain the Brooklyn Botanic Garden—for years it has been my sanctuary, and its quiet beauty has nourished my imagination, producing this novel (and countless haiku!). I urge everyone to take the time to rediscover Brooklyn—claim its rich history, visit its dynamic cultural institutions, and honor those who sacrificed so much to put down roots in this place.

Zetta Elliott
August 26, 2008
Brooklyn, NY

PART I

1.

I turn my back, close my eyes, and toss the penny over my shoulder. I hear it slap against the water, but I turn around just the same and watch it sink to the bottom of the fountain. It lies there with all the other glittering coins. Money unspent. Wishes waiting to come true.

Slowly, I walk away from the fountain and wonder if any of my wishes will ever come true. I wish for lots of different things. Sometimes I make wishes for other people, like my mother. I wish she didn't have to work so hard, and I wish she didn't always have that knot between her eyes from worrying about how she's going to pay the rent and buy food and clothes for all of us. I wish my *abuela* still lived with us, but she went home five years ago. Abuela said *living* in America was hard enough; she wanted to go home to die. Sometimes I wish my sister Toshi didn't act so evil all the time. And I wish my brother Rico would stop trying to mess with me. But mostly I make wishes for myself. I wish my hair was long and wavy like those caramel-colored girls in music videos. I wish I had nice clothes to wear instead of knockoffs or bargains from the ten-dollar store. I wish I wasn't so tall. Being tall's okay if you look like a model. But I don't. I'm just plain, and dark, and too tall, and too smart, and too shy to talk to anybody. Except I'm not shy, really. I just don't fit in.

I always have pennies in my pocket whenever I come to the garden, and I come here a lot. It's real quiet, and pretty. No one notices me, not even the security guards. Because I'm so tall, they think I'm old enough to be in here alone. They don't know that I'm only fifteen. They don't know anything about me—where I live, or what my family's like. I feel free when I walk through the garden gates, like I'm somebody new. I wish I could always feel that way. I wish I could go somewhere different, another country, someplace far away. A place where I don't have to feel ashamed of my home, and my clothes, and my short nappy hair that just won't grow. I toss a penny into the fountain and wish I could live inside someone else's body, even for just one day. But that wish—like all the others—hasn't come true yet.

2.

I miss my grandmother, but sometimes I'm glad she left. I know Abuela would have been real upset if she saw us living this way. There's five of us altogether: Mama, me, Toshi, Rico, and my baby brother Tyjuan. We used to live in a two-bedroom apartment, but Mama couldn't make rent, so the landlord put us down here on the first floor. He tried to act like he was doing us a favor, but we're doing *him* a favor by living in this dump. Nobody likes living on the first floor. If you're up front, then you have to listen to the sound of cars honking and people talking and shooting and blaring their stereos all night and day. But it's worse if you're out back. People in the apartments upstairs throw garbage out the window instead of bagging it and putting it in the trash cans around the side of the building. Mama says people are ignorant and ought to go back to the bush if they don't know how to live in the city. The back alley fills up with cats and rats and all kinds of nastiness because the super won't clean up the mess. He says there's no point 'cause people will just throw stuff down again. We keep our blinds closed so we don't have to look at that mess. In the summertime it's even worse, because the junk starts to smell real bad.

With the windows shut and the blinds always closed, it's dark in our apartment. Not that there's much to see. We got five people living in two rooms. One tiny bathroom, and a kitchen that's so small we can't even eat in there together. I think we all hate living here, all of us except Tyjuan. I think Tyjuan could be happy anywhere so long as he's got me or Mama around. When it's my turn to sleep in Mama's bed, Tyjuan crawls into the space between us. He holds his bottle with one hand and puts the other hand on my face. Tyjuan's little fingers touch my short, curly eyelashes and my short, hard hair. He tugs at my ears and presses my nose like it's some kind of button. He giggles and gurgles while he's doing all this, and I just lie there, smiling at him. Happy I got at least one person in this world who thinks I'm beautiful. Worth touching. Worth smiling at.

After Tyjuan falls asleep, I stroke his soft baby hair and wish I could take him somewhere far away from here. I wish he didn't have to grow up like I did, here in this building where drug dealers stand out front all day, and the super doesn't fix anything like he's supposed to, and the porter won't clean stuff up but leaves vomit and empty bottles and chicken bones on the stairs. I wish Tyjuan could grow up in a house, on a block where there are big trees on both sides of the street and flower boxes in all the windows. A block where people pick up after their dogs instead of leaving piles of dog shit all over the place. A block where people go to sleep at night instead of blasting music from the open windows of their apartments or cars. A block where people get up in the morning and go to work, and they do stuff that's legal, and they go to church on Sunday, and have block parties in the summer where nobody gets shot.

I think all this while Tyjuan sleeps in between Mama and me. Toshi and I take turns sleeping in Mama's bed. Rico says he prefers sleeping on the couch, and Mama says that's better because Rico's a boy, and he kicks too much anyway. When I'm not sleeping in Mama's bed, I have to sleep on the floor. We got an old cot mattress that smells funky and feels all lumpy. I hate sleeping on that mattress because it's too short for my body, so I have to curl up in a ball. Rico's supposed to switch with me, but he never lets me sleep on the couch. So every other night I curl up on the floor and pull a blanket over me to keep the roaches out.

Abuela would cry if she knew we were living this way. So even though I miss her, I'm glad she went back to Panama. Sometimes I wonder if she ever found my father there. We think that's where he went. Mama says Papi couldn't handle the way black folks are treated here in the States. He wanted all of us to move back there with him, but Mama said no. Mama's not from Panama. She's American. She said she didn't want us growing up in a Third World country where people go hungry and die of diseases, where folks live without clean water and electricity. I don't blame her for feeling that way, but sometimes I wish she had said yes. I think about the way we're living here, and I think the First World isn't all that great.

Mama tries to do what's best for us, but it's hard 'cause she's all alone. When Abuela lived with us, she used to do all the cooking and the laundry. My grandmother always made sure the house was neat and tidy by the time Mama got home from work. She kept us neat and tidy, too—Abuela didn't speak much English, but she still didn't take no lip. If any of us kids ever got out of line, Abuela was real quick to beat our behinds.

But I still loved my grandmother. Once Papi left, it got harder and harder to remember what he was like. But Abuela would often talk about my father—what he was like as a boy growing up in Panama. Sometimes Abuela would slip into Spanish, and I couldn't always understand everything she said. I speak a little Spanish, but not much. Just what I learned at school. Mama always told us we were black, not Hispanic. She says in America, it doesn't matter where you're from or what language you speak. Black is black, and you might as well get used to it. And if you *are* black, then you better speak English, 'cause that's what white folks speak.

I think that was one of the things Mama and Papi used to fight about. They were happy for a long time, but then Papi lost his job and Mama had to work double shifts at the hospital to make ends meet. Toshi, Rico, and me were just kids back then. But I can still remember a lot of what went down. Each morning Papi would go out looking for a job, and each night he'd come home looking more and more frustrated. He'd talk about all the things he hated about America, and he'd get angrier and angrier, and his voice would get louder and louder. Mama would tell my father that he was just one man, and one man can't change an entire country. And Papi would say, in America, a black man can't even *be* a man.

Papi didn't like it that Mama worked so much. But if Mama hadn't worked so hard, we wouldn't have been able to eat or pay rent. Mama would get real quiet when she tried to explain this to Papi. She didn't want him to feel bad about losing his job. She'd tell Papi the same thing she's been telling us kids all our lives: "Don't worry, baby, trouble don't last always." But Papi would get mad anyway. Sometimes he'd throw things against the wall. One time he even hit Mama.

That was more than ten years ago, but I can still remember the sound of my father's palm slapping my mother's face. Abuela had taken us kids into the other room, but we could still hear what was going on. Things got real quiet after that. Abuela told us to stay in the bedroom while she went to check on our folks. But we followed her into the living room anyway. Mama was standing in the corner, facing the wall. She was holding her cheek with one hand. Papi was sitting on the sofa. Both his hands were covering his face, and his shoulders were going up and down. I had never seen a grown-up cry before. Abuela went over to Mama first to make sure she was okay. She led Mama into the kitchen and got her a cold wet cloth for her face. Then Abuela went over to the sofa and sat down next to Papi. She put her arm around him and spoke to him softly in Spanish. Eventually Papi stopped crying. He took his hands away from his face and looked at us. We were huddled against the living room wall 'cause we didn't know what else to do. Papi wiped his eyes, looked at us, and tried real hard to smile. I had never seen my father look so miserable. I wanted to smile back, but instead I started to cry. Papi got up from the sofa and slowly walked over to the front door. Abuela called to him in Spanish, but he didn't turn around. My father opened the door, closed it behind him, and he never came back again.

Tyjuan's daddy is different than mine. But I don't care. I love my little brother more than anything in this world. When we're in Mama's bed, I pull him close to me and feel his warm baby breath on my neck. Before I go to sleep, I say a prayer and kiss him goodnight. I don't know what I'd do without Tyjuan. He's the other half of my heart.

3.

Toshi's two and a half years older than me. Even though we have the same daddy, Toshi and I are like night and day. I'm tall and thin and dark. But Toshi's the exact opposite. She's short and curvy, with long brown hair and skin the color of butterscotch pudding. Abuela used to say Papi's Indian blood came out in Toshi. Abuela was fair, too, but that's 'cause her daddy was a white man. My grandmother told me that in Panama, almost everybody has mixed blood. It used to be only Indians living in Panama. Then white people came over from Spain, and then black people from Africa and the Caribbean. I guess Papi's African blood came out in me.

Toshi and I don't just look different; we act different, too. I'm really good at school and almost always get straight As. Toshi says she's going to drop out and work full-time at this clothing store downtown. She already works there evenings and weekends. I want to go to college and become a psychiatrist. Toshi says college is a waste of time and that only a nutcase would pay money to sit and talk to someone as ugly as me. Toshi can be real evil sometimes.

It wasn't like that when we were little. We used to get along. But once Papi left, everything started to change. Mama says not to worry, Toshi's just jealous 'cause school is easy for me. Mama thinks Toshi might be dyslexic, but I'm not so sure. Seems like the only thing Toshi's got mixed up are her priorities. Clothes and shoes and boys are pretty much all she cares about. Toshi only goes to school to show off her latest outfit. Every weekend she gets her hair and nails done, then she puts on one of her way-too-tight outfits and heads out to the clubs. Mama tells Toshi to stay home, but no one's around to *make* Toshi stay home. Just like no one's around during the day to make sure Toshi's butt goes to school.

Toshi acts like she doesn't ever want to leave this building. She says, "If it's good enough for my friends, it's good enough for me." I want something better, and I know Mama does, too. That's why she works so hard at the hospital. Mama's a nurse's aide.

Sometimes when I come home from school, Toshi's just sitting there in front of the television. She doesn't even say hey, she just keeps on watching those dumb talk shows or music videos. Sometimes a song will come on that Toshi likes, and suddenly she'll jump up and start dancing all over the place. My sister may not be that smart, but Toshi sure thinks she's *all that*. Most of the boys on the block think so, too. Toshi's got big breasts, a big butt, and those thick legs that make men turn and watch her as she walks down the street. When Toshi dances, there's a whole lotta shakin' goin' on. She sticks her butt out, puts her hands on her knees, and grinds her hips like she's one of those video 'hos dancing on the beach wearing nothing but sunglasses and a thong.

Toshi thinks I'm jealous of her. And maybe, in some ways, I am. I'm not as pretty or as popular as she is. But I know I'm going to do something with my life. I'm going to finish high school, go to college, and help people deal with their problems. I don't need a big butt or light skin to be a psychiatrist. All I need is a chance.

4.

Most days when I get out of school, I go straight to the library. If I have any money on me, I might stop for a slice or a patty with coco bread. But usually I just go straight to the library and sit in my favorite spot. I like the library. Partly because it's air-conditioned, and the wide windows let in lots of light. It's usually stuffy and dark in our place with all the windows shut. Plus somebody's always there making all kinds of noise, and there's no place for me to spread out my books.

At the library, everybody's quiet. I sit at a big black desk near all the reference books. I sit there because it's quiet enough for me to focus on my homework, and I have to concentrate if I'm going to get good grades. And I have to get good grades because that's the only way I'm going to get a scholarship. And I have to get a scholarship because that's the only way I'll be able to go to a really good school. My guidance counselor, Mrs. Freeman, says if I do well on the SAT, I might even get into an Ivy League school. I can't exactly remember what Ivy League means, but I know those are the top schools in the country. Mrs. Freeman says a degree from an Ivy League school will take you far. I just want it to take me far away from here.

There's another reason I like going to the library. His name's Judah. He works at the checkout counter. Judah and I go to the same high school. He sits behind me in my English class, but Judah never notices me. He's a bit older than the rest of us, but not because he got left back. Judah moved here from Jamaica, and they put him in the tenth grade. He doesn't talk much in class, but I listen closely whenever he does. Judah's words have a rhythm—not quite like music, but something real close. When he talks in class, Judah always sounds real serious. Maybe it's because he's older than us, but I think it's deeper than that. He's got something going on inside.

I only ever talked to Judah once. I was standing in line at the library, waiting to check out some books. There were three people working behind the counter. Judah was at the far end. One by one the people in front of me got called up to the counter. I was kind of hoping Judah would help me when it was my turn, but I didn't really figure it would happen 'cause stuff like that never does happen to me. I was looking in my wallet, trying to find my library card, when I heard Judah's voice calling me. "Next, please step down."

I was so nervous I couldn't even look up. I just dumped my books on the counter and started tugging at my library card. It was stuck inside my wallet, and my hands were shaking so badly I couldn't get it out. I glanced up at Judah, but he wasn't looking at me. He was opening all the books and scanning them with his laser. Finally I got the card out and slid it across the counter.

Judah picked it up, scanned it, and then handed it back to me. "Genna, right?"

I wanted to smile real cool like and say, "Hey, Judah, what's up?" But I was too nervous. I couldn't believe he knew my name. So I just nodded and tucked my card back inside my wallet.

Judah stamped the cards, then slid them one by one into the pocket of each book. I could tell he was watching me, but I kept my eyes on the counter. I wondered why he was taking so long. The other clerks had called new people up to the desk. I didn't have that many books. Just one book for my social studies class, and a few picture books for Tyjuan. When he was done with the cards,

Judah closed my books, demagnetized them, and handed them back to me.

"You're kind of old for these, aren't you?"

I looked down at the picture books. "They're for my little brother." I tried to smile as I said this, but my mouth felt like it was crooked.

Judah nodded and kept on looking at me. I tried to think of something else to say. He spoke before I could.

"Is Toshi Colon really your sister?"

I pressed my lips together and tried to keep all my good feeling from draining away. Judah was only talking to me so he could get to Toshi. I should have known. It happened all the time. With most guys, I didn't really care, but this time it hurt. I wanted Judah to be interested in *me*. I just nodded and put my books in my bag.

"You like reggae music, Genna?"

This time I looked at Judah, hard. What did he want from me? Was he trying to play some kind of game? I shrugged and put my bag back on my shoulder. "It's alright, I guess. I haven't heard all that much, so I couldn't really say."

Judah glanced at the long line of people waiting to check out books. "Maybe I'll play some for you sometime."

I looked in his face and tried to find the truth. Judah is about the same color as me, maybe a little bit darker. He has dreadlocks that hang down past his shoulders—not the little ones that look all neat, but thick chunky ones that look like he just stopped combing his hair one day. There was a very small smile on Judah's lips. His dark eyes were serious.

The longer I looked at Judah, the more I wanted him to like me.

"See you later, Genna," he said, and then called the next person in line. I tugged at the strap of my book bag and walked away.

5.

I walk through the garden on my way home from the library. Things are always changing in there—it's like magic, almost. Every time I visit the garden, I see something new. And every time I go to the garden, I find something old. The garden's got a lot of history, and I like that because I'm into old things. Not just any old things—not my crappy building, for instance, or the old hand-me-down clothes I sometimes have to wear. I like *really* old things, things that were made thirty, fifty, or a hundred years ago. In the garden, all the old things still look new because people take care of them. Nobody sprays graffiti all over the place, and you almost never see trash lying on the ground. The garden's always clean and tidy 'cause they got people who pull up weeds and rake the leaves and cut the branches off trees when they start growing out of control. It's hard to believe those gigantic trees were once skinny and only as tall as me. Now they're so wide I can't get my arms around them. There are trees in the garden that are older than me, Mama, and Abuela put together. The weeping hemlock is one hundred and twelve years old, and the Armistice maples were planted in 1918 after World War I. If those trees could speak, I wonder what they would say. Sometimes I sit still and listen as the wind whispers through their leaves.

Everything in the garden has a place, and I like that, too. Somebody really put a lot of thought into it. Each plant has a name, and a special place to grow, and somebody to look after it full-time, all year round. Mrs. Charles tried growing roses out front our building, but those ignorant Negroes threw trash on them, ripped off the leaves, and let their dogs pee all over them. That poor rose-bush couldn't even stand up. Mrs. Charles had to tie it to the fence, and even then it still fell down. Whenever a rose finally did bloom, somebody would snatch it off or mess with it so bad all the petals fell off. Mrs. Charles finally gave up. The tenants' association broke up, and nobody else bothered trying to make our building look good. What's the point? You can't do nothing when the folks around you just don't care.

Mama says people who have nothing of their own don't know how to take care of other people's things. Maybe that's so. I think people are just selfish. They got no problem making a mess of the train or the schoolyard or this building, but they wouldn't scribble on the walls or throw trash all over their own apartment. Mama says, don't be so sure.

I think sometimes people want to own something so bad that they just can't help themselves. I know kids at school who carry markers with them wherever they go just so they can leave their tag someplace. To show that they've been there, or maybe to pre-tend that that space is theirs. If you don't got anything of your own, you might as well pretend other folks' stuff is yours. 'Course, that just messes up everything for everybody else. You can't hardly see out the train window, Negroes got it scratched up so bad. And sometimes they don't leave just their tag, they write dirty words all over the building, and then little kids got to grow up looking at that mess every day. You're waiting for the elevator and there's curse words scratched onto the door. Then you go inside the elevator (when it's working) and the doors close, and more curse words are scratched in there. Folks use a lighter to burn their initials onto the ceiling. They use whiteout if they don't have a pen. And I just think, *damn*. You only in that elevator about half a minute, but you got time to do all that? I don't get it. I think people need to find better things to do. Like learn to spell, 'cause half the time they don't even spell the curse words right.

Last week I was in the garden and I noticed a group of kids hanging out. I guess they were older than me, old enough to get past security. They were laughing and fooling around and being loud. And eating, too, which isn't allowed. I steered clear of them, 'cause I knew they were going to get tossed. Sure enough, before too long, security rolls up in their little golf cart and tells the kids they got to go. I don't know if they're allowed to do that, throw you out just 'cause you brought in food. Other times they just make folks throw the food out, then they're allowed to stay. But that's not really why those kids got tossed. They got kicked out 'cause they were acting *too black*—too *ghetto*, and the security guards probably got orders to keep the ghetto *outside* the garden gates.

After they were gone, I passed by the bench they'd been sitting on. Someone had used a black marker to leave their tag on the wood. That made me kind of mad at first, but then I looked closer and I saw it wasn't a tag at all, it was two people's names inside a heart. Tony loves Keisha, or something like that. And I thought, great. Now people got to look at this every time they walk past this bench. And then I thought about it for a minute, and I realized that that was the point. Tony may not always love Keisha, but in a way they own this bench now. They claimed it by leaving their mark, and maybe the rain will wash it out over time, but it's still gonna last a while. Then I felt kind of sad inside, 'cause even though I hate graffiti, I'd like to have somebody do that for me.

In the garden there are little blue plaques everywhere telling you who donated money to pay for certain benches or bridges or statues. There are only a few statues in the garden. One's a white girl wearing a long flowing dress. She's holding a sundial and a bunch of roses in her arms. I like that one. Another one's a young girl (she's white, too), buck naked, riding a giant fish that shoots water out of its mouth. That one seems kind of weird to me, but I guess if you got all the dough, then you can make things look any way you want. All the statues I've ever seen are of white folks, although there is one brother in the group of soldiers on that big arch at Grand Army Plaza. And I heard once that the Statue of Liberty was supposed to be a black lady, but the Americans didn't want her that way, so the folks in France made her white. But I don't know for sure if that's true. It could just be one of those urban legends.

Since I'm not in any hurry to get home, I just walk along the pathways, listening to the birds. Lots of rare birds live in the Botanic Garden. I know because I followed a tour one time. I wasn't sure if you were supposed to pay or not, so I just trailed along at the end, listening to everything the guide had to say. He said the garden was like a sanctuary for all kinds of birds that couldn't live anywhere else. It's hard for birds to find a safe home in the city. "The urban environment isn't hospitable for most species." That's what the guide said. I think he's right, and not just about the birds.

When I'm inside the garden, sometimes I imagine that I'm a bird. A rare, beautiful bird from somewhere far away. I imagine that I have flown hundreds and hundreds of miles just to get here, and the garden is my sanctuary. I pretend that I am only staying here for a little while, gathering strength for the long journey home.

That might sound kind of corny, but I really do like birds. There are all kinds of them in the garden. I catch them looking at me, sideways, 'cause that's how birds see. They turn their heads and watch me for a minute, and then they fly away or hop across the grass like one of those wind-up toys. Sometimes when I'm on my way home I see my friend, Mr. Christiansen. Whenever I'm with Mr. Christiansen, he'll hear a bird singing and he'll get real still and listen. Then he'll turn his head and look at me—out of one eye, just like a bird—and he'll say "robin" or "cardinal" or "warbler." Mr. Christiansen knows all their names. Sometimes I see people with binoculars looking up at the trees. It's real hard to see the birds when they're way up high. But you can still hear them, loud and clear. If I were a bird, I'd have a beautiful song, and whenever I sang, people would stop what they were doing and listen to me. I asked Mr. Christiansen which bird had the most beautiful song. He said the mockingbird. That's the kind of bird I want to be.

6.

Last night there was a fight outside my building. Mama knew all about it because it happened just as she was coming home from work. We live at the back of the building, so we don't always hear what's going on out front. And that's usually a good thing, 'cause a whole lot of stuff goes down in our building that I'd rather not know about. But last night, Mama came in laughing so hard she had tears running down her face. She sat at the kitchen table and told me about it while I heated up her supper. I'd already put Tyjuan to bed, and Toshi was still at work. I didn't know where Rico was, and I really didn't care. It was nice having Mama all to myself.

Mama wiped the tears out of her eyes and pulled her chair up as I set down her plate. "Thank you, baby," she said and closed her eyes to say a quick prayer. Then she put one forkful in her mouth and chewed while chuckling to herself. "Genna, honey, the Negroes in this building are something else." Mama calls black folks "Negroes" when she doesn't approve of the way they act. She won't use the word "nigger," and won't let any of us say it, either.

Mama shook her head for a moment, then went on. "I knew something was up as soon as I turned the corner. There were a whole lot of folks out front—more than usual, and more than just the usual suspects. A lot of those folks I'd never seen before. They were lined up all along the front of the building like they were waiting for somebody—I'm glad that somebody wasn't me!"

When Mama stopped laughing, I asked her if she was ready for her tea. "I don't feel for anything hot just now, baby. A glass of water will do me fine."

I got up to get a drink for Mama, and she went on telling her story.

"Now, I'm the last person to put my nose in somebody else's business—" Mama paused and winked at me. "But Mrs. Charles happened to be sitting out front, and she sort of filled me in. Apparently, Shiree up on the fifth floor has been going around talking about Mrs. Johnson's granddaughter. You know the one—not much older than Toshi, just had a sweet little baby girl not too long ago. So Peeter's got this baby, and she's got this big old stroller, too. Now, the stroller was sitting in the hallway—there's at least eight of them living in that studio, so I don't know where else the stroller could have been. Anyway, Shiree went by and kicked the stroller, and something or other fell off."

"The baby?"

"No, not the baby. Peeter had the baby with her inside. But you know they keep their door open a crack, and she saw Shiree kicking the stroller. So Peeter goes out and the two of them have words, and next thing you know there's a posse waiting outside to beat the stuffing out of Shiree. And that's just what they did, too. I only stood there and watched because I couldn't get into the building 'til the cops came and shut them all down. If it was me, I'd have called the fire department—let them turn the hoses on these backward Negroes. Swinging and punching and clawing and biting like a bunch of animals."

I looked at Mama. She was shaking her head like she was disgusted, but her mouth kept sliding into a smile. "Poor Shiree tried to run away, and one of them grabbed her by the back of the head and tore out half her hair—and that was her own hair, not some tacky old weave!"

I laughed along with Mama even though inside I felt kind of bad for Shiree. But she should have known better than to mess with Peeter. Nobody messes with the Johnson family. They've been living in this building for more than twenty years. Some folks say even Mona had to get their permission before she started running her business out of here. And some of the Johnsons work for her— protection, stuff like that. Mama doesn't like us to hang around out front, but I see them all as I'm coming and going. The super hangs signs all over the place telling folks not to loiter. But they stand out there every day and night, and he doesn't do a damn thing about it. Shoot, Mona and them even got chairs they stash somewhere, and by three or four o'clock in the afternoon, they're out there sitting on the front step, waiting for their regulars to stop by. Peeter seems alright, and her little girl really is sweet. But I leave them Johnsons alone. Rico, he's tight with one of Peeter's brothers, and I think both of them might be working for Mona. I've never told Mama this. She's got enough to worry about already.

Once Mama's done eating, I take her plate and start to wash up. Mama pushes her chair back from the table and goes to check on Tyjuan. During the day, Tyjuan stays with our neighbor, Mrs. Dominguez. Mama drops him off there on her way to work each morning, and I pick him up as soon as I get in from school. I wish it didn't have to be that way. Mrs. Dominguez is a real nice lady, but she takes care of a whole lot of kids. She doesn't have time to sit and read to Tyjuan. Basically she just gives him his bottle and makes sure his diaper's dry. Tyjuan loves playing with the other kids, but sometimes he learns words from them that no kid his age should know. I'm trying to teach Tyjuan his ABCs and 123s, but I don't get to see him all that much. I bring Tyjuan home, feed him, and give him his bath. Sometimes I read him a bedtime story before he falls asleep. Mama only gets to see Tyjuan when he wakes up in the morning and on her day off. He cries every time Mama knocks on the door and hands him to Mrs. Dominguez. That makes sense because Tyjuan's just a baby. But sometimes I think Mama wants to cry, too. And that's not right, 'cause Mama's grown.

When Mama comes back into the kitchen, she's wearing her nightgown and robe. I wish I had enough money to buy Mama a new robe. The one she has is so old it's got holes around the collar and the fabric's worn thin at the elbows and on the behind. Mama wouldn't let me get a part-time job after school. She says I have to focus on my schoolwork. There'll be plenty of time later for me to hold down a job. Mama says she always hoped all her kids would graduate from high school, but right now it looks like I'm her best bet.

"I sure do appreciate the way you help out around here, Genna." Mama gently squeezes my shoulder as she puts the kettle on to boil. "I don't know how I'd manage without you."

I turn around and smile at Mama. She smiles back before sinking into a chair. Mama holds her head up with both her hands. I can see how tired she is, and I know that she's already got a lot of things on her mind. I don't want Mama to start worrying about me, too. But then I see her elbows pushing through the thin fabric of her robe. I dry my hands and sit down at the table.

Just as I'm about to speak, Mama opens her mouth. "I was thinking about your daddy today. A song came on the radio at work, and I remembered the time he taught me how to dance all those tricky Spanish steps." Mama's talking to me, but she's looking at the kitchen table. I want to ask Mama about getting a job, but I think right now she just wants me to listen. So I wait for her to finish and silently mash a baby roach that is crawling up the wall.

"I'm real sorry your daddy left us, Genna. And Lord knows I'm sorry we've had to stay in this place so long. I always hoped I'd be able to move us out of here before you reached high school." Mama sighs and rubs her eyes. "I guess I'm running a bit behind schedule, huh?"

I reach across the table and put my hand on Mama's arm. "Don't worry about it, Mama. We'll get out of here someday. I was thinking maybe this summer I could get a job, and we could put half of my paycheck in your savings account. Then when we have enough for first and last month's rent, we'll tell Mr. Kurzner we don't want to live here anymore, and he can rent this dump out to someone else. Maybe we could get a floor in a brownstone, one of those houses over on Carroll Street." The more I talk about it, the more excited I start to get.

Mama sits and listens to me, a small smile tugging at her lips. Then she shakes her head, and her eyes look like they're happy but a little bit sad, too.

"You're such a dreamer, Genna. Just like your daddy used to be."

I want to tell Mama more about the brownstones on Carroll Street, but I think maybe now's not the best time. I saw a sign in one of the windows last week, a red "For Rent" sign tucked into the corner of a tall first-floor window. I want Mama to come with me next time, but Mama's tired right now. I decide to go back on my own tomorrow and write down the phone number and the address. Maybe there'll be a backyard that Tyjuan can play in and a garden where Mama can plant her herbs instead of leaving them on the windowsill where they hardly get any light. Toshi and Rico might not want to move, but I don't really care. *I* want to get out of here, and that's more than just a wish. It's going to take more than a few pennies to find us a new home. It's going to take a lot of hard work and a real good plan. I may only be fifteen years old, but I know I can make this happen. Like Mama always says—I'm her best bet.

7.

I guess I should say something about my other brother, Rico. I would call him my big brother, except he isn't even bigger than me. Mama always told us to keep our mouths shut if we didn't have anything good to say about somebody. But if I did that about Rico, I'd have to stop right now. Rico and me, we've never really gotten along. Toshi might act evil now, but we were tight when we were kids. I don't know what happened to Toshi, but Rico's been a pain in the butt ever since I can remember. Maybe it's 'cause he's the middle child, or maybe it's 'cause he's a boy. He's Mama's favorite, I know that much. And maybe I'm a little jealous of Rico because of that. He doesn't do anything around the house to help out. He's selfish and loud and rude to me all the time. He acts nice in front of Mama, but that's only when he needs money. But Rico doesn't do that anymore. Like I said, I think he's working for Mona, and that really is bad news. Rico thinks he's real tough, but he's no match for Mona and the other dealers on the block. If he doesn't watch out—watch *his own* back instead of his boys'—he's gonna land himself in juvie. Again.

It's hard to understand sometimes how Rico can be Mama's favorite. He's always getting into trouble—with the police, the neighbors, his teachers. He's been suspended from school at least a half dozen times, and he's in most of my classes, too, because his dumb behind got left back. But Rico doesn't care. He just uses it as an opportunity to make life miserable for me. Him and his homeboys, Eddie and Lydell.

When they're not hanging out in front of the building, Rico and his boys hang out on the stairs. We live down on the first floor, but Eddie lives with his grandmother up on fourth. Sometimes when I'm going up to get Tyjuan, I pass them all sprawled out on the steps. I take the elevator sometimes just so I can avoid them, but the elevator hardly ever works. Plus, one time I got stuck in there with this creepy old man, and he tried to get fresh with me. He asked me if I wanted some money, and before I could even say no, he had his hands all over my body. I may be kind of skinny, but I still got *something* to grab. That was one time I was actually thankful for being so tall. I lifted my knee and rammed it into that nasty man's crotch, just like Mama told me to. I think I might have heard something snap, but I didn't stick around to find out. I busted out of that elevator as fast as I could, and I haven't been back in it since. Which isn't surprising, really, 'cause like I said, that elevator hardly ever works.

Last week I was going upstairs to pick up Tyjuan, and I found Rico and his boys hanging out on the stairs. They were passing a brown-bagged bottle between them, and I could tell they'd been smoking, too. There were shreds of tobacco all over the steps, which means they ripped apart a cigar and rolled it back up with weed inside. Rico's eyes were ugly and red. Smoking weed makes some people mellow, but it just makes Rico mean.

I stood on the landing and waited for them to move out of the way.

Lydell nudged Eddie and smirked at me. "Where you going, Genna?"

"Mind your business, Lydell, and get out the way." I put one hand on the railing and one foot on the stairs.

Eddie and Lydell cracked up like I'd just said something funny.

Rico took a swig from the bottle and glared at me. I decided I was just going to have to crawl over them. There's another stairway at the front of the building, but Mrs. Dominguez lives at the back. These stairs are closer, and I didn't think I should have to go out of my way just 'cause these dumb Negroes got nothing better to do.

I was halfway up the stairs when Lydell grabbed my hand. "Why you so bitter, Genna? Huh? Why can't you be *sweet*?"

I snatched my hand away like I didn't want to catch whatever Lydell's got. Eddie laughed and slit his eyes at me. "She's dark like chocolate, but she sure ain't sweet."

Rico snorted and pulled the bottle away from his mouth. "Chocolate, my ass. Genna's black like licorice. Mama's little tar baby."

Lydell held his hand up to check their laughter. "Now wait a minute, y'all. Licorice is black, but it still tastes sweet. But Genna— she walks around with her face all screwed up like somebody stuck a lemon down her throat. Tell you what, Genna. I'll give you something real good to put in your mouth. How 'bout it, Genna? You want me to give you something sweet? I'll bet you ain't never tasted nothing like what I got."

Lydell's hand was on his crotch, and he was looking at me like he thought he was real slick. I looked at Rico to see if he had anything to say. He doesn't care if they talk to me like that. He'd probably sell me to those fools for twenty dollars, maybe even less. A girl at my school got raped that way. She had a pass to go use the bathroom, but two boys dragged her into the stairwell and attacked her. Then when they finished, they threw a couple dollars at her. I guess the girl took the money with her when she went to the principal's office. When the cops showed up, those two boys told them she was a prostitute. They said she offered to suck their dicks for a dollar and that she was lying about being raped. The cops almost believed them, too.

That girl shouldn't never have picked up that money, and she should've stayed out the hallways, too. I'm not saying it's her fault or nothing. Just that it's not safe being out there alone. Me, I go to the bathroom before I leave the house, and then at lunch if I can't hold it any longer. I think I could probably handle myself if anyone tried to mess with me. But then I look at Eddie and Lydell, and I think about how scared that girl must have been.

I turned to Rico and tried to sound as disgusted as I felt by Lydell's proposal. "Why you always let them mess with me? These fools disrespect me all the time, and you never do a damn thing about it."

Rico shrugged and let an oily smile slide across his face. "So what you gonna do, Genna? Run to Mama? Who you think she's gonna believe?"

I looked at Rico and all I felt inside was hate. I know he's my brother, and blood is thicker than water, they say. But all I wanted to do just then was kick his ass down those hard marble stairs. I wanted to mash his face into the wall so I wouldn't have to see him laughing at me.

Instead I crawled over them and headed upstairs, stomping real loud and hard, hoping their fingers would get caught beneath my feet.

8.

Mr. Christiansen is pretty much the only white person I know. That sounds like a dumb thing to say, but it's true. I have a couple of teachers who are white, but I wouldn't really say that I *know* them. And they sure don't know *me*.

But Mr. Christiansen is different. For one thing, he's old, and that makes him pretty harmless. I see him in the garden sometimes, perched on this collapsible stool that looks like it's about to collapse alright. He squints at the flowers and trees, then leans forward and dabs his brush against the canvas. I like to watch him paint, and he says he likes the company. He even painted me one time. I thought the picture would look ugly, but it turned out alright. Actually, it was kind of nice.

Mr. Christiansen is Danish. He says America is the greatest country in the world. Sometimes he talks about the city and what it was like when he came here as a little boy. He still remembers stopping at Ellis Island. "America is a great melting pot," he says before winking at me.

I've heard that before. People say it all the time, and it's in every social studies textbook I've ever read. But that doesn't mean it's true. I haven't seen much of America. I've spent my whole life here in New York. But in this city, people are separate. Blacks and Latinos mix sometimes, but Asians mostly keep to themselves. Whites might live *near* us, but they don't live *with* us. At least that's how things used to be. When I took the train, most of the white people used to get off before me. But these days more and more of them are staying on the train. Mama says they're pushing deeper and deeper into Brooklyn. So far no white people have come to live in our neighborhood. Mama says that's the only good thing about living in such a crappy building. White folks are too scared to move in.

Mama doesn't like white people. She says when I get older, I'll understand why. I haven't told Mama about Mr. Christiansen. Like I said before, he's just a harmless old man, and he's been real nice to me. One time he asked me why I only came to the garden on Tuesdays. I said, " 'Cause that's when it's free." Mr. Christiansen looked at me for a minute. Then he got up off that crazy stool, packed up all his art stuff, and told me to follow him. He took me to the visitor center and told the lady behind the desk he wanted to buy me a visitor's pass. The old lady frowned at me, then she gave Mr. Christiansen a real funny look. He just put his money on the counter and waited for her to give me my card.

When we were outside again, Mr. Christiansen smiled at me. "Now the garden is yours—*every* day." That was one of the nicest things anyone had ever done for me.

Mr. Christiansen's a really sweet man. So I just bite my tongue and listen while he talks about America being "the land of opportunity" or "the great melting pot." I want to ask Mr. Christiansen what happens to the folks who get left at the bottom of the pot. I'm thinking whoever's down there probably gets burned. Not just black people, either. A while back they executed a white man for blowing up a government building in Oklahoma. I was just a kid when all that happened, but I remember seeing pictures of what the place looked like afterward. The front half of the building was gone, and you could see all the guts hanging out—wires and hunks of concrete and clouds of dust everywhere. People were screaming and holding their heads, and little babies were being carried out covered in blood. It takes a whole lot of hate to do something like that. Papi, he didn't like America and that's why he left. But that white man, he made a bomb and killed 168 people. And never said he was sorry. They injected him with poison, and the people who watched said he died without showing any remorse. They said he looked like if he wasn't strapped down, he'd have jumped up and done it all over again.

Mr. Christiansen sees things differently. Sometimes I sit beside him while he paints. I look around the garden, and then I look at his canvas. Half the time he's painted something that doesn't even exist. Mr. Christiansen says he paints what's in his "mind's eye." I'm not sure what that means. Maybe he just sees what he wants to see. Maybe he can do that 'cause he's old and white. All I know is when I look around me, I only see what's real.

9.

Our building's right across the street from the garden, but I'll bet half the people living here have never even been inside. Some of the kids have—most grade schools drag you there at least once a year. It makes an okay trip, I guess, but it's different when you can explore the garden on your own. I'm almost always alone when I visit the garden. Sometimes I take Tyjuan, but that can get complicated 'cause I got to push him in the stroller and it's a cheap, tacky old thing that won't even go straight. Plus I don't like it when folks stare at me. I might look older than my age, but I still don't want folks thinking that Tyjuan is my son. And that's exactly what they do think when they see a black girl like me pushing a broke-down stroller: *baby mama.*

Now, if the kid in the stroller was white, that would be something else altogether. Then they'd figure I was the nanny, and everything would be alright. I see them in the garden sometimes, brown-skinned women pushing little blond kids in deluxe-type strollers, or talking to each other on benches while the babies shove handfuls of dirt in their mouths. Some of the women seem like they really care about those kids.

Sometimes I wonder if they have kids of their own, and who takes care of them while they're looking after these white kids. Most of the nannies sound foreign, like they come from the Caribbean or someplace where people don't speak much English. Sometimes they get together in the garden and talk in their own language, and I wonder if they knew each other before they came here, or if they're just looking for a way to not feel homesick. It seems like a pretty good job, but I guess it can get kind of lonely, 'cause no matter how much you like the kid, it isn't yours, and the people you live with aren't your real family. You're like a servant, really. But it still seems like a pretty cushy job to me.

I'd do it part-time, or maybe during the summer once I'm in college. Most times the family wants you to move in, and so you have your own room and your own keys to the place. And people who have nannies have money, so you know they got nice houses full of nice stuff. I wouldn't mind living in one of those brownstones over in Park Slope. Like I said before, I really dig things that are old, and all old buildings aren't crappy like mine. I know because one time this white lady let me come home with her and I saw how nice her building was. That doesn't sound right. She *invited* me to come home with her and her little boy, Chad. I met them in the garden one time. I was standing by the lily pool keeping a real close eye on Tyjuan. I didn't bring the stroller that time. I just carried him over and let him toddle along beside me while I held onto his hand. He likes watching the goldfish, and so he knelt down by the water and tried to touch them with his little finger. I just held onto him and made sure he didn't fall in.

Hannah—that was the white lady—she was standing by the lily pool, too, except her little boy was in a stroller—a real nice one that had a little umbrella on the side to keep the sun out of her kid's face. Well, Hannah, she thought Tyjuan was just the cutest thing she'd ever seen. And he is—I'm not just saying that 'cause Tyjuan's my brother. He really is a beautiful child, and I always feel real proud when other folks pay him all kinds of attention.

Anyway, Hannah asked how old he was, and I told her. Then she looked at me, not in a hard way, just like she was trying to guess my age as well. And so I told her that Tyjuan was my little brother, and that I just brought him here sometimes to see all the flowers and the fish and the turtles that swim around the Japanese pond. Then she introduced herself and pushed the umbrella out the way so I could meet her little boy. He was cute. Kind of doughy, but a nice enough kid. He and Tyjuan hit it off right away, and next thing I knew, I was sitting next to this white lady on one of those hard stone benches with the two babies laughing and pointing at each other. She asked me all kinds of questions, and I didn't mind answering most of them. I told her how I wanted to become a psychiatrist one day, and she told me she had some old psychology textbooks at home from when she was in college.

Next thing I knew, we were walking through the garden, heading toward the entrance that's up on Eastern Parkway. We went out and just kept talking and walking until we reached this real nice building. It was made of smooth white stone, not bricks, and the fire escapes had been painted a real pretty turquoise blue. There were bars on the first-floor windows, but they curved out so whoever lived there still had enough room to plant flowers in their window box. Inside the building, everything was spotless. The elevator didn't smell like urine, and it didn't bounce when it came to a stop. Hannah unlocked her apartment and told me to make myself at home. I couldn't do that at first—everything was just too nice, too clean, and too expensive. I kept a real close eye on Tyjuan 'cause I didn't want him to break anything. I put him down on this fancy rug so he could play with Chad. Then I sat on the edge of this soft leather sofa and took a good look at the apartment. One whole wall of the living room was covered with books. I mean, *covered*, from the floor all the way up to the ceiling. There was lots of light coming through the windows, and there were plants everywhere. The apartment was so neat I could hardly believe Hannah and her husband lived here with a baby. Plus there was a dog—a big shaggy brown thing that didn't bark or anything when Chad started climbing all over him.

While I was looking around, Hannah was standing in front of the wall of books. Finally she pulled two real thick books off the shelf and handed them to me. Then she plunked down on the sofa next to me and talked while I flipped through the books. She told me she used to be a social worker, but she quit her job after having the baby. I asked her did she know Chad was the name of a country in Africa. She laughed and said that she met her husband while they were both working in the Peace Corps over there. She said if they had a little girl, they were going to name her Kenya. That made me laugh, 'cause I know about five girls named Kenya, but none of them's white.

After a while Chad started to yawn and I knew Tyjuan was getting tired, too. Before I left, Hannah said maybe I could babysit for her sometime, and I said sure. I gave her my phone number and thanked her for the books. Then I picked up Tyjuan, told him to say bye-bye, and we left. When Mama got home that night, I was looking through one of the psychology books. She asked where I got it from, but when I told her about Hannah, she screwed up her mouth and got real nasty with me. Mama said I ought to know better than to go around taking handouts from white folks. I told her it wasn't like that, that I was going to babysit for Hannah. And then Mama said oh no I wasn't, that she didn't raise her daughters to play mammy to Miss Anne and her little white brats.

I'd heard Mama talk about white folks before, but never like that. Never about someone she'd never even met, someone as nice and friendly as Hannah. That's why I never told Mama about Mr. Christiansen. Whenever I ask Mama why she hates white people so much, she just sucks her teeth and says, "You'll find out soon enough." I know Mama puts up with a lot of crap on her job. I know she gets tired of having to clean up after old folks all day long, and most of them are white. But I don't think it's right for her to talk about all white people that way. That's like white folks saying all black people are on welfare or doing drugs. It's not like that, but you'll never know unless you give people a chance.

Mama told me I could keep the books, but she said I wasn't allowed to babysit for Hannah. Which isn't fair, because Mama can't always afford to give me pocket money, and she lets me babysit all the time for people in our neighborhood. Mama said Hannah's place was too far, but I knew what the real reason was. So when Hannah called a couple nights ago and asked me to watch Chad this weekend, I said sure. She said I could bring Tyjuan if I wanted, and that I could use their computer if I had homework to do. Hannah's a real nice lady. And Mama will be working anyway, so she doesn't even have to know. Rico and Toshi do stuff behind Mama's back all the time. I don't like lying to my mother, but I got to do what I got to do. Sometimes I feel like Mama's got one set of rules for Toshi and Rico, and another set of rules just for me. And sometimes that makes me feel special, but other times it's just not fair.

10.

Sometimes I feel like there's a tattoo on my forehead that says "ghetto." And I don't know if it'll ever go away, not even if I change my clothes, move out of this neighborhood, and graduate from college. Mama says ghetto isn't just a place, it's a mentality. She says if you let it get inside your head, you'll never leave the ghetto behind. It'll live inside of you, no matter where you go. Mama says, "You can take the girl out of the ghetto, but you can't always take the ghetto out of the girl." I try not to let any of my ghetto ways show when I'm over at Hannah's. Sometimes I feel like she's proud of me for talking right, and working hard at school, and for having plans to go to college. Other times, I feel like she thinks I'm just acting, like she wishes I'd just be myself around her. More ghetto. More black. The thing is, everyone who's black ain't ghetto, and everyone who's ghetto ain't black.

To prove this, Mama brings lots of magazines home from work. The hospital subscribes to all kinds of different ones, but nobody really reads the magazines about black folks. So Mama comes home with copies of *Essence*, and *Ebony*, and *Black Enterprise*. And sometimes if it's not too late and all my homework's done, she'll tell me to read some article about a black banker, or a lawyer, or a doctor—Mama doesn't really care about the celebrities, and she doesn't want me to care, either. She says we already got too many black folks singing and dancing and rapping and playing sports.

Mama says it's a good thing I'm going to be a psychiatrist one day, 'cause black folks in this country have been brainwashed—*miseducated* is what she likes to say. She says we can't trust what they teach us in school, we got to supplement our education. Mama says, learn everything they teach you, and then go out and learn even more. She says kids in white schools get taught different stuff than us. She says white schools get more money and have better teachers, and that's why their kids get higher grades. I say, what about *Brown v. Board of Education*? Back in 1954, the Supreme Court said that wasn't fair. But Mama just looks at me and says, "You still got a lot to learn, baby."

I know that a lot of what Mama tells me is true. I know she wishes she could have gone to college when she was young, but she met Papi first and then all of us started coming along. Mama always made sure we had books to read when we were little. She didn't buy us fun books like *The Cat in the Hat*; she bought us books about black inventors and Frederick Douglass and Sojourner Truth. Mama made sure we all got library cards, and she used to take us over there once a week. But then Mama started to work a double shift, and Rico and Toshi kind of got lost, and it was just me doing all the reading, making up for all the things none of us learned in school.

Hannah's not like the white people Mama talks about. She helps me because I need the help, and I guess she thinks I deserve it. But sometimes I get the feeling she wishes I was more messed up—like that Tyjuan really was my baby, or that I couldn't read or write. She wants to do more for me—that's what it is—and I won't let her. Not 'cause I don't need the help, but 'cause I want to do some things for myself.

One time when Hannah came home from yoga, she paid me and then hauled this big bag of clothes out of her bedroom. "These are for the Salvation Army," she said, "but there are some nice things in here. Want to take a look?"

I looked at the big garbage bag full of clothes, and I wanted to say, "No, thanks." But Hannah had that look on her face, that shiny-eyed look that lets me know she's trying to be nice, that she wants something good to happen for me. I thought, maybe Hannah knows something I don't, like that you have to wear a certain kind of clothes to go to an Ivy League school. So I agreed to take a look, even though I was okay with the clothes I had on.

She opened up the bag and started pulling out these clothes. Everything still looked brand-new, and I recognized the names on all the labels. Hannah kept pulling things out and handing them to me, and I was just standing there holding the clothes like the salesgirls who stand outside the fitting room while you try things on. Finally, Hannah stopped and looked at me, and she could tell by my face that I wasn't interested in her preppy designer clothes. She sighed and pushed her hair out of her face, and she said, "I guess these aren't really your style, huh?" And I kind of smiled and shook my head. Then as I handed her back the clothes, she said, "What about your mother?"

And that's when I got mad. It's okay that Hannah wants to help *me*, but I don't need her to help my family. I don't need her to put clothes on my back, and I definitely don't need her to dress my mother. Sometimes people give you things, and they don't know when to stop. They give *too much*, 'cause they want to fix all your problems but sometimes you got to fix your own problems, your own kind of way. Hannah's already paying me, and that's what I said.

"You paid me already, Hannah." And her face got kind of flushed, and her eyes lost all of that shine, and I kind of wished I hadn't said it, but I knew it needed to be said. Mama says that's the problem with white folks—they're always crossing the line. "They want to keep you in *your* place," says Mama, "but they don't know how to stay in *theirs*."

I don't want to think like Mama. I try not to lump Hannah and all white people together, 'cause that's exactly what I don't want people doing to me. I want people to accept me for who I am, with my own ways, and my own ideas, and my own future that's separate from everything else that's going on. Separate from Rico dealing drugs and Toshi acting fast and Papi walking out on us. Separate from where I live or how I dress or the color of my skin. I'm not ashamed of none of those things, I just want people to see *all* of who I am—and not just the messed-up parts.

When I left Hannah's that day, I didn't go to the garden. Instead I walked over to Carroll Street and took another look at that house. The red FOR RENT sign was still in the window. I went halfway up the stoop and wrote down the number so Mama could call later on. I had just written down the last digit when the front door opened and caught me by surprise. I hadn't been doing anything wrong, but I was on somebody else's stoop and that somebody sure didn't look happy to see me. This little old white lady with a shriveled-up face said, "What do you want?" Her voice was a lot bigger than her body, and a couple people on the street turned to see what was wrong. I started going down the steps backward and said I was just writing down the number to call about the apartment for rent. She looked at the sign like she wished she could make it disappear, then she turned those same eyes on me. "You're too young," she snapped. I said I was looking for my family, not for myself. Then she screwed up her mouth and said, "No kids allowed. No kids, and no pets." And before I could say anything else, she slipped back inside and slammed the door behind her.

When Mama says white folks are evil, that's the kind of person she's talking about. I was real polite to that lady, but she treated me like I was a stray dog trying to bring fleas into her house. I bet she made that up about no kids and no pets. There was a rubber toy in the front yard that must've belonged to somebody—if not the old lady, then someone who lived on the top floor or in the basement. I walked home thinking of ways I could prove the old lady had lied.

If I could prove it, then we could threaten to sue her for discrimination. I'm only in the tenth grade, but even I know you can't kick someone out of an apartment because of the color of their skin.

What I really wanted to know, though, was how come Hannah saw me one way while that old lady saw something else—some*one* else. Maybe it's like Mr. Christiansen and his mind's eye that sees things that aren't even there. Or maybe it's that tattoo on my forehead that just won't go away.

11.

Rico, Eddie, and Lydell are lying face down on the ground. Their hands are cuffed behind their backs. Cops stand over them, laughing like they think this is some kind of joke.

The cops know they can't touch Mona. They've tried to arrest her dozens of times, but Mona's too smart to get caught. She lets the people who work for her take the fall, and each time she walks away clean. Then she finds a new group of suckers and starts her business up all over again. Even though Mona's the actual dealer, she never has any drugs on her. She keeps them stashed in an apartment inside, so whenever there's a sweep, the person living in the apartment gets busted, not Mona.

A police van pulls up, and the swirling lights seem to remind the laughing cops of what it is they're supposed to be doing. Each cop bends down and hauls one of the boys to his feet. One by one they are pushed into the back of the van. Before Rico gets in, he turns and looks at me. For the first time, I can tell my brother is scared. His eyes plead with me to help him. I run inside the building and call Mama as fast as I can.

When Mama gets home, she's real upset. She opens the front door and shoves Toshi inside, then slams the door behind her.

"What did I tell you about standing out front? Prancing around all made up like some kind of whore. Is that what you want people to think—that you're a prostitute? Nobody out there is up to any good, so you just keep your behind inside the house, young lady. You understand me?"

Toshi turns her face away and sucks her teeth. Mama hears her, and for a moment I think Toshi's gonna get hit. But Mama presses her lips together and tries to stay calm. She doesn't want to waste energy on Toshi when Rico's the one in real trouble. Toshi flops onto the sofa and aims the remote at the TV. Mama snatches it out of her hand and turns the TV off.

"What's happening, Genna? Tell me everything from the very beginning."

I tell Mama all I know, and Toshi fills in extras that she got from the people out front. When we're through, Mama sinks onto the sofa and holds her head in her hands. Her eyes are shut tight, and I can tell Mama's trying to think of what to do next. We don't have enough money to hire a good lawyer. Like last time, Rico will have to depend on a court-appointed one, and most of them don't care whether you're guilty or not.

I put Tyjuan to bed hours ago, but I guess he can tell something's wrong, because now he starts to cry. I want to stay with Mama, but I go into the bedroom instead. Tyjuan crawls into my arms, and I carry him back to the living room. Mama is standing up now. She looks real tired, and she's moving kind of slow. Mama takes up her pocketbook and her keys. She turns to Toshi.

"Come on, girl, let's go find out where they've taken your brother."

Toshi doesn't move. She gets all pouty and stares at the blank TV. "Why can't Genna go? I got plans tonight."

Mama's head swings around, but once again she keeps her cool.

"Genna's got to look after Tyjuan. Now get your ass up off the sofa and come on."

Toshi hears the edge in Mama's voice, and this time she does as she's told. After they leave, I sit down on the sofa and try to read a story to Tyjuan, but he's feeling fussy tonight, and after a while I set the book aside. Tyjuan rolls off my lap and gets down on the floor. He finds his little xylophone and starts hammering away.

I try to block out the noise and think about what's going on. I wonder what's going to happen to my big brother this time. Rico's just sixteen, so they can't send him to prison—I think. How could they put a kid like Rico in a jail that's full of grown men? I've heard about the messed-up things they do to you in prison. Even if he was with Eddie and Lydell, Rico couldn't handle all that.

I look at Tyjuan who's yawning now, and I wonder if this will happen to him one day. I think about the house on Carroll Street. I know Mama's got a lot on her mind, but we've got to get out of this place. At least with Rico gone, that's one less mouth to feed. Plus I won't have to sleep on the floor anymore. I feel kind of guilty thinking this way, but people have to pay for their mistakes. Rico knew what he was getting into. And he sure wouldn't have listened to me if I'd tried to tell him what Mona was about. I didn't try, but Rico should have known better anyway. Then I think, maybe I wanted Mama to see that her favorite son isn't so perfect after all. Maybe deep down I actually wanted this to happen.

Tyjuan crawls over to the sofa and stretches his arms toward me. I lift him up and begin rocking him to sleep. *Maybe I wanted this to happen.* That's a real ugly thought to have inside your head. Rico's never been nothing but a jerk to me, but that doesn't mean I don't love him. That doesn't mean I wanted him to get locked up, sent to prison, or juvie, or wherever he's going to end up this time. I just wanted things to be different between us.

Pretty soon Tyjuan's sleeping soundly in my arms. I lay him down on Mama's bed and go back into the living room to wait. That's really the only thing I can do right now. Think, and wait.

12.

What I want to know is, why is Mama yelling at *me*? She's got one son locked up for dealing drugs. Toshi's about to drop out of school, and she's gonna get herself in trouble if she don't stop switching her butt like that. I'm a straight A student, I help out at home, I'm working part-time so I can move us out of here, and Mama's yelling at *me*?

There are so many things Mama just doesn't understand. I could fight back, I could yell and blame *her* for everything instead of just taking it like I do. But that wouldn't change anything. And we'd still have to live together in this tiny, crappy apartment that feels even smaller now that Rico's gone. I'm glad I don't have to sleep on the floor anymore, and I don't miss those boys messing with me, but other than that, things aren't so great around here. Mama won't talk about anything other than the trial, and she's taking off work more and more so she can be home when the lawyer calls. I come home from school some days and she's just sitting there on the sofa clutching Tyjuan like she don't ever want to let go. Sometimes he doesn't want to be held, and he'll start kicking and crying for her to put him down. Other times he just does what I do. He gets real quiet and takes it, 'cause he knows it's what Mama needs right now.

Lately I've been feeling like Mama's lost. And part of me wants to draw her a map so she can see where she is, so she can see how far apart we are, the mountains she's putting between us. But Mama's stubborn. All the women in this family are a little hard-headed, including me. That's why I've been babysitting for Hannah even though Mama said I wasn't allowed. Hannah has yoga on Tuesdays and Thursdays, so I go over there after school and watch Chad from three to five. Hannah always asks if I want to stay for dinner, but I tell her I have to get home and look after Tyjuan. And that's partly true, although there's less for me to do these days now that Mama's always around. Mostly I just want to come here, to the garden, for a little while before the gates close at six. I come with Hannah's crisp bills folded up in my wallet, and I stand in front of the fountain with my pennies, wishing things didn't have to be this way.

Times like these I wish Aleesha was still around so I'd have someone to talk to. She was my best friend from third to eighth grade. Then Aleesha's parents bought a house out in Jersey, and she left. We kept in touch for a little while, but it wasn't the same. Aleesha's folks got her a voucher to go to one of those charter schools, some academy where everybody wears a uniform. Not a prep school or anything, but Aleesha knew she was on her way. Out of the city, out of the ghetto. Out of my life. And she never looked back.

I've never been popular, but I thought maybe I'd make new friends once I started high school. But soon as I got there, kids started asking me if I really was Toshi Colon's little sister. If I lied and said no, they'd just turn and walk away like I wasn't worth talking to anymore. And if I said yes, then they'd stare and whisper and point at me in the hall. I'm in my second year of high school, and I still haven't made a single friend. The popular girls hate me 'cause they're jealous of Toshi, and they can't get to her so they try to get to me. If Toshi knows what's happening, she never lets on. She hardly even looks at me when we pass each other in the hall. The teachers like me 'cause I'm quiet and smart, and I don't cause any trouble like Rico. Problem is, kids hate a teacher's pet. So even though that's not what I'm trying to be, that's how the other kids see me. And that's why I'm always alone. At least I think that's the reason. Maybe I'm wrong. Maybe it's something else.

I got a book from the library once, a picture book about a little black boy who had wings. All the other children teased him, and he had nowhere safe to land, and only one little girl tried to protect him because she really thought he was beautiful. I read that story to Tyjuan over and over again. Tyjuan loved the pictures, but he hardly understood the words. Mostly I was just reading that story to myself.

That's how I feel about Judah. And how I want him to feel about me. When you're different, people treat you like you're some kind of freak. They're afraid, maybe, and people who are scared can be cruel. They don't know what to do with you because you don't fit into any of the boxes they're in. You're not *this*, so you don't fit into *this* box, and you're not *that*, so you don't fit into *that* box, either. And sometimes people hate you for not fitting in 'cause they think that you think you're better than them. But I don't think I'm better than anyone else. I'm proud of the fact I'm smart, and I'm glad that I do well in school. But at the end of the day, I'm not so different. I'm just a regular person, except that I'm always alone. I wish I had real close girlfriends like Toshi has. I wish I had someone to hang out with all the time, like how Rico had Eddie and Lydell, even though they were stupid and got him into trouble. But I don't have anybody, really. I have Tyjuan, but he's just a baby, and he needs *me* to take care of *him*. It can't be the other way around.

Sometimes I think if my Papi was still here, I wouldn't feel so bad all the time. People think only boys need their fathers, but girls need a daddy, too. I know deep down Mama blames herself for what happened to Rico, even though it isn't her fault. She talks about Papi and how she wishes he had stayed, because boys can't grow up right without a man in the house. Maybe that's true, but what about girls? Sure, we still have Mama but she's hardly ever around. She's there, but she's not really *there*. I think everybody needs at least one person to love them. Somebody who thinks they're special, worth taking care of, worth sticking around for.

All these thoughts are in my head today as I stand in front of the fountain. I reach into my pocket, pull out a handful of change, and sift through it, picking out the pennies. Then I put the silver coins away and launch the pennies into the fountain, one at a time.

Once I've thrown all my wishes away, I just stand there staring into the water. I think about how still and peaceful it must be at the bottom of the fountain. I think about stories I have read to Tyjuan about beautiful mermaids who try to lure people into the sea. I think about that Greek guy from long ago who thought he was so beautiful that he tried to kiss his own reflection and fell into the water and drowned. I think about news reports and all the warnings I've heard about babies drowning in just a couple inches of water, how careful I always am when I'm giving Tyjuan his bath. The water in the fountain is shallow, it wouldn't even come near my knee. Still, I think about how nice it would be just to lie there at the bottom, with the cool water from above trickling over me like rain. I think about floating in that fountain the way I used to do in the tub when I was little. But I'm too big for that now.

Then I hear something that doesn't sound real, even though I know that it is. I freeze and wait to hear it again, the way I listen for birdcalls I don't recognize.

"Genna."

This time I spin around. I know I'm wide awake but I've had this dream before, so at first I'm not sure this is real. Things like this don't happen to me. I can feel my cheeks burning up but I try not to look as flustered as I feel. My heart's racing and I want to smile because it's Judah, and he is sitting on the stone bench that circles the fountain looking like he wants me to come and sit next to him. But instead I frown because I know he's been watching me, and I don't like being watched. I know people can't see inside my head, but sometimes when they stare at me, I feel like my thoughts are naked.

Judah doesn't smile at me. He just nods, and I know that that means come here. I walk over to where he is sitting in the shade. His eyes are dark and hard to read, but I don't think he is laughing at me. Then, just as I sit down, Judah stands up and starts to walk away. I'm already feeling kind of messed up inside, and this makes me want to cry. I don't want him to play games with me. But Judah looks at me over his shoulder, and there is a soft smile tugging at his lips. His half-smile is like an apology for so many different things, so I sit back on the bench and try to pull myself together.

Judah sits down at the far end of the bench. We are sitting at opposite ends of a quarter of a circle. There is so much space between us, lots of shade and silence and leaves moving in the breeze. I'm not sure what I'm supposed to do, so I look over at Judah. He smiles at me then, and his teeth look like pearls under water. I smile back at him and wonder again what's going to happen next. Then Judah says something to me real quiet like, and I figure maybe I'm going to have to read his lips because he's so far away. But his words come to me, they press up against my ear, and my eyes open wide in surprise. Judah laughs, and I turn around to see if someone's behind me because the laughter is right there beside me, but I'm still sitting all alone.

"How did you do that?"

Judah grins at me with all those pretty white teeth, and then he puts his finger up to his lips. I get real quiet and look at the curving circle of stone we're sitting on. It looks like an ordinary bench. I figure if anything's magic, it must be Judah. I get a tingly feeling inside.

"Don't look at me," says Judah in his regular voice. "Just close your eyes and see if you can hear what I'm going to say."

I close my eyes and try to keep my lips from twitching into a smile. For a moment there's only silence, then a soft voice whispers in my ear.

"Genna, you're different."

I open my eyes, but I don't look at Judah right away. I want to make sure I believe what I have heard. I stare at the moss growing between slabs of stone on the ground, and Judah slips words in my ear once more.

"I'm different, too."

"I know." I speak quietly, to the moss, but my voice travels just like Judah's, around the bench and into his ear. I want to look at him so I can know that my words really did arrive. But like the moss, my gaze has grown attached to the stones on the ground.

"I like you, Genna. Because you're different. Not like the rest."

Now I have to look at Judah because my heart is pounding real hard and I can't let him play me like that. If this is a joke, I have to know *now*, because I *really* want this to be real.

Judah isn't smiling. His face is solemn but sincere. I feel my eyes filling up with tears but I try to blink fast so they will be gone before Judah can see. But I cannot blink fast enough and they're still pooled in my eyes when Judah stands up and comes to sit next to me. He waits for me to look up, and when I do, I know my eyes are shining like two bright coins. I can feel my wet eyelashes curling against my dark skin.

Judah puts his hand on my shoulder and looks straight into my face. "Your eyes are silver," he says.

This makes me want to cry even more, but I can't because Judah's lips are pressed against mine.

13.

Sometimes the kids at school tease me. Mostly they just ignore me and leave me alone, and I like it that way. I mind my business and keep a low profile, and the cute girls with their cute hair and cute clothes, they get all the attention. I'm fifteen now, and Mama says I'll fill out once I get a little bit older. But I know I'll never look like the women in all those raunchy music videos. I'll never have light skin, or blue eyes, or long, curly blond hair. Not unless I buy it. You can buy almost anything these days—fake breasts, fake nails, fake hair (although some of it is real human hair you just pass off as your own). Some of the girls at school wear those contact lenses, the ones that turn your eyes green or purple or light brown. I think it looks kind of freaky, but I guess it might be kind of fun, too. To look like somebody else for a day. To be yourself, but look different on the outside.

I feel like I'm just a shadow at school, but sometimes kids mess with me just the same. Like in English class. That's one of my favorite subjects, and I like our teacher, Ms. Harraway. Sometimes she asks for volunteers to read stories and poems out loud. I don't ever raise my hand, but she chooses me anyway. Ms. Harraway likes the way I write. She kept me after class one day and talked to me—*to* me, not *at* me, like most teachers do. Ms. Harraway thinks I should major in English when I go away to college. I told her I want to be a psychiatrist, so

I'll probably be a psychology major instead. She said maybe English could be my minor, and I told her I'd think about it.

So like I was saying, sometimes Ms. Harraway picks me to read things out loud during class. I don't do it to show off, but I do like the way the words sound when they're coming out of my mouth. Especially old words, things people wrote a long time ago. Sometimes I'm so nervous I don't even hear myself speaking. But the kids in my class, they hear me. Afterward, some of them come up to me in the hallway. They say I'm trying to talk white 'cause I don't say "ain't" or "we be going to the store." I do say that sometimes, just not all the time. And *definitely* not in class.

My guidance counselor, Mrs. Freeman, says it's important to be yourself, but it's also important to know how to blend in. I don't see how that's possible for a black girl like me—I'm more likely to stand out. But Mrs. Freeman says that when you go into the real world, you've got to learn how to adapt to your environment. She says you can't go through life thinking you can just dress and talk and act any way you want. Mrs. Freeman says it's okay to do that when you're at home, but not when you're at work or at college or a fancy restaurant. She says you've got to be like a chameleon. Mrs. Freeman calls that a survival skill. Most of the kids I know call that selling out. Mama says if you're going to learn another language, you might as well learn how to talk white. Mama says in America, that's the only language that really counts.

Right now in English class we're reading Shakespeare's sonnets. Ms. Harraway says some scholars believe that Shakespeare was in love with a black woman. I never knew there were black women in England way back then. There's a Shakespeare corner in the garden. It's full of the flowers and strange plants he talks about in his plays. That part of the garden's kind of messy, and some of those plants look like regular old weeds. I wonder if that's really how things look over in England. Someday I'll go there and find out.

Today Ms. Harraway doesn't call on me. Instead she starts reading one of Shakespeare's sonnets herself. I like the way she reads. When Ms. Harraway reads poetry, it sounds like it's coming from somewhere deep inside of her. Like it's her feeling those things and not some old white guy who died hundreds of years ago.

My mistress' eyes are nothing like the sun;
Coral is far more red than her lips' red;
If snow be white, why then her breasts are dun;
If hair be wires, black wires grow on her head.
I have seen roses damasked, red and white,
But no such roses see I in her cheeks …

Ms. Harraway is halfway through the sonnet when a fight breaks out in the hall. We can hear bodies slamming into lockers. Ms. Harraway sighs and puts down her book. She tells us to finish reading the poem and leaves the room. Kids crowd around the door trying to see what's going on. I don't bother to get up. It's probably just my brother or some other reject cutting class and fooling around. Then I remember that Rico's locked up. I focus on the poem so I don't have to think about that.

I'm sitting at my desk reading the sonnet when all of a sudden, fingers scratch the top of my head and my scarf is gone. I clap both my hands over my hair. I want to scream, to hide under the desk, but instead I try to stay cool. I look around to see who has it, but there is so much movement and laughter, so many pointing fingers, I don't know where to look. Then my eyes fix on Malcolm. Malcolm's one of those kids who cuts up all the time to hide the fact that he doesn't know how to read. Or maybe I'm wrong, 'cause right now he's standing on his chair, an open book in one hand and my scarf in the other.

"Hey, y'all, listen up. This poem's about Genna. 'If hair be wires, black wires grow on her head.'" A handful of people laugh. Encouraged, Malcolm goes on. "Damn, girl, you get your finger caught in the socket this morning? Why's your hair standing up all over your head like that?" More people laugh this time. I tell Malcolm to give me back my scarf. He balls it up in his hand and tosses it to his homeboy Godfrey.

I wish Judah was here, but the desk behind me is empty today. Normally I can handle myself, but right now I don't know what to do. I don't want to stand up or walk out of the room. I am too tall, and everyone will stare at me. So instead I swivel in my seat while the boys howl. The girls curl their mouths into ugly sneers, even the ones whose hair is wrapped like mine—as hard and short and nappy as mine. Finally, I put my head down on the desk and try not to cry. Then I feel someone standing beside me. It is Peter, one of Judah's friends. He hands me my scarf with a silent nod. I tie it back on my head as best I can and force myself not to cry.

After class ends, I race to my locker. I want to get out of that school as fast as I can. I go straight to the garden, past the Shakespeare corner, past the Japanese pond, and over to the cherry esplanade. I find an empty bench and sit down. For a while I just sit there, staring at air, trying to delete from memory what happened in class this afternoon. I feel for loose change in my pockets, and then I think, what's the point? All this money I've been throwing away, and none of my wishes have come true. I think maybe I should save my pennies from now on, save up so we can move out of this neighborhood. Maybe then I could transfer to a different school. Then I wouldn't have to deal with Malcolm and Godfrey and kids who tease me 'cause I don't speak Ebonics all the time.

After a while I don't feel so upset anymore. Everything in the garden is quiet and calm. I start to feel that way inside, too. I sit on my bench and look out over the grass that's so soft and thick it looks like plush green carpet. The cherry trees have lost nearly all their blossoms, but a few final petals drift to the ground like snow. A couple of people are laid out under the trees, sleeping or reading a book. I search for the black nannies with the pudgy white babies, but can't find any today.

I am feeling so calm inside that I don't hear Judah until he sits down beside me on the worn wooden bench. Suddenly I'm feeling all hectic inside, and my cheeks are burning like fire. I want to ask him how he knew I was here, but I am too ashamed to say anything. Peter must have told him what happened. All I can think of is how awful I must have looked with my hair sticking up all over my head. My scarf is back on my head now, but it can't cover up the way I feel inside. I don't want Judah to look at me. I turn my head and pretend to stare at something that's real far away.

Judah says, "Sorry I couldn't be there today. Something came up at home."

I shrug so he'll think it was no big deal. But I really wish Judah had been there.

We sit without talking for a little while. Then Judah says, "Why you always cover your hair, Gen?"

I want to say because it is ugly, because it is short and stiff and does not swing when I walk. Because I cannot afford to get braids put in, or a weave. Because I will never look like Toshi or the girls in music videos.

Judah says, "My Aunt Marcia could show you how to lock your hair. You'd look good with dreads."

I want to look in his face and make sure there is no laughter there. Judah sounds serious. I think of how I would look with locks. Judah's hair is already way past his shoulders. It would take a long time for my hair to get that long, if it grew at all. But if I did have dreadlocks, Judah and I would look alike. We'd look like we belonged together. I want to smile at Judah. Instead I stare at my feet.

Judah promises to take me to see his aunt next week. I want to tell him that I cannot afford to pay anyone to do my hair. But then I think, Judah knows that. And then I start to feel good inside, and my lips curl up into a smile. There are a lot of things I don't have to tell Judah. Because he already knows.

14.

I can't stop touching my hair. And for the first time since I was a little kid, I actually like how it feels. It's going to take a while for me to get used to how it looks, though. Right now my scalp is shiny 'cause Judah's Aunt Marcia put a whole lot of this nice scented oil on it. Then she showed me how to wrap my hair with a piece of African cloth, instead of just tying a scarf on any old way. She had to cut some of my hair 'cause it was messed up from the home perm I used on it a few months back. But what's left is my own real hair—and it doesn't look ugly. It looks neat and shiny and natural—I've got tiny little coils of hair all over my head!

When I first saw them, I thought they looked like plain old bumps, but then Judah touched my hair and he said these baby locks are like seeds, and I have to take care of them—feed my mind with positivity and shower them with love—so that the seeds take root. His Aunt Marcia showed me how to put oil on my scalp and twist the locks before I go to bed at night. She even gave me a bottle of that special oil to take home with me, along with some pretty pieces of African cloth. I tried to give her the little money I had, but Judah's aunt wouldn't take it from me. She said this was an early birthday present—Judah told her that I'll be turning sixteen next month.

Before we left, Judah pulled me over to a mirror and made me stand there next to him. He looked at my reflection and told me to look as well. "What do you see?" Judah asked me.

For the first time, I really looked at myself in the mirror, and for once I didn't feel ashamed. With Judah there beside me, and the African cloth wrapped around my head like a golden crown, I felt beautiful. But I couldn't say that out loud. Judah gave me his words instead.

"You look like a queen," he told me. "This is who you are, Gen. Beautiful—natural." Then Judah turned my face toward his and kissed me—on the lips, right there in front of his Aunt Marcia.

When Judah talks to me like that, I can never think of anything to say. I just blush and try not to act all stupid and shy, like I'm not used to compliments. But the truth is, I'm not. I'm used to Rico and his boys with their scissor tongues, always cutting me to shreds. I'm used to the kids at school teasing me, and guys on the street ignoring me when I walk by. I'm used to avoiding mirrors so I don't have to see how much I don't look like Toshi and all the other pretty, popular girls.

Now, with Rico gone and Toshi out most of the time, I spend more time in front of the mirror alone. Each morning I wrap my hair the way Judah's aunt taught me to, and each night when I get ready for bed, I unwind the cloth and sit on the edge of Mama's bed, oiling my scalp and twisting my little locks—tending my garden so the seeds will take root and grow. But Judah says it's not enough to just care for my locks on the outside. He gives me books about African history and teaches me about his faith in Jah, the twelve tribes of Israel, Haile Selassie I, and red, gold, and green—red for the blood of martyrs, gold for the riches of Africa, and green for hope and all growing things.

Judah's hair is thick and wild, like a lion's. And that's where he gets his name, from the Bible—Judah was the son of Jacob, and in Revelations it says the seven seals shall be opened by "the lion of the tribe of Judah." Some of this makes sense to me, 'cause even though

Mama never took us to Sunday school, she used to make us read Bible stories on Sunday. But a lot of this is new to me, and I try hard to keep all the facts straight, but that's a whole lot of information to fit inside my head—along with everything we learn in school each day. It's June already, and that means final exams are coming up. Judah's smart, but he doesn't try that hard in school. I ask Judah doesn't he worry about his grades, his GPA, and getting into a good college. But Judah tells me he doesn't plan on going to college. Soon as he gets his diploma, Judah wants to leave New York—go to Africa to travel, work, maybe even live. I ask Judah what's so important about Africa, why can't he wait 'til he's done with school. And Judah says he's already done with school, that he won't learn anything in an American college except lies and misinformation. So then I ask why he doesn't just go back to Jamaica if he doesn't like it here. And Judah says, "Sankofa, Gen. Return to your source." Then he shows me a wooden figurine he keeps on a shelf that's crammed full of books. It's a bird with a long, pointy beak that's looking back over its shoulder.

"But you're Jamaican," I argue.

Judah takes back the wooden bird and shakes his head solemnly. "*African*, Gen. All of us—no matter where we're born or where we are now—we come from Africa. We're African."

I don't really like it when Judah talks that way. Most times when Judah hangs out with me, we talk about all kinds of different things and we both sound the same. But when Judah starts talking about Africa, his Jamaican accent returns—it's like he becomes somebody else, someone who's not like me. I want Judah to know that I respect his religion and the ideas in his mind. But I got my own ideas and my own plans, and I want Judah to respect those, too. More than that, I want Judah to think about how we can be *together* someday—not a thousand miles apart. 'Cause I *know* I'm going to college. And things may not be perfect here in the U.S. of A, but they're not so great over in Africa from what I see on TV. Judah says that's a distortion—it's like how black people only make the news here in America when they've committed some crime, which makes people think all of us are criminals. Judah says the only way to find out the truth is to go to Africa and see for ourselves what's going on. I tell Judah some colleges have a study abroad program where you can be an exchange student in another country for a semester or even a year. But Judah just shrugs like nothing I say is going to change his mind, like an exchange program might be okay for someone like me, but it's not good enough for him. "Don't really matter how you get there, Gen. So long as you get there."

Judah says this real casually, like it's no big deal and he could care less either way. But Judah's eyes are always serious, and I know he is challenging me—daring me to change my plans and go to Africa like him instead of staying here in the United States. Fact is, I'd really like to go to Africa someday. I want to see the pyramids and Gorée Island—the last place slaves were kept before being shipped across the Atlantic. I know all about Nelson Mandela and how he ended apartheid in South Africa. I may not know everything about the continent of Africa, but I'm not ignorant—at least not as ignorant as Judah seems to think I am. Judah acts like there's something wrong with me just 'cause I don't hate the United States. I *do* hate living in the ghetto, and I *definitely* want to get out of here someday, but I'm not ashamed of being American. And I'm not ashamed of being African, either. That's why we call ourselves *African Americans*—'cause we're both, not just one or the other. But Judah doesn't see it that way.

I'm taking good care of my baby locks, and a couple of girls at school even said they liked how I wrapped my hair. I'm starting to get used to compliments, and I guess I have Judah to thank for that. But when I sit on Mama's bed and look in the mirror each night, I see myself through my own eyes. I see Genna Colon, a girl with a past *and* a future. And I'm not sure which matters more—where the seed comes from, or where it takes root and grows.

15.

Judah nods at a group of girls talking on the corner. They're wearing designer gear—short, tight skirts, and skintight jeans, and little baby tees with glittery decals on the front. I watch those girls and I think about Toshi and all the looks she gets from men. Even with my new locks, sometimes I wonder if Judah wishes I was more like Toshi and those loudmouth girls—cute like them, dumb like them.

Judah sucks his teeth and shakes his head. "Pimper's paradise," he says and his accent turns the words into tiny spears that Judah spits at the ground.

I look at Judah, not quite sure what that means.

"It's a song," he tells me, switching back into the voice he normally uses with me. "I'll play it for you sometime."

We walk for a while without talking. Judah checks on Tyjuan now and then, and finally takes him from my tired arms. I watch Judah holding my little brother, and he's so gentle I can't help wishing he was ours—that we were a real family, like Hannah, Mark, and Chad. I know it's not right to want other people's stuff, but for just a moment I think about what it would be like if Judah, Tyjuan, and I lived in an apartment like theirs, in a building and a neighborhood that was safe and clean. We're too young to be getting married, but I still think about it sometimes. Especially when I see Judah with Tyjuan.

It's Tuesday, so today the garden's free. We can go any day, really, 'cause I have a pass and Judah's cousin works security at the side entrance, and he lets Judah in for free. Today the garden's full of families so no one looks at us twice. I open the stroller and Judah puts Tyjuan in it. He's sleeping soundly, so we don't bother with the seat belt. Judah squats in front of the stroller, just watching Tyjuan sleep. His eyes are dark, and I've learned that that means Judah's got something on his mind. When he stands up again, Judah puts his hand around the back of my neck but he doesn't look at me. I start pushing the stroller along the path but the front wheel's all messed up, and I can't make the stroller go straight. Judah sees me struggling and suggests we just sit for a while on a shady bench.

Without looking at me Judah says, "I never knew my father. But if I ever have a kid, I'm gonna *be* there, no matter what."

The leaves overhead shield us from the sun, but there is heat coming from Judah. His body is pressed close to mine, and I can feel anger in the tightness of his arm and leg. I can see his hurt even though Judah keeps his face turned away. I have told Judah what I know about Papi, but he has never mentioned his father before.

Judah changes the subject suddenly. His muscles relax, but his eyes stay hard. "Cops swept Franklin again last night. You hear the guns going off? Pop pop pop." Judah makes a gun out of his hand and aims it at the innocent robins hopping around looking for worms. "Sometimes those helicopters feel like they're right outside my bedroom. It feels like they're coming for *me*."

Since we live down on the first floor, the police helicopters sound real far away and that's if we hear them at all. But I know what Judah means. He means they treat us like we're *all* guilty, all the time. I remember the look Rico gave me before he crawled into that van, and I know it could have been Judah lying face down on the ground, and one day it could be Tyjuan.

"We got to get away from this place, Gen." Judah shakes his head and whistles softly. "*Babylon*."

I look around us at all the green, growing things. I breathe in the scent of lilacs and early roses. I see the dragonflies zooming over the grass, and I hear the birds calling to each other. It is hard to believe there is so much life, *so much life* here inside the garden. Here, in the city, in the heart of Brooklyn, with the ghetto waiting just outside the gates. In biology class we learned that the heart has chambers. Inside mine is a room full of flowers and trees and dragonflies and roses. I look at Tyjuan sleeping peacefully in his stroller, and I take Judah's hand and say, "This isn't Babylon. This is heaven."

Judah turns to me and smiles that small smile. He looks like he wants to believe what I am saying, but a voice louder and wiser than mine says it just isn't true. Judah squeezes my hand. "C'mon, I want to show you something."

Judah gets behind the stroller, and his strong arms force it to go straight. We walk toward the Japanese pond, and Judah starts talking about tranquillity and serenity, harmony and balance, and how the Japanese design their gardens so you get a perfect view from every angle. Judah studies jujitsu, so he's really into all this Asian stuff, but whenever he starts talking about Zen, I start to tune out. "What's Japan got to do with you and me?" is what I want to ask him. But instead I nod and try to act like I'm into the things he's talking about.

Right now I'm mostly listening to Judah, but part of me is looking at the turtles as they bob their heads above the murky green water. Part of me is looking for the great white egret that sometimes stands near the shore, his long rubberband neck ready to snap forward and snatch a fish out of the water. Part of me is still thinking about that room in my heart that only special people like Judah can enter, so I'm not really ready when Judah stops pushing the stroller and asks me a question.

"You know what a haiku is, Genna?" Judah presses a small piece of paper into my palm and walks on ahead with Tyjuan. I trail behind, wanting to be alone. I stop in front of the purple irises growing next to the pond and open Judah's note. At first I feel disappointed 'cause there are only a few words written inside. But then I read them and my eyes fill up with water and my heart aches with that sweet kind of pain, and I wonder if I'm always going to feel this way whenever someone does something nice for me. Inside the note is a poem. Judah has given me these words:

> my love is the sun
> and you are a blue lotus
> turning toward me

Later Judah explains that a haiku is a Japanese poem that has to have a certain number of syllables on each line. Five-seven-five. I count them over and over and read that poem again and again until I don't need the paper anymore because the words are printed on my mind. I see them when I close my eyes at night, I see them when I'm trying to study at the library, I see them when I'm staring into space and thinking about Judah instead of concentrating during class.

One day on my way home from babysitting at Hannah's, I stop at the garden and go straight to the lotus pool. I look at the big flat lily pads that float on top of the black water, and I check the color of every lotus I see. Lots are different shades of pink, but there are yellow and white and purple ones, too. I don't see any that are blue. A woman dressed all in green is on her knees, pulling weeds out of the flowerbed. Since she works at the garden, I go over and ask her if she's ever seen a blue lotus. She says, "Sure, the Blue Goddess is farther down. It's tropical, though, so it blooms later than all the others." She takes off her glove and points to a closed green fist that is rising out of the dark water.

I thank her and leave the garden smiling, whispering Judah's poem to the sky:

> my love is the sun
> and you are a blue lotus
> turning toward me

16.

The moment I walk through the door, Mama starts up with me.

"And YOU! Don't think I don't know what *you've* been up to. The two of you make me *sick*. Is this what I've been working my ass off for all these years? To have all three of my children throw their lives right back in the gutter?"

Mama glares at me, and maybe she sees the confusion in my face, or maybe she sees Tyjuan sleeping in my arms. Either way, her angry voice drops to a low rumble. She turns her back to me but keeps on muttering while she scrubs at the grime caked onto the wall behind the stove. I stand in the doorway for a second, wondering if Mama found out about me babysitting for Hannah. What else could I have done? I decide I'd better put Tyjuan to bed, then come back and figure out what's going on.

The light is on in Mama's bedroom but the door is mostly closed. I push it open with my hip and then jump back as Toshi dumps an armful of clothes onto the bed. She heads back to the closet, then stops and spins around. Toshi's got a real evil look on her face, and she spits her words at me.

"You better not touch none of my shit while I'm gone."

"Gone? Where you going?" I avoid Toshi's clothes and find a spot for Tyjuan near the top of the bed. Then I turn around to face my sister. Her face looks hot and flushed, and she's sucking in her lip the way she does when she's trying not to cry. I'm starting to piece it all together. I'm guessing there must have been a fight, Toshi sassed Mama and got hit. But Mama said she's sick of the *both* of us, and I need to know what that means. So I ask, "What happened, Toshi? What's going on?"

Toshi stops shoving clothes in her bag and leans in close to me. She lowers her voice so Mama can't hear, but she doesn't whisper, she hisses instead. "Don't act like you don't know. *Bitch*. You think I don't know you the one been telling Mama 'bout me and Troy?"

Right about now I'm so confused I don't know what to do. Toshi's always got all kinds of boys sniffing around her, but I don't know any particular one named Troy. Part of me thinks I should leave Toshi alone and go ask Mama for the truth. But part of me doesn't trust Mama right now, and if my sister's leaving home, I need to know why.

"Who's Troy?" I ask with a real serious face so she knows I'm not trying to front.

Toshi squints up her eyes and watches me for a minute. "You really don't know, huh. 'Course not, you don't know shit. You never did know shit, Genna. You always thought you was better than everybody else 'cause you get them grades in school. Well As and Bs don't mean nothing in the real world, and one day you're gonna find out."

Toshi grabs a handful of panties out the drawer and crams them into her duffel bag. Then she tries to zip it up, but the zipper won't go. I reach over and pull both ends of the bag so the zipper goes in a straight line. Toshi takes my help but doesn't say thanks. She just slings the bag over her shoulder and looks around the room. Her eyes rest on Tyjuan for a second, and I think maybe she's going to go over and kiss him goodbye. Instead she looks at me like she feels sorry for me. Or maybe like she wishes I was coming, too.

I ask her one more time. "Where you going, Toshi?"

All the softness goes out of her eyes. "Never mind where I'm going," she snaps. "I'm getting the hell out of here. And if you got any real sense, you'll get out of here, too. Mama done lost her mind."

17.

I follow Toshi out of the bedroom and over to the front door. She turns the top lock and it snaps real loud. Before she can undo the bottom lock, Mama comes into the hall.

"You walk out that door, young lady, don't think about coming back. If you're too grown to live by my rules, then you best find yourself someplace else to stay—permanently. I've worked too damn hard to keep a roof over your head. I won't be defied or disrespected in my own home. You think you know what you want, but you *don't* know what you need. *I* know that, 'cause I'm your mother. I know you, and this world I brought you into. It ain't perfect, I ain't perfect, and neither are you. But *I* make the rules in this household, Toshi, and if you can't follow them, you best change your address."

Toshi's eyes are glistening with tears, but she's shaking her head too softly for them to fall. "I hate you" is all she whispers.

Mama doesn't say another word. She just turns around, takes up her sponge, and goes back to scrubbing the kitchen wall.

Inside, my heart is beating fast. I want to reach out and touch my sister, I want to tell her to stay. Toshi's been nothing but evil to me all these years, but I don't want her to leave me here alone. Bit by bit I've watched my family fall apart. People walk out that door and they never come back. First Papi, then Abuela, then

Rico, now Toshi. My lips fall apart but my throat's almost closed. "Toshi, *please*—"

My sister looks into my face and sucks in her bottom lip so she won't cry. "You need me, leave a message with Peeter. She'll know how to find me." Then Toshi flips the bottom lock, swings open the door, and walks out of the apartment.

I stand there for a moment, my forehead almost touching the closed door. I hear the click of Toshi's shoes as she walks down the short hall, goes down the three steps, and then crosses the wide foyer. I wonder if she is heading for Troy. I wonder when I'm going to see my sister again.

Finally, I turn away from the door. I leave both locks open in case Toshi changes her mind, even though I know she won't. I keep my eyes out of the kitchen. I can't stand to look at my mother right now. But Mama won't let me just walk on by. She stops scrubbing, puts her hand on her hip, and stares sternly at me.

"Don't you go anywhere, young lady. I need to have a word with you, too." Mama nods at the kitchen table. I shuffle over and sink into one of the chairs.

"I never would've thought it would come to this, Genna. I didn't expect this—not from you."

I look up at Mama but her face is so hard I have to look away. She looks like she doesn't even care about Toshi. I wonder if she cares about me.

"You been spending a lot of time outside this house, Genna. Where you been?"

I listen to the sureness in Mama's voice and try to figure out what she knows. She's trying to catch me in a lie. I tell her half of the truth. "I been at the library. I stop at the garden sometimes."

Mama and I eye each other. Neither of us wants to play games. I look past Mama to the clean white oval she has scrubbed off the greasy wall. It looks just like a hole, a hole that has swallowed up Toshi. A hole that is waiting for me.

Mama tosses the filthy sponge into the sink and folds her arms across her chest. "Mrs. Charles tells me she's seen you with some boy—a Rasta, some pot-smoking fool."

I press my lips together to keep my anger inside. Prickles of electricity are running up my spine. I want to stand up and walk out of the kitchen, but I sit and glare at Mama instead.

"So it's true, then. Have you lost your mind? How many times do I have to remind you about your priorities, Genna?"

"I don't need you to remind me about anything, Mama." My voice is cool and hard. "I know what my priorities are."

Mama leans back against the counter and watches me. I'm thinking maybe she's going to let it rest. And I hope she does, 'cause otherwise it's going to get ugly. I won't let her talk about Judah that way. He's mine, and I have to protect him. I got a snake coiled in my belly, and if Mama pushes me, I'm going to let it out.

Mama takes a deep breath. She talks softly this time. "You know I got plans for you, Genna. You know that you're my best bet."

"I got my own plans, Mama. It's *my* life. I got my own plans."

Mama sighs and starts nodding her head. "You're right, it is your life, Genna. I just don't want to see you mess it up. Your sister, she's always been too headstrong. Too fast—her body matured before her mind could catch up. But you're not like that, Genna. You've always been smart, different than the others—"

"Then why are you grilling me, Mama? Why can't you trust me? You listen to other people, you believe what they say. Why can't you believe *me*?"

"I want to, baby. I really do." Mama sighs again, and I think maybe it's over. Mama looks tired, like she's ready to surrender. "So tell me about this boy," she says.

I keep my mouth shut and look at the hole on the wall. I don't want to talk about Judah. But then I think about all the things Mama's probably heard from Mrs. Charles. I decide to set the record straight.

"His name's Judah. He's from Jamaica. And he's not a fool, he's really smart. He's in my English class, and he writes poetry. I like him a lot …" I stop there because I can't think of anything else to say. Mama doesn't look like she's listening, anyway. Her eyes are glued to the wall above my head.

When she finally pulls her eyes away, they look real dark and sad. "You're so young, Genna. You don't know what the world is like."

I feel Mama trying to wrap her words around me, I feel her trying to keep me close. But I am not a child anymore, and Mama's got to understand. So I say, "Yes I do, Mama. I *live* in this world. I live in this building. I see all the messed-up stuff that goes down. But I'm not a part of that, Mama. And neither is Judah. We're looking for a way out. We're going to help each other find a way out."

Mama looks at the floor. She's still trying to hold onto me, but she knows I'm slipping away. "I don't want you hanging around people who do drugs."

I stop a minute and think about what I really want to say. I feel the snake in my belly start moving. I say, "Rico does drugs, Mama."

This is the wrong thing to say, and I know it. Mama's head tips up and her eyes flash danger at me. "Don't you say that about your brother."

"Why not? It's true. He used to hang out in the stairwell smoking weed, and then he started working for Mona, so he was selling it, too, and who knows what else. Rico didn't get *set up*, Mama. He got *caught*."

Mama takes two quick steps across the kitchen floor, but I'm faster and already on my feet. Mama's eyes only reach my chin. She puts her face real close to mine.

"Take it back."

I look down at my mother and feel the snake slithering inside. Why does she have to protect him? Why can't she see that it's true?

Mama clutches my arm and says it louder this time. "TAKE—IT—BACK!"

I know I'm heading for trouble, but somehow I can't slow down. "Why won't you believe it, Mama? You believe the worst about me and Judah. You throw Toshi out like she's some kind of trash. You're so caught up saving Rico, you can't even see how worthless he is—"

Even though I am looking right at my mother, I don't see her hand flying at me. She slaps me hard, right across the face. The only reason I don't fall down is 'cause Mama's gripping my arm.

I don't say a thing. Mama has knocked all the words out of my mouth. She shakes me, but still I say nothing. Then Mama grabs my other arm and shakes me even harder. And that's when I realize that I am stronger than my mother. I realize I am no longer a child. With all my strength I wrench myself free and shove Mama away from me. She slams into the counter. A strange, awful sound comes from inside of her.

I feel like the last piece of my family has just broken in half. I feel like Mama's to blame. "I hate you," I whisper, just like Toshi. Then I walk out the unlocked door.

18.

I take a minute out in the hallway to pull myself together. The right side of my face is tingling, but I don't think anyone can tell I got hit. I can hear Mama crying on the other side of the door. Part of me wants to go back inside and tell her everything's going to be alright. But another part of me is stinging, and I need someone to put their arms around *me* and tell *me* it's going to be alright. I take a deep breath and walk across the foyer. I stop again, take an even deeper breath and push my way out the door, through all the Negroes standing out front. I hold my head up but keep my eyes on the ground. I watch the sidewalk until there's no one around, then I lift my eyes up and blink at the moon. Everything's blurry 'cause I got tears in my eyes. My face is burning and my lips feel like rubber, they keep bouncing apart, and I just want to disappear inside Judah's arms, but Judah isn't home. I go straight to his building, but nobody answers the buzzer, and an old lady sitting by the first-floor window tells me the whole family went out.

"They had those drums and things with 'em," she adds as I'm walking away.

I thank her and wonder if maybe Judah's drumming in the park. It wouldn't take long to walk over there, but I don't want to show up looking all pitiful, like a dog that's been chased away from its home. And that's just how I feel right now.

So instead I keep on walking. I walk down the blocks, over, and back up again until I reach the garden. It's late, but the Palm House is lit up and there's music coming out into the street. I stand on the sidewalk and look up at the tiny white lights that go all the way up to the top of the glass dome. I decide to get a little bit closer, even though this brings me closer to my building. I know I'm not going back there tonight. But that means I need someplace else to go.

People in fancy clothes are standing around, smoking ciga-rettes and laughing kind of sloppy, like they've had a little too much champagne. The good thing is, these folks are black. If it was a white wedding, I'd never get in, but I'm dressed alright, and I look kind of grown. So I go up the steps real casual like to see who's work-ing behind the desk. It's Samuel, Judah's cousin. He recognizes me right away and starts to say hey when the phone on his desk rings. Samuel picks it up, and someone on the other end starts shouting at him. I step back from the desk and try to keep out of the way. A group of loud, tipsy wedding guests pushes past me, and Samuel is trying to talk to whoever's on the phone when his walkie-talkie goes off. A big man in a tuxedo staggers into the lobby, his cummer-bund and bow tie undone. "Where's the toilet? I gotta take a piss." The other wedding guests laugh, then groan in disgust as the man unzips his pants and stands in front of a big potted plant. I glance over at Samuel, who has started shouting into the phone. "Lady, I can't help you right now. The garden's closed. I can't help you right now, you gotta call back on Tuesday. Not Monday, we're not open on Mondays—yo, man, *what are you doing!?*"

I see my chance and take it. I walk through the open glass doors and out onto the terrace. A security guard is standing by the lotus pool, but he's holding his walkie-talkie up to his mouth and he just pushes past me and heads straight for the lobby. I can see more security guards farther down the terrace, their white shirts and gold badges glowing in the dark. More wedding guests are standing in clusters around the lotus pool. The bass from the stereo system throbs through the glass conservatory, the tiny white lights flash like diamonds against the black surface of the lily pool. A breeze ruffles the sheer hems of elegantly dressed women. I would look too out of place if I tried to mingle with this crowd. I look over my shoulder once, real quick, then dart up the steps and into the shade of the magnolia trees.

I've never been in the garden at night, but I know these paths like the back of my hand. I could walk them with my eyes closed and not miss a turn, but right now my eyes are open wide. There are shadows everywhere—hanging above me, shifting beside me. Black shadows are pooled like water on the ground. I tell myself these are only bushes and trees—green leafy things that look so innocent during the day. But now it is nighttime, and despite the nearly full moon shining overhead, the garden feels sinister and strange. A wave of laughter suddenly ripples up from the terrace, and I decide I'd better leave the visitor center behind. I turn left, and the glowing white triangles of the giant compass tell me I am heading west.

I pass the weeping hemlock, and for a moment I consider hiding beneath its drooping canopy. But I haven't come to the garden to hide. I need to be someplace quiet, someplace safe. The garden is a refuge for birds and other animals that have no place else to go. Tonight I am like a wounded bird. I just need someplace to rest.

The whir of an engine makes my feet pick up speed. Security is focused mostly on the party by the terrace, but I need to be careful just the same. I don't know what they'd do to me if I got caught, and I don't plan to find out. I swim through the shadows without making a sound.

I reach the cherry esplanade, and the long, open field glows as though it's covered in frost. The moon is so bright that I squint up my eyes and search for the safety of shadows. I decide to cut through the rose garden, and when the scent of rotting petals reaches my nose, I realize why I am here. I walk quickly, no longer unsure of my destination. I know where I am going. Some part of me must have known this was where I needed to be. Like the instinct Mr. Christiansen told me about that tells birds how to find their way home.

I pass through the white wooden gate of the rose garden and climb the steps that lead to the fountain. It waits for me in the moonlight, its water murmuring softly. Beyond the fountain and past the long stretch of grass, I can hear the faint sound of engines and horns as cars race along the parkway outside the garden gates. A rabbit bounding across the pale field stops and stares at me, its nose twitching nervously. But I am like a statue frozen beside the fountain, and within seconds the rabbit disappears.

It is only after I have spent several minutes staring at the silvery surface of the water that I realize I have no coins. I fish deep into the pockets of my jeans, but my nails dig up only lint. I stare at the water again. The fountain is like a round mirror held up to the night sky. I step closer and peer into the water, hoping yet fearing to see my own reflection. Before I can catch a glimpse of myself, a cool breeze ripples the water and the liquid mirror loses its image. I feel like I must be invisible, and my eyes start to well up. I tell myself it is only the wind, but the tears are falling freely and my cheek is still stinging and it feels like Mama hit me all over again. I stumble over to the whispering bench. I cry as softly as I can, even though I am alone.

My tears empty out of me, but the hurt doesn't go away. I sit on the curved bench and think of all the wishes I have made at this fountain. I'm still waiting for them to come true. I remember the first time Judah kissed me, and the salty tears make my lips burn. I wish Judah were here beside me, or down at the other end of the bench. I wish he were here to tell me everything's going to be alright. His words would slide around the bench in a whisper, just like they did that time before when Judah told me I was different. I am different. When Judah said it, he meant it in a good kind of way. But right now I don't feel special. All I feel is lost and alone.

After a while, the tears stop falling and I lean back against the hard stone bench. I wonder if Tyjuan's still asleep in the bed, or if Mama woke him up just so she'd have something to hold. Tyjuan is all she has left. And what do I have? Nothing—not even a penny to waste on another worthless wish. I look over at the fountain and consider scooping coins out of the water. But that doesn't seem right somehow, stealing other folks' wishes. It would be like robbing a grave, disturbing the dead. I lean forward and search my back pockets for change but find a scrap of paper instead. The words are faded and the light is dim, but I have no problem reading Judah's haiku. The words echo and swirl around me. Five-seven-five. The poem is short, yet when I finish reading, the whispering goes on. *Please don't leave me take me with you don't look back stay with me hold my hand I'm frightened don't let go they're coming run …*

Startled, I stand and look around, worried that I am not alone after all. In the distance, another rabbit stops halfway across the field. He rises up on his haunches, sniffs the air suspiciously, then continues on his way. I want to trust the rabbit, but my own instinct tells me something is wrong. I look along the bench, but it is empty. I check the shadows nearby but find only leaves shifting in the breeze.

Cautiously, I return to the bench. I perch on its edge like a bird ready to take flight. There is only silence around me. I turn and check the bushes behind me, then ease further onto the bench. Despite the hard stone, my tired body relaxes. I close my eyes and try once again to conjure Judah. I picture him sitting across from me at the other end of the bench, his full lips broken apart in a smile, his teeth shining like pearls. Then the voices return. *Don't trust anyone look for the signs sleep during the day run at night don't look back help others if you can but help yourself first I'll meet you there I'll find you I will I promise just don't look back …*

Despite the warning, I do look back. I turn and look over my shoulder, and what I see there shocks me so much that I scream.

Something strong and sudden like a jolt of electricity hurls me from the bench. I fall on the hard, flat stones that circle the fountain, too stunned to feel any pain. I clamp my hand over my mouth to keep from screaming again.

On the bench, in the exact spot where I was sitting just a moment ago, is a child. Though the bench is smothered in shadows, this little boy is glowing like a statue of ice. He watches me with his dark, frightened eyes, and then he whispers, *Don't leave me ...*

The air in the garden chills suddenly. I shiver as fear and a cold wind raise the hairs on the back of my neck. My eyes are fixed on the ghostly boy, but another voice pulls my gaze away. A silver-white woman emerges from the black shadows beneath the wisteria. She has a shawl wrapped around her shoulders and a long skirt that touches the ground. She whispers, *Don't tell*, and takes a step toward me. Terror chokes the scream that is rising in my throat. For we are no longer alone. The terrace around the fountain is crowded with children, women, and men. The shimmering ghosts all wear clothes that come from another time. All glisten in the moonlight just like silver coins under water. All plead with me to stay, to go, to help them, to take care. They move silently across the cold, flat stones. *Please ... please ... please ...*

The ghosts look desperate but not unkind. I try hard to swallow my fear. Questions whirl inside my mind—*Where did you come from? Why are you here? What do you want from me?* But before I can utter a single word, a nearby tree starts to shake violently and a swarm of starlings descends without warning. I cover my head with my arm and stay close to the ground. In the chaos of flapping wings and frantic cries, the cluster of ghosts disintegrates and the silvery figures disappear.

Silence and shadows surround me. I pull myself up from the ground and try to think of an explanation for what I have just seen. I quickly scan the garden for traces of silver, but instead a flash of red catches my eye. Something small is lying on the ground a few feet away from the fountain. It glints in the moonlight and I move toward it, but a cloud covers the moon and I have to fumble for it in the dark. My fingers feel only the cold, hard stone, and so I stop, stand back, and wait for the moon to return. The cloud doesn't budge, but then I see it shining again—what else could it be besides a penny? A worthless coin someone dropped and never bothered to pick up. I reach for it again, but once again it disappears in a darkness that wasn't there just a moment ago. Now I am determined. I can feel a wish trembling on my lips.

The moon slides out of the clouds like a hand pulled from a glove. The penny glows and then dies like a fiery spark. I reach for it, and this time I feel it beneath my fingertips. Though it is strangely hot, I pick it up, then move closer to the fountain, into the light of the moon. The penny cools in my palm. It grows dull and old even though it was flashing like a new coin just a minute ago. I stare at the penny and the longer I stare, the less certain I feel that my wish will ever come true. I close my hand into a fist and squeeze the round, hard piece of copper. I want to hurl it into the still water, but it weighs in my hand like a rock. The longer I hold it, the heavier it becomes, and I have to struggle to raise my hand up to my shoulder. For a moment I stand frozen, the penny in my hand, my hand poised beside my head. The fountain blurs, and I blink back my tears. Then with all the strength I can muster, I throw the penny up into the air.

Everything happens at once.

The penny cuts through the air in a slow, silent arc. I hear a motor humming behind me and I know security has found me at last. I am ready to run, but I have to wait until the penny hits the water. Headlights slice through the darkness and shine bright in my eyes. The penny is still falling, the air is thick and cool like gel. Then the voices return. Voices, too many voices, and they are not whispering softly any more, they are telling me to RUN, they are telling me to HIDE, they are ordering me to FREEZE. This time the voices come with hands that tug at every inch of my body. TAKE ME WITH YOU WAIT FOR ME DON'T LOOK BACK JUST RUN RUN RUN. My heart is pounding and the penny is still falling and I'm begging them to let me stay just until my wish hits the water. I am blinded by the headlights and the voices keep getting louder and the penny is still falling and then one sound rises above all the others—a single shot is fired and my body sinks to the ground. The last thing I hear is a tiny splash as my penny slips beneath the silvery surface of the water.

PART II

1.

I am alive.

But it hurts to breathe. Every inch of my body is screaming with pain—I feel it, and this is how I know I am alive. I want to cry, but my eyes are so dry they burn. Fine dust covers my lips, lines my throat and lungs, and clings to the rims of my eyes. I blink and try to swallow, but my mouth feels like an empty well. I can feel the ground beneath me. Through the dust I can feel its solid warmth pressing against my body. The air around me is smoky. The air is smoky and the ground is warm and bits of ash are falling from the sky. *There must have been a fire.* I close my eyes and imagine flames devouring the garden—the hundred-year-old trees, the lilacs, the roses. With my mind's eye I see the fountain licked dry, the coins at its bottom scorched by fire. I think of all the birds left homeless, without a refuge in the city. I blink and this time tears wet the dust powdering my eyes. I cannot tell if my body is burnt. I try to reach up and touch my face but I don't know where my arm is, and it will not move. I try to lift my head to see the damage around me, but my body will not respond. I lie still. The ground beneath me is still warm, but the air above me is cold, and the damp in my clothes makes me shiver. I cough and it feels as though every bone in my body is broken. I close my eyes and remember that building in Oklahoma. *A bomb?* The idea forces my eyes open, and I try again to lift my head. I can see nothing through the haze of smoke, but in my mind I see shattered glass and concrete rubble, wires hanging out like guts, and babies being carried away covered in blood and dust. My heart thuds against the ground as I think of Tyjuan, of Mama and Judah, our building, our home. I take a deep breath and dust fills my lungs. I choke, cough, try again.

help

The word is a red siren blaring inside my head, but barely a whisper passes through my lips. Another try. Another lungful of dust and smoke. Another coughing fit. The sky crushes my body into the warm bed of earth. I am too weak to resist. The agony of not knowing is too much to fight against. I sob quietly, close my eyes, and let my body sink into the dust.

The sound of a man's voice somewhere above me makes me open my eyes.

"It's a wench—a nigger wench!"

That one word makes me want to stand up and fight, but right now I can barely move. I lie there on the smoldering ground and wait for the face to appear, the face that goes with the mouth that just spat that word at me.

"Charlie—come take a look at this!" His boot knocks against my shattered ribs, and the dust muffles my groan. "She must be hurt or somethin'. I'll betcha she's a runaway! Think there might be a reward?"

A second, heavier white man approaches. The ground shakes with each step he takes. "Only one way to find out. Put 'er in the wagon 'n let's take 'er to Captain Gaines. He'll know what she's worth."

"Well, gimme a hand here, Charlie. She's a big gal. I can't lift 'er on my own."

Charlie mutters something under his breath, then I feel his

hands digging into me and the two white men toss me up onto some hard wooden boards.

"Goddamn, niggers sure do stink. Why they all gotta smell so bad?"

"'Course they stink, stupid. What barn animal you know of that don't stink? Now get up here 'fore I leave you behind and claim that reward myself."

The wagon slowly eases forward, and for the first time I am able to see the sky. What I thought before were bits of ash are actually flakes of snow. *Snow.* It falls gently from a gray, sullen sky, brushing against my skin like cold feathers. *Snow.* What about the fire? What about the garden? The roses, the lilacs—how could there be *snow*?

Tin cans rattle beside me, and I can hear the two men talking up front. I learn that the smaller man is called Lester. A whiff of liquor drifts my way each time he opens his mouth. "Ain't no rush, really. She's bad off, but she ain't gonna die. We could pull over, have a little fun with 'er. Then take 'er to the precinct 'n claim our reward."

Charlie says nothing for a moment. Then I hear him smack his lips, and another draft of whiskey blows over me. "Ain't you the one said you can't stand niggers 'cause they stink? Sounds like you ain't too partic'lar after all." Both men laugh at the crude joke. I lie quiet in the back of the wagon, trying to will my limbs back to life. If they do try to start something with me, I won't be able to fight back. I close my eyes against the falling snow and pray they will leave me alone.

Charlie takes another swig from the bottle. "Soon as we get that reward, we'll go visit the gals at Sally's place. I ain't too picky when it comes to color, but at least those gals got soap!"

Lester laughs loud and long. Charlie swells with the liquor and the attention and starts listing all the things he's going to do with his share of the reward money. I listen and try to understand why my broken body is worth any kind of reward. How long had I been lying on the ground? Hours? Days? Maybe Mama had called the police and reported me missing. That had to be it. But who were these men? They didn't talk like they were from New York. They talked like a couple of country bumpkins. Maybe I wasn't in New York anymore. Maybe we were out in the country somewhere. Why else would they be driving a wagon?

I turn these questions over in my mind as the wagon rolls along the bumpy road. My bones rattle like the empty tin cans around me. I listen for a while longer, but it doesn't seem like Charlie and Lester are going to mess with me. I close my eyes and drift into a wakeful sleep.

After what feels like a long time, the wagon comes to an abrupt stop. From where I am lying, I can see a brick building. It has no bars in the windows, but over the arched doorway are words carved in stone: Police Precinct. White people move along the sidewalk in order to stay out of the street, which is full of wagons, carriages, and piles of reeking horseshit.

"Should we bring 'er in?" Lester asks.

Charlie heaves himself off the wagon and it rocks unsteadily. "Naw, leave 'er there. I'll get the captain to come and take a look. If he don't want 'er, I know a feller who'll take 'er off our hands for cash."

Lester leers at me over his shoulder. I want to sit up and look around, but my limbs still feel like lead. With a great deal of effort, I manage to lift my head up for a few seconds—just long enough to catch the eye of a black man who is leaning against a nearby lamppost. My head slams back against the boards, but a prickly current of hope electrifies my limbs. A black man. *A black man.* He won't let them hurt me—will he?

A door opens and I hear Charlie's heavy step lumbering across the paving stones. The police captain is beside him. A long row of brass buttons runs down the length of his navy blue coat. The butt of a cigar is stuck in one corner of his mouth. A sheet of paper held in one of his hands is flapping in the breeze.

"Well, let's see what we got here. Sure looks like a runaway—shoes worn down, clothes tore up." The captain peers at me over the edge of the wagon. "Phew! Sure smells like a runaway." Charlie and Lester laugh and ask how much I am worth. The captain holds up the piece of paper and squints at it for a moment. "Hold on now, boys. I only got one notice 'bout a female fugitive, and this don't sound like her. 'Wanted: Negress, twenty-nine years of age, answers to the name of Betty. Has a large birthmark on her left shoulder and a missing tooth in the front.' This gal looks too young to be our Betty. Either o' y'all check her teeth?"

Just as Lester reaches for my mouth, the black man I saw earlier coughs loudly and comes over to the wagon. I can see him clearly now. He is an older man judging from the threads of gray in his hair and beard. Before speaking, he pulls off his hat, clears his throat, and nods solemnly at me.

"'Scuse me, Cap'n, I needs to have a word with you."

The captain doesn't even bother to turn around. "Not now, Sam, can't you see I'm busy?"

"Yessuh, Cap'n, suh, I can see you's busy, suh. It's jus' 'bout that gal there, suh."

This time the captain turns and gives the black man his attention. "Well, what about her?"

"Cap'n, suh, I knows that gal. She ain't no runaway."

Charlie pushes past the captain and tries to use his massive weight to intimidate the meek old man. "What you say, boy?"

The man named Sam lowers his eyes and continues to address the police captain with the utmost respect. "I said I knows her, Cap'n, suh."

"Get down here, Sam. You sure you know this gal?"

The black man carefully steps around Charlie and eases himself down the stairs. He pretends to inspect me for a moment and then turns back to the captain. "Yessuh. I knows for certain that there is Reverend Macklin's niece. She been visitin' them for the holidays. Reverend Macklin gon' be real upset when he see what been done to his niece."

"Done? We ain't done nothin' but brought 'er in here, prob'ly saved the gal's life. Captain, you gon' stand there and let this ol' nigger talk to us like that?"

"He ain't talkin' to you, Lester, so just shut your trap and let me do my job. Now look here, Sam. These two gentlemen say she was like this when they found her."

"That's right, she was layin' out there in the ash dump wearin' just what she got on—woulda froze to death we hadn't a come along," Lester adds sulkily.

The old black man nods his head and twists his cap in his hands, keeping his eyes on the ground while he speaks. "I'm sure Reverend Macklin be real grateful to both these gen'l'men soon as he find out. I best take her over there straightaway."

Charlie folds his arms across his sizable belly. "Well, *I* say she's a runaway. Any fool can see this gal's been runnin'. She may not be the wench they lookin' for on that piece o' paper, but that don't mean she can just go free. You ain't gon' take the word o' this nigger over the word of a white man, are you, Captain?" The tone of Charlie's question makes it seem more like a taunt, and the police captain rises to the challenge.

"You got anybody white who can vouch for this gal, Sam?"

Like an actor in a play, Sam rolls his lips together and scratches his gray head to make it look like he's thinking real hard. His performance almost makes me want to laugh, but the white men take him very seriously. "Yessuh, Cap'n, suh. Mr. Harrington—he know Reverend Macklin. I'll go get him straightaway, Cap'n, suh."

"Harrington!" Charlie bellows. "That nigger-lovin' lawyer?"

"Yessuh, that's the one. You wait here, Cap'n, I'll go fetch 'im and bring 'im back." Sam acts like he's anxious to leave, but the police captain grabs his arm.

"Not so fast, Sam. I don't want no trouble 'round here. I know what you're thinking—you'll go get one and come back with twenty. Tomorrow's Christmas, and we don't need no crazy abolitionists starting a riot over some runaway."

Sam feigns innocence and repeats in his childlike way, "But I told you already, Cap'n, that gal ain't no runaway. She Reverend Macklin's niece."

The police captain chomps on his cigar and searches both our faces for signs of a conspiracy. "You swear on it, Sam? You telling me the truth?"

"Bring the Good Book, Cap'n, 'n I'll swear to it right now. That gal ain't no runaway."

The captain eyes the old man carefully, then grunts and spits several inches from the wagon. "I guess you better get her back to her folks then. And you best be telling me the truth, Sam Jenkins. 'Cause if I find out that gal got a price on her head, I'm a come and get the both of you and sell you to the highest bidder. That clear?"

Sam nods and keeps his eyes on the police captain's boots. "Yessuh, Cap'n. Thank you, suh, and thanks to these here gen'l'men what brought 'er in. I'm sure Reverend Macklin be real grateful, real grateful indeed."

The captain saunters back over to the sidewalk and leans lazily against the lamppost as Sam struggles to get me into his wagon, which is parked nearby. When we're about ready to leave, he plucks the cigar stub from his mouth and says, "Reverend's wife's pretty handy with pies and such, if I 'member correctly. You tell her apple pie'd go real nice with my Christmas dinner." The police captain chuckles to himself, spits again, and then heads back inside the jailhouse. Charlie and Lester follow him, still loudly complaining about their lost reward.

Though now he really is anxious to leave, Sam takes a moment to make sure I'm comfortable. He eases a small sack of flour under my head and tucks a woolen blanket around my body. The pain is changing, it is draining out of my limbs and concentrating in my center. It feels like barbed wire is wrapped around my spine. I bite down on my lip so I won't cry out. Sam watches me with concern. "That's alright, missy, we be home soon. Sam gon' take care of you now, so don't you worry 'bout a thing. You safe now," he whispers. "You safe with ol' Sam." Then he takes off his glove and gently touches my cheek. My grateful tears spill over his fingers, but he just smiles softly and brushes them away. "I'm gon' take you home now. You jus' hold tight. We be home soon."

2.

"A pie? What you need a pie for?"

Sam stands in the doorway of the kitchen, hat in hand, and tells the cook his story. She listens to him with both hands on her hips and disapproval stamped all over her face.

"They was blackbirders you say?"

"Naw, they looked like reg'lar white trash to me—just sniffin' 'round the ash dump. Said they found 'er over there and brung her to the precinct lookin' for a reward. They'd a turned 'er over to slave catchers, though, if I hadn't piped up."

"That's you alright—always pipin' up."

Sam sighs and tries not to lose his patience with the woman. "Well, I had to tell 'em somethin', so I said she was Reverend Macklin's niece."

"Sam Jenkins, have you lost your mind? Cap'n Gaines ain't the sharpest tool in the shed, but he sure 'nough knows how to ask a simple question. What you gon' do when he asks the Reverend 'bout his so-called niece?"

"I ain't gon' do nothin'," Sam replies testily.

"That's right," Esther shoots back, "you done done too much already. So where is she?"

"Out back, in the wagon. I'm gon' need a couple o' boys to help me bring 'er in."

Esther sticks her head out in the hallway and calls for Willis and Jake. Two tall youths come into the kitchen, listen to Esther's instructions, and then head out the back door. Sam starts to follow them, then turns and looks at Esther. "You best start boilin' some water, gather up some clean rags. There's blood."

Esther nods wordlessly, and begins preparing the back room for the newest arrival at the Howard Orphanage in Weeksville, Brooklyn.

I can no longer hide my pain. The boys try to be gentle as they ease me out of the wagon, but their hands dig into my body like forks. Through my tears I can see Sam's familiar face. He is trying to comfort me, but his words open and close like the wings of butterflies. Everywhere around me I see yellow butterflies. I reach for them, and for a little while the pain disappears. The butterflies float around the room. I try to gather them in my arms, but one by one they drift into the fire that is burning in the corner. I, too, am drawn by the light, by the warmth of the orange flames. I can smell their wings being singed by the fire. I reach in and try to pluck the butterflies from the flames. My fingers catch fire, then my wrists, my forearms, and my elbows. By the time the fire reaches my shoulders, I cannot control my screams. The butterflies are dying and I can't save them. I can't save them and I can't save myself . . .

Esther tears an old pillowcase into strips. She pats her apron pocket to make sure the scissors are still there, then pulls in a deep breath and takes hold of the situation.

"Willis, go find Miss Holme and tell her come quick. Jake, put a coat on and go get Dr. Brant. Tell him it's an emergency. Sam Jenkins, don't you dare sneak outta here. I'm gon' need you to help me. We got to tie her down. Fever's got her actin' out of her mind, and I'm gon' have to cut this dress off. You hold her, and I'll tie her down—Sam Jenkins, you listenin' to me?"

For just a moment, Sam looks as though he is about to bolt out of the room. Instead, his jaw tightens and he steps forward to follow Esther's orders. After a difficult struggle, they manage to bind my wrists and ankles to the four iron posts of the bed. Breathing heavy, Esther wipes the sweat from her own brow and pulls the scissors from her pocket.

I am lying face down on the bed. The entire back of my dress is dark and sticky with blood. Esther hands Sam a cloth, tells him to dip it in the bucket of cold water and hold it over my face. "Child, forgive me, there just ain't no other way." Esther grasps the back of my collar and starts cutting. The screaming starts again.

Three hours later, Sam stands outside the orphanage. It has stopped snowing, and the night is crisp and clear. In one hand he holds a pipe that has long since grown cold. In the other, he squeezes the half-frozen rag he had been using to wipe my brow. "Jesus, Lord," he whispers to the stars, "where do white folks come from?"

Esther sidles up behind him, her itching fists pressed into her narrow hips. "Same place they goin' back to. Wish I could be there to watch 'em burn, but I'll be with the righteous. God help 'em come Judgment Day."

Sam turns to Esther, certain she can't see the shine in his eyes. "How she doin'?"

Esther grunts and tries to keep her hands busy so they don't jump out and punch someone. She tugs at her apron, adjusts the kerchief on her head. " 'Bout as well as can be expected. Dr. Brant give her somethin' for the pain. You can go back in if you want. She passed out a while back, 'n she's sleepin' now. Not sure how we'll manage once she wakes up. Can't have all that hollerin' on Christmas morn. She's already scared the other children half to death."

They stand together in silence for a moment. Then the back door opens, and Dr. Brant steps out into the yard. "I haven't seen a case like that in quite some time—thank God. They used a paddle on her, I suspect. It's a long, thick piece of wood that has about a dozen holes drilled through it. Each time it hits the skin, just as many blisters are raised. Judging from the blood and the amount of skin she's lost, I'd say they beat her off and on for at least a couple of hours. Maybe more." The doctor stops and squints up at the stars. It's Christmas Eve, and his wife and infant son are waiting at home. But he is glad he came. It is in keeping with the spirit of the season.

Dr. Brant looks down from the stars and realizes the two Negroes are waiting for him to go on. He clears his throat to alert the driver and begins pulling on his gloves. "I've given Miss Holme strict instructions regarding the care of this poor girl. She's not to be moved for several days, and the dressing on her back should be changed twice a day to prevent it from sticking to the newly formed skin. The fever should pass by morning—if it doesn't, send for me again." The coachman opens the door of the carriage and Dr. Brant climbs inside. Once he is seated, he pushes down the window and tries to sound as festive as the circumstances allow. "Merry Christmas to you both. I'll see you in the new year, God willing."

Esther and Sam return the greeting and watch as the carriage pulls out of the yard and disappears down the street.

"He's a good man, that doctor." Most of the bitterness has left Esther's voice.

Sam nods in silent agreement, and they both go back inside.

3.

This isn't happening to me. Even though I am in my body, and my body is in pain, I know that none of this is real. It's a dream, and soon I'm going to wake up in the bed next to Mama, and Tyjuan will be sleeping in the space between us, and everything will be just like it was before. The question is, before *what*?

Every time I close my eyes, I hope that it will be the last time. But every time I open my eyes, I find myself still trapped in this messed-up dream.

I open my eyes. Invisible fingers try to shove a corner of the pillow into my mouth. My back feels like it has been scorched by fire and then splashed with salt—it stings and burns as the blisters swell and burst. I cry out and the pillow fills my mouth. I grind linen and feathers between my teeth until my jaw aches and falls slack. Those same invisible fingers lift my chin and bring milky water to my lips. The cool fluid spills into my mouth, over my lips, down my neck to my bare breasts. I fall forward onto the pillow and close my eyes.

I open my eyes. I am tied to a bed in a small, hot room. My head is facing a blank white wall. I turn and see a black iron stove in the corner. A girl comes in, opens its mouth, and feeds it a hunk of wood. She closes the stove door, then comes closer and looks at me. Her eyes are much too bright. I try to ask her for a drink of water, but no sound comes out of my mouth. She leaves suddenly as though her name has been called. I close my eyes.

I open my eyes. A young, slender woman hovers over me. Her voice is a cross between a whisper and a song. I try hard to pick out her words while she changes the cloth that covers my back. Each time I wince, she sings an apology. She puts a spoonful of white powder into a glass of water, stirs it, and holds it to my lips. Then she unties my ankles and wrists and sits by the bed with my hand inside of hers, singly softly. I start to cry, not because of the pain, but because Mama used to sing to me when I was a little girl. Shame turns my face toward the wall. Before the young woman finishes her song, my eyes are closed again.

I open my eyes. There is a tiny brown bird perched on the windowsill. I watch it and wait for it to fly away, but the tiny bird doesn't move. I reach out to touch it and still the bird sits frozen on the sill. My fingers run over the grooves in its wings and the smooth polished surface of its breast. I hear a sound on the other side of the door and scoop the wooden bird up with my hand. I hold it under my pillow to keep it safe.

A short, wiry woman bustles into the room and draws a chair up to my bed. The girl with the too-bright eyes comes in to feed the stove. She stands in the corner and watches as the older woman tries to spoon something into my mouth. I hide my lips in the pillow. I have no appetite. I am waiting for the whispersong woman to return with her spoonful of white powder.

The wiry woman takes it personal when I don't eat her food. She sets the bowl on a nearby table and leaves in a huff. The girl with the too-bright eyes is still standing in the corner. She takes a quick look out the door, then comes closer and sits down on the chair. She starts talking to me, but her words are so thick and round

I can't tell what she is saying. I watch her and wonder what makes her eyes burn so bright. Then she reaches over and takes the bowl and spoon off the table. She puts a spoonful of soup in her own mouth first. Then she ladles out a bit of broth and offers it to me. Refusing it will hurt her feelings, so I open up my mouth. She feeds me seven more mouthfuls before the wiry woman comes back in. "Well!" she says before turning and stomping out of the room. The girl with the bright eyes giggles and dips out another spoonful of broth. I take three more then close my lips for good. The girl with the bright eyes holds the bowl in her lap and starts talking about money. I try to listen but the story makes no sense. Finally she says something I can understand: *Rest now.* She takes up the bowl in one hand and pushes the chair back against the wall. She watches me for a while longer before leaving the room. I close my eyes.

These are my days and my nights. I don't know how long I have been trapped in this dream. But I know this *is* a dream because everyone looks and acts and talks like they all belong together, like they've been knowing each other a long time. Everything that happens makes sense to them, but it doesn't make sense to me.

One morning I open my eyes and the room is full of a different kind of light. The girl with the too-bright eyes comes in to feed the fire. She closes the stove door and then hurries over to me.

"Guess what?" she says, and then rushes on without waiting for a reply. "We got snow—a whole lot of it, everywhere! Money, he too scared to go outside, but I went out and touched it. It's so cold and clean—you can even eat it! Miss Holme say it was okay, so I put some in my mouth—"

She is interrupted by a sudden commotion out in the kitchen. It sounds like people are laughing and crying at the same time. I hear someone shout, "Praise the Lord!"

The bright-eyed girl forgets all about the snow and starts telling me a different story. She has a thick accent that tells me she's from down South. "Guess what else? We's free! Ain't that somethin'?" She is beaming, her face only inches from mine. She wants me to do or say something, but my blank eyes tell her I don't understand. She tries again. "Massa Lincoln—I mean, President Lincoln, he give us the 'mancipation Proclamation. It say all us runaways is free. Ain't that good news? We ain't slaves no more!" She waits for my face to mirror her excitement. "You happy, right? On the inside?"

She is trying so hard, but all I can give her is a slight nod of my head. I think back to my history class and the books Mama used to make us read. The Emancipation Proclamation—Lincoln issued it *when*? I lick my lips and manage to ask her what year it is.

"Eighteen sixty-three," she says proudly, and then remembers to add, "Happy New Year!"

4.

One day my eyes are already open when the whispersong woman comes into the room. She closes the door behind her this time and lays some clothes over the back of the chair. "You have a visitor," she says in that feathery voice. Then she helps me roll onto my side. "We've got to get you dressed."

The girl with the too-bright eyes always wears a long white apron over a plain gray dress. It falls just below her knees, right at the top of her high lace-up boots. The girl might be as old as me, but that outfit and the way she plaits her hair make her look like a little kid.

The young woman helps me sit up for the first time. My back is sore and the skin feels tight, but the pain is much better than it was before. As she lifts the dressing to check underneath, I ask: "Is there any more powder?"

The young woman gently pats the cloth on my back and begins sorting through the clothes she has brought along. "Dr. Brant only left enough for two doses. Morphine's expensive, you know, and we have to save as much as we can for the poor soldiers. Right now I'm afraid they need it more than you."

I nod to show I understand and wonder what soldiers she's talking about. Then I remember what year it is, and I realize the country is at war.

The whispersong woman looks at me like she is seeing me for
the first time. I guess I look different now that I'm sitting up. I have
only a square piece of cloth covering my breasts. It is pinned at the
shoulders to the dressing on my back. I feel kind of embarrassed
facing her this way. I wonder how long I have been lying face down
on that bed. I wonder if she was the person who bathed me. My
heel kicks the empty chamber pot that is underneath the bed. The
room, as always, is hot, but I feel my cheeks growing even warmer.

The young woman seems to understand the way I am feeling
right now. She turns a bit to the side so I have some privacy. "What's
your name?" she asks.

The days and nights of silence have left my throat feeling tight
and dry. I cough a bit, still hoping she'll bring me a glass of water
mixed with a spoonful of that powder. "Genna."

"Pleased to meet you, Genna," she says, and holds out her
hand. When I take it, she says, "I'm Miss Holme—Lenora Holme.
I'm head teacher here at the orphanage. And I also happen to be
Reverend Macklin's niece—his *real* niece," she says with a little
tinkling laugh.

At first I'm not sure what she's talking about, but then I remember the police captain and the story Sam Jenkins made up. I smile a
little and try to figure out how long ago that happened. A few days?
A few weeks? Can a dream really last that long?

The whispersong woman sees me staring off into space and
keeps talking to keep me alert. "My uncle is coming to see you
today. We're all very curious about your history, Genna. You mum-
bled some things while you were still feverish, but we'd like to hear
your story in full. But first, we have to get you dressed. Do you
think you can stand up?"

Getting dressed takes a long time. Not just because my back's
still tender, but because there's so much stuff to put on. Thick
woolen stockings that almost reach my knees but don't stay up on

their own. I have to tie them to my leg with a piece of string. These long, baggy cotton pant things that have a stupid frill at the bottom of each leg. Then another cotton skirt over that. Miss Holme even brought a corset, but I can't wear it because of my back. She helps me put on a loose camisole instead, one that buttons up the front. Then I have to step into the dress itself. It doesn't reach all the way to my ankles because I'm taller than Miss Holme. She tells me this dress once belonged to her. It has long sleeves and a high collar and more buttons to do up on the front. Either she didn't wear it much or somebody ironed it with starch. The fabric is stiff and scratchy and a drab shade of blue.

There is no mirror in the room, so I have to take her word for it when Miss Holme says I look okay. They don't have any lace-up boots that are large enough for my feet, so Esther, the cook, gives me her slippers instead. They look funny, especially since my dress is too short. But Miss Holme says the Reverend won't mind. She gives me a clean kerchief to tie over my hair. I can tell she wants to ask me about my locks, but she's holding all her questions until the Reverend arrives. Before we leave the room I slip my hand under the pillow and grab my little bird.

Reverend Macklin is waiting for us in a large room that looks like it serves as a classroom and a dining hall. There are no children in the room right now, but through the window I can see a long line of boys and girls marching around the yard. Their breath freezes as it meets the cold air, but they seem happy to be outside. The sound of a chair scraping on the wooden floor pulls my attention back inside the room. Reverend Macklin gets up from the desk he is sitting behind and offers me his hand. He has thick black sideburns that would make a beard, except his chin has been shaved clean. He's bald on top, but the hair above his ears is long like a brushed-back Afro. He's wearing a plain black suit and a white collar. His friendly brown face makes me think he'd make a good uncle.

Reverend Macklin's smile is as warm as the large hand he wraps around mine. "It's a pleasure to finally meet my long-lost niece. How are you feeling?"

"Better," I say, as I take back my hand and sit on a chair Miss Holme has set behind me. The Reverend nods at his niece, and she goes around the desk to stand beside him.

"Well, Genna, what can you tell us about yourself?" she asks.

Both their faces are full of kind curiosity, but I don't really know how to answer this question. So I say, "What do you want to know?"

The Reverend looks surprised when I say this, but he just laughs and tries again. "Well, where are you from?"

Without thinking, I say, "Brooklyn."

Miss Holme frowns sympathetically before coming over and putting her hand on my shoulder. "You're in Brooklyn *now*, Genna. The Reverend wants to know where your people are from—your family, your master."

Brooklyn sits like a pill on the tip of my tongue, but I swallow it back down. They watch me closely. I remember how Sam Jenkins's performance fooled Charlie, Lester, and the captain, and decide to give it a try. I suck in my lower lip, scrunch up my forehead, and try my best to look confused.

The Reverend softens his voice and tries to ease the truth out of me. "Do you remember anything about where you lived before? Do you remember how you got here?"

I keep my blank look on and shake my head. My amnesia act appears to be working. The Reverend and his niece glance at each other, and then the Reverend moves on.

"Do you know how old you are, Genna?"

Before this dream started, I was about to turn sixteen. But we are far from July now. There is snow on the ground outside. I tell the Reverend I'm about sixteen years old.

He hears the uncertainty in my voice and nods as though he

understands. "Many former slaves are unsure of their exact age. Our enslaved brothers and sisters have been kept in a shameful state of ignorance. Do you know when you were born, the season perhaps?"

I tell him the exact date so he won't think I'm just another ignorant slave. The Reverend frowns and glances at Miss Holme. "Hmm. We'd like to help you, Genna, but I'm afraid you're too old to stay here at the orphanage. But I'm sure we could find you a suitable position somewhere in the city."

I want to tell him this is just a dream and that I plan to wake up soon. But I know that won't make sense. Instead I tell him I don't need a job because I won't be staying here long. I use my good English and try to act real polite so he won't take offense.

The Reverend's eyebrows go up toward the ceiling. Miss Holme kneels down beside me and looks into my face. "Where are you going, Genna?"

"Back home," I tell her.

"And where is home, Genna?" The Reverend watches me with his deep black eyes. I look away, but I can still feel his eyes on my face. He is trying to decide whether or not I'm crazy. I can tell they both feel sorry for me.

Miss Holme puts her hand on my arm and shakes it a bit like she's trying to get me to join some game. "Perhaps you could take a temporary position. Just for a little while, until you're ready to go."

She is talking to me like I'm one of those kids outside, caught up in a game of make-believe. This makes me angry, but there's nothing I can do. They just don't understand.

The Reverend starts playing along. "What kind of work did you do—at home?"

I think for a moment and decide it's safe to tell the truth this time. "I used to babysit for this white lady named Hannah. I took care of her little boy."

The Reverend's face lights up. "Do you like children, Genna?"

I nod quickly, and the Reverend sees an opening. "Do you have many brothers and sisters?"

I nod again, slower this time.

"Do you know where they are, Genna? Did you run away together?"

I shake my head and fight back tears because this really is the truth. I don't know where Rico, Toshi, and Tyjuan are. They didn't come here with me. I got sent back alone.

Miss Holme squeezes my arm again and tells her uncle I need to rest now. Reverend Macklin stands up and the interview comes to an end. Miss Holme asks me to wait outside the classroom. She and the Reverend talk for several minutes behind the closed door. I stand by a window in the hallway, watching the children outside form a long line as they prepare to come back inside for lunch. Aside from their different clothes, these kids look just like the ones I used to see playing in the schoolyard near my building. But these children are orphans, and this isn't Brooklyn. Not the Brooklyn I know.

I am so caught up in my own thoughts that I don't hear the classroom door open. I jump a little when Miss Holme slips her arm around my waist. She asks me if I can help out around the orphanage until they find a job for me. She says the Reverend is confident they'll find a placement soon. Until then, she says I'll have to sleep with the other children so Esther can have her room back. I don't have any belongings to move, so Miss Holme just takes me upstairs. The large, cold room smells faintly of urine. About forty beds are arranged in two long rows that are separated by a main aisle. Miss Holme walks to the far end of one row and tells me this is where I will sleep. The bed is narrow and much too small for my body. I look at the thin blanket I will be sleeping under and shiver at the thought of spending long, cold nights in this room.

Miss Holme can tell I'm not looking forward to sleeping up here. She tries to cheer me up by reminding me that it will only be for a little while. "There are plenty of charitable people in the city who are working hard to uplift our race, Genna. I'm sure the Reverend will find you a wonderful position. We'll pray on it, won't we?"

I nod so I don't seem disrespectful, but I am starting to get tired of her singsong voice. I don't need anyone to take pity on me, and I don't want their charity. Right now all I want is to be left alone. "My back still feels sore," I tell her. "Is it okay if I lie down now?"

"Of course," Miss Holme says in her whispering way. She says she'll send one of the children upstairs to tell me when supper is ready.

Once she is gone, I sit down on the bed. The mattress is lumpy and the springs creak noisily. I slowly ease myself onto the bed, lying on my side to protect my back. I have to curl up in a ball so my feet don't hang over the end.

I am alone in this large, empty room. The pillow beneath my head smells musty, and I can tell that the mattress I'm lying on once held a bedwetter. Some poor little kid probably slept here before me, and maybe he was scared of the dark, or homesick. Maybe he cried himself to sleep wondering where his folks were. Maybe that little kid is me.

I close my eyes and think of a song Mama used to sing when things got really bad. *Sometimes I feel like a motherless chile, a long, long ways from home* ... My eyes start to fill up with warm tears, and for the first time I wonder if this really is a dream. If it isn't ... but it has to be. *It has to be.* I close my eyes and rock myself back and forth until the pillow grows damp beneath my cheek and I finally fall asleep.

5.

I wake up to two surprises. First, I am not cold. There are two blankets draped over me, and these keep out the icy drafts coming in through the large windows. The day is nearly over, and the room is dimly lit. But there is enough light for me to see the second surprise: the girl with the too-bright eyes is sitting on the bed next to mine. A younger boy sits beside her, holding a small tin cup.

"We figgered you might be thirsty," she says. The boy hands her the cup, and she holds it out to me. I take the cup, drink the water it contains, then wipe my mouth and say, "Thanks." She smiles shyly and gives the empty cup back to the boy. He accepts it without a word.

"You feelin' better? Miss Holme say your back be healed up 'fore too long."

She is sitting on the bed with the boy pressed up beside her, but somehow she can't sit still. Her fidgeting makes the springs in the bed creak. The little boy sits as close to her as he can. He looks like he's about ten. I watch him, but he keeps his eyes hidden from mine.

"I'm Mattie, and this here's my brother, Monroe. That's his proper name, but he don't mind if you call 'im Money."

I want to ask Mattie how old she is, but I am too tired to speak. Instead I just watch the two of them with drowsy eyes.

Mattie squirms on the bed and rolls her lips together, trying to keep her questions inside. I can tell she has waited a long time for this moment. I watch her until my own body becomes restless. Then I throw back the blankets and sit up so that we are facing each other in the dim room.

Mattie unrolls her lips. "Money 'n me, we thought maybe you was a African."

I slit my eyes at Mattie, then remember what Judah told me about our ancestors. I think of Papi and his African blood, the same blood that's inside of me. Even if she meant it as a diss, I refuse to be insulted. "Why'd you think that?" I ask.

Mattie nods at the kerchief I have tied around my head. "Africans always got all kinds of funny marks and bumps on they skin, and sometimes they teeth is pointy like a animal. Your teeth ain't like that, but you got funny little knots all over your head. I never seen a slave with hair like that before. You from Africa?"

Without thinking, I let my hand roam over the kerchief. I can feel the locks underneath, taking root. Then I remember that Mattie is staring at me, and I answer her question. "My people came from Africa, but I was born here."

"Down South?" she asks. Mattie's accent's so thick, it sounds like she said "down Souf." I know kids at my school who say it that way, too.

"No," I reply. "Here, in Brooklyn."

Mattie nods at me but her eyes show that she doesn't quite understand. The welts on my back press against the coarse fabric of my dress, and I realize Mattie has probably seen those, too. I wonder if everyone here knows how my body looks underneath these clothes. My cheeks start to burn, and I feel naked even though I am wearing all those underclothes and a borrowed dress. I want to tell Mattie that this body is borrowed, too. But I'm not sure she would believe me. I'm not sure I'd believe myself.

Mattie shifts on her bed so that our knees are almost touching.

"That's what Miss Holme figgered. She figgered you was raised up North somewheres 'cause of how you talk. But if you from New York, you musta been born free, 'cause slavery ain't 'llowed in this state no more. Miss Holme figgered maybe you got catched by slavers, and *they* beat you, but you got away 'fore they could sell you down South."

Mattie waits for me to confirm Miss Holme's story, but I just look away. I cannot correct her because I have no story to tell. A story has to have a beginning, a middle, and an end. And right now I don't know where to begin.

Mattie accepts my silence and moves on. "You don't have to say nothin'. Lots of folks don't like talkin' 'bout they past. My mama always used to say, nothin' good's waitin' for us in the past, nothin' but salt. She was talkin' 'bout Lot's wife. You know 'bout Lot's wife, right?" My blank face pushes Mattie on. "The angels told her not to look back, but she did and got turned into a pillar of salt! So it's best to look at what's comin' up ahead."

I wonder what's waiting for me "up ahead." Are Mama and Tyjuan and Judah somewhere out there—in the future? In the past? Do they even know I am missing? Have they noticed I am gone? My eyes fill up again, and Mattie rushes on, thinking she has said something to upset me.

"Me, I'm glad I left my past behind. If I don't never see the South again, it'll be too soon." Mattie laughs behind the hand she keeps close to her mouth. I smile at her because she reminds me of a child. She reminds me of Toshi when she was still a girl and not evil all the time. I reach over and pull Mattie's hand away. She looks at me, and then her eyes flutter and her smile trembles like she is nervous or afraid. Mattie is like a bird, like a sparrow that flaps in the dirt and pecks at crumbs in the gutter but can still sing better than any fancy bird in a cage.

"Can you fly, Mattie?" The words come out of my mouth, and

I know that they are strange, but in this dreamworld, I figure I can say whatever I want.

Mattie laughs again and takes back her hand. I can tell she doesn't trust me yet, but I think she wants to. I think Mattie needs a friend.

"I reckon we should go back downstairs," she says. "Miss Esther be needin' help in the kitchen. You comin' to supper?"

I don't feel like eating with a bunch of little kids, but my stomach feels real empty right now, so I nod. Mattie and her brother stand together at the same time, like Siamese twins. "You can sleep more if you's tired. Money and me, we come get you when supper's ready."

I lie back down and Mattie pulls the blankets up to my chin the way Mama used to when I was little. Mattie smiles at me, then takes her brother's hand and heads down the long aisle. Inside I'm hoping I won't be here when they get back. But I close my eyes knowing that I probably will.

6.

I spend the next few days working as a teacher's assistant in Miss Holme's classroom. I started out working with Mattie and Esther, but within an hour I burned myself twice on the big iron stove. Esther frowned, put lard on my burns, and banished me from the kitchen. Esther looks mean, but she helped me when I was sick and I wanted to return the favor. But when I kept on burning myself, Esther said Mattie was all the help she could handle, so Miss Holme suggested I work with her. Now I tutor the littlest kids, teaching them their ABCs. It's cold in that classroom, and we don't have many books—no pencils or paper, either. The children share a piece of chalk and write on a small square slate. But each day I come up with new ways to make learning fun. I teach them nursery rhymes and simple songs, and I let the children sit close to me so we can keep each other warm. I'm not getting paid, of course, but I don't mind, really. In fact, having something to do keeps my mind off the fact that I'm trapped in another century.

Problem is, once the children have been fed, bathed, and put to bed, there's nothing else for me to do but think about the past. Or is it the future? Everyone goes to bed early around here. It's wintertime, so the sun sets by five, and Miss Holme says we can't afford to waste candles (which Esther and Mattie make by hand).

That means by eight o'clock, it's lights out. No television, no radio, no telephone. Lights *out*.

When all the other kids have gone to sleep, I take the kerchief off my head and work on my locks. I don't have the scented oil Judah's aunt gave me, but Mattie snuck some grease out of the kitchen, and I've been using that instead. Not a whole lot—I don't want to walk around smelling like a piece of fried chicken. Just enough to keep my scalp from getting dry. Mattie can't get enough of my locks. She sleeps in the bed next to mine, and Money's right across the aisle with all the other boys. He usually falls asleep as soon as the lights go out, but Mattie stays up and watches me twist my locks. I tell her what I know about the Rastafarians in Jamaica and Haile Selassie in Ethiopia. I try to fix some of the messed-up ideas Mattie has about Africa. I can't blame her for being so ignorant, 'cause Mattie's been a slave all her life. I just feel bad sometimes 'cause until I met Judah, I used to think that way myself.

"I hear them folks over in Africa eat each other up. I seen a feller once and he had real pointy teeth."

"That's got nothing to do with eating people, Mattie. Africans mark themselves so they know who belongs to which tribe."

"What's a tribe?"

"It's like a big group of people. They practice the same religion, and they all live a certain way. It's like how here in America we're divided into different states. Some people are from New York, and some are from Virginia. In Africa, some people belong to the Yoruba tribe, and some belong to the Ashanti." I look at Mattie and know she doesn't really understand. "Anyway, the point is, Africans aren't a bunch of savages who run around naked and eat each other for lunch. White people just want you to believe that so you'll be ashamed of who you are."

Mattie's neck snaps back. "I ain't no African!"

"Yes you are, and so am I. We're *African American*—we're from there, but we live here. And we live here because somebody stole us from there. If it weren't for slavery, we'd still be in Africa right now."

I finish twisting the last coil of hair and wrap the kerchief back over my head. Mattie watches me, her eyes shining even in the dark.

"That why you wear your hair like that? So folks know you's from Africa?"

I want to tell Mattie what Judah told me about roots. I want to tell her I decided to grow locks so that folks would know I belong with Judah. But saying Judah's name out loud right now would hurt more than it would help. So instead I just nod and wrap my blanket around me to help keep out the cold. Mattie does the same. We are sitting cross-legged on our beds. Our frozen breath hangs in the air between us each time we speak.

Across the aisle, Money moans and turns over in his sleep. Mattie's eyes flash in his direction and stay there until he is quiet and still once more.

"You tired, Mattie?"

"Naw."

I think Mattie's got insomnia. I've never seen her sleep. Two nights ago I got up to use the bathroom—I mean, the tin bucket they keep in the corner—and Mattie was sitting straight up in bed, watching her little brother. I asked her if she was feeling okay, and she said Money had been talking in his sleep and that was what woke her up. But she was still sitting like that when I crawled back into bed, and Money hadn't made a sound. Mattie never looks tired in the morning, but I'm starting to wonder if staying up all night is what makes her eyes shine so bright.

I smother the yawn that's about to pull my mouth apart. Working with little kids all day wears me out. But Mattie is wide awake, and I figure I ought to keep her company. "What else you want to know about Africa?"

"Those folks over there—can they really fly?"

"Fly? Where'd you hear that?"

"When we was too little to work in the fields, the old folks lookin' after us used to tell us stories. They used to tell us 'bout the very first slaves what worked on the farm. They was from Africa, and the old folks said they could fly. Soon as they got here and took a look around, saw all the black folks workin' for the white folks, they just lifted up into the air and flew back to Africa. 'Cross the ocean, just like that. When I was littler, I believed 'em. I used to wish my whole family could fly—Mama, Papa, and all my brothers and sisters. I wished we could fly away together, leave Massa far behind. But we didn't have no wings. All we had was feet. So we ran."

I watch Mattie. Her eyes are fixed on the floor, and the hand that normally hovers around her mouth has slid down to her throat. Mattie has forgotten what her mama told her. She has gone back. Her body is here beside me, but she is somewhere in the past.

"You ran away by yourself?" I ask quietly.

Mattie keeps her eyes on the floor and shakes her head. "We ran together. Mama planned it, and we left late one night when every-body was asleep. We all ran together, but we moved real quiet like 'cause Papa, he was part Seminole, and he knew how to walk through the woods without makin' no noise. He taught us that 'fore he left, 'fore he got sold away."

I want to ask Mattie why she is here alone if they all ran together, but I don't think I have the right. After all, when I wouldn't tell her about my family, she just left it alone. I wait to see if she will go on.

Mattie's hand keeps circling her throat. She squeezes her neck but the words don't stop. They come out anyway.

"We ran together. Mama held onto Jackie, and I had Sophie and Monroe by the hand. We ran through the woods, and it was black as pitch, and Sophie, she's scared of the dark, but Mama told us to run, so that's what we did. She said don't never stop, don't never stop 'til I say so. So we ran as fast as we could. Sophie and Monroe, they held onto me, they squeezed my hands tight 'cause they was afraid.

I was scared, too, but Mama said run, so that's what I did. Then we heard the barkin' and we knew the dogs was after us. We knew, but we kept on runnin'. Mama said go in the water. She said get your feet wet. We kept runnin', but dogs got four feet and we only got two. Wasn't long 'fore they catched up with us...."

Mattie's eyes are shining with tears that will not fall. She is staring at the floor between us, but she is seeing something else, something evil from the swamps.

"They catched Mama first. One got her by the ankle so she couldn't run, and another jumped on Jackie. That dog tore into my baby brother and Mama, she screamed. She tried to pull that dog off Jackie, but his teeth was in too deep. He wouldn't let go. Blood was flyin' everywhere and Mama was screamin', but Jackie never made a sound. We could hear them comin' and the last thing Mama said to me was RUN! She screamed it at us. She said, RUN! And so that's what we did. We didn't stay and help them. We ran, and we didn't stop. We didn't stop 'cause we was waitin' to hear it from Mama. And Mama said don't never stop...."

I suck in my lip so I won't cry, but my lip tastes salty and I realize my face is already wet. I want to ask what happened to Sophie. There's no little girl by that name at the orphanage. But when I look at Mattie, I realize I really don't have to ask. She's frozen like Lot's wife. Her eyes shine with tears that refuse to fall. I reach over and grab Mattie by the shoulders. I shake her gently, then I shake her harder, again and again, until the tears spill over her eyelids and stream down her face. After a while I stop shaking her and hold Mattie in my arms. She sobs like a little girl, and I realize this is why she cannot sleep at night. I hold Mattie and I remember Toshi as a girl and I wonder where she is right now and I wonder if Mama and Tyjuan are okay.

When Mattie stops crying, I tell her to lie down and I pull the blanket up around her chin. Then I crawl into my own tiny bed and try to get warm again. I watch Mattie's breath rising above her like a small white cloud. I can tell she is still awake, so I ask her one more question. "Mattie, how old are you?"

She turns her head toward me and whispers, "I don't know."

I remember what Reverend Macklin said about slaves being kept in the dark. I wonder if he ever sat Mattie down and listened to her story the way he listened to mine. "Give me your hand," I tell her. Mattie pulls her arm out from under the blanket and wraps her cold fingers around mine. I hold onto Mattie's hand until we both fall asleep.

7.

"So, how is our patient coming along?"

Miss Holme starts talking to the doctor before I can even think of what I want to say. She gushes on about how easy it was to follow his instructions, and how kind it was of him to venture out in the cold on Christmas Eve. She tells him my back is healing just fine. I'm even able to change the dressing by myself now.

"Is that so? Well, let's take a look, shall we?"

We are standing in the kitchen. A closed door in the far corner leads to Esther's bedroom. Miss Holme looks at me expectantly, then gently pushes me in that direction. I stay where I am and steal a quick glance at Dr. Brant. He's a tall man with a kind face that's partly hidden by a bushy mustache. I know he's a doctor and he's treated me before, but right now I don't feel like getting naked in front of a white man. Miss Holme titters nervously and puts her hand on my elbow. She tries to steer me over to Esther's room and she still has that sweet smile on her face, but I can see a tiny knot forming between her eyes. She gets that knot whenever one of the children dares to step out of line, and that doesn't happen too often around here. I know Miss Holme doesn't want me to embarrass her in front of Dr. Brant, but I am not a child and I am not ready to move.

Miss Holme tightens her grip on my arm. "Hurry along, Genna. I'm sure Dr. Brant has other patients to see."

Dr. Brant smiles like he understands what I'm feeling inside. He pulls out a chair from the kitchen table, sits down, and crosses his long legs. "There's no rush. Why don't you sit down, Genna, and we'll get to know one another. You weren't quite yourself the last time we met."

I jerk my arm free from Miss Holme's grasp and move closer to the table. But while I'm taking a moment to figure out what I want to say, Miss Holme starts blabbing again. She tells Dr. Brant what a help I've been, working with the younger children in the classroom during the day. This bit of information seems particularly interesting to the doctor. He untangles himself from Miss Holme's singing whisper and takes a closer look at me.

"Can you read and write, Genna?"

I nod and Dr. Brant squints at me from behind his tiny round glasses. He is starting to have the same effect on me that he seems to have on Miss Holme. I feel a sudden need to impress this white man. Without being asked, I blurt out that I plan to go to college one day.

Dr. Brant starts to laugh and Miss Holme follows his lead. "You're quite an ambitious young woman," Dr. Brant says finally. Miss Holme just shakes her head and looks at me like I'm a cute little dog that just performed an amusing trick. "Of course, it isn't such an outrageous idea. Your people have taken mighty strides in the direction of progress and civilization. I firmly believe that education is the key to the advancement of colored people. What would you study if you did go to college, Genna?"

"Psychiatry," I say with calm determination.

Miss Holme is clearly amazed, but Dr. Brant doesn't seem shocked at all. He studies me closely, then abruptly asks to see Reverend Macklin.

Miss Holme sings him her sweetest apology. "I'm afraid my uncle isn't here, Dr. Brant. Is there some message you'd like me to convey?"

"Yes. Tell him I'd like this young woman to come and work for me. My wife, as you know, has not been well this past while, and our housekeeper is getting on in years. We could use a bright girl around the house to serve as a nurse for our son, and to help me with my practice from time to time. I daresay Genna would be the perfect candidate since she knows how to work with children and has an interest in medicine. I'll have to consult with my wife, of course, but in the meantime, please mention it to your uncle, Miss Holme. If he has no objections, I'd like her to start first thing next week."

Though somewhat surprised, Miss Holme nods obligingly. She flicks her eyes at me and I think I see envy there. Then Dr. Brant surprises us both by clapping his hands together and saying, "Right then—on to the matter at hand. Let's take a look at your back, shall we?"

This time I go into Esther's room without waiting for an escort. I'm kind of glad, though, when Miss Holme follows me inside and helps me peel off some of these clothes. I sit on the bed with a shawl held over my breasts while Dr. Brant gently presses his fingertips into my back. Most places where he does that I hardly feel a thing, but then he touches a spot somewhere near the center that sets my spine on fire. I try to clamp my hand over my mouth, but part of a scream slips out anyway. Dr. Brant makes sure I'm alright before he touches my back again. Miss Holme tells me to hold onto her hand, but I just shake my head and hold my mouth shut instead.

After a few more minutes, Dr. Brant tells me I can get dressed. He goes back into the kitchen and Miss Holme hurries after him. She closes the door between us, but I can still hear some of what they are saying. I press my ear as close to the door as I can, but I can't make out all of the words. Dr. Brant is explaining something to Miss Holme, but he sounds just as confused as her. I open the door a crack and catch the tail end of their conversation.

"You mean to say that she may continue to feel pain even after the sores have healed? How is that possible?"

"Some people—children in particular—never fully recover after suffering such cruel maltreatment. I'm afraid scars inflicted on the body heal much faster than the scars inflicted on the soul."

Miss Holme sighs sympathetically but stops wringing her hands when I walk back into the kitchen. Dr. Brant smiles warmly when he sees me and assures me my back is healing just fine. I don't ask him about the streak of pain he sent shooting up my spine.

"Well, then, I'll be on my way. Miss Holme, please do inform your uncle of my interest in employing this young woman. I'm certain Genna would be a wonderful addition to our family."

Miss Holme escorts Dr. Brant out to his carriage, and I go back into the empty classroom. I take a rag out of the bucket kept in the corner and start wiping the chalkboard clean, all the while smiling to myself. It doesn't make sense, but for some reason I feel proud that Dr. Brant chose me. Then I think about leaving Mattie behind, and bit by bit my smile disappears like the chalk words beneath my wet rag.

8.

I am sitting at the kitchen table, waiting for the Brants to arrive, waiting for my new life to begin. Esther is scouring the stove, determined to impress Mrs. Brant with the order and cleanliness of her kitchen. The rest of the orphanage has already been scrubbed from top to bottom. Everyone talks about this woman as if she were a queen. The children have been given strict instructions to be on their best behavior, and Miss Holme has reminded me several times that I am to curtsy when I meet the doctor's wife. Earlier this morning, Reverend Macklin took me aside. His face was serious, and his voice was stern. "This is an important opportunity, Genna, not just for you, but for our people. The Brants are one of the finest families in the city and true supporters of the abolitionist cause. You should feel honored that they have chosen you to care for their infant son. Be diligent and dutiful, and above all things be humble. Be a model for the child by keeping the model of our Lord, Jesus Christ, ever before you." The lecture ended with Reverend Macklin giving me a Bible. I put it in the bag that held my other belongings: a nightgown, some underwear, a spare kerchief for my hair, and the wooden bird Sam carved for me.

We expected the Brants around ten that morning, but they arrive closer to noon. Dr. Brant climbs out of the carriage and shakes hands with Reverend Macklin. It is cold outside, but Miss

Holme keeps a perfect smile on her face as the two men begin talking about the progress of the war. I try not to shiver as I clutch my bag, wishing Mrs. Brant would appear so I could curtsy and get inside the carriage already. Finally, Reverend Macklin changes topics and thanks the doctor for giving me this job. He assures Dr. Brant that I am honest and obedient, and will serve his family to the best of my ability. Reverend Macklin doesn't invite the Brants to come inside. He seems to understand without anyone saying a word that the honor will have to be postponed. I can tell that Esther and Miss Holme are disappointed, but their perfect smiles are frozen in place.

We are all waiting for Mrs. Brant to make an appearance. It is understood that her approval is needed before the transaction is complete. Somewhat embarrassed, Dr. Brant explains that his wife is recovering from a cold and so must stay inside the carriage. "She was determined to accompany me, so anxious was she to meet Genna." He pauses to chuckle good-naturedly. "As her physician, I couldn't allow it, but my wife simply insisted, and so we took the carriage instead of the sleigh." The adults around me nod and smile sympathetically. I fight the urge to roll my eyes. Dr. Brant clears his throat and taps on the carriage's glass windowpane. It looks as though it slides down from the inside, but Mrs. Brant doesn't move. "My dear, this is the young woman I told you about. Would you like to come out and meet her?"

Mrs. Brant sighs before leaning forward and peering at me through the carriage window. After one quick glance up and down, she sinks back against the plush velvet seat and says with a careless wave of her hand, "She'll do."

Dr. Brant clears his throat again and smiles awkwardly at me. "Well, then, it's settled. Have you packed your things? Good, Adams will take your bag." The black coachman appears, takes my bag, and holds open the carriage door. Dr. Brant shifts his weight from foot to foot, pats his pockets as though he's forgotten something, and looks up at the sky. Then he leans into the carriage and says, "My dear, it looks as though it might snow again, and since Genna is still recovering, it might be best if she rode inside with us. Would you mind terribly, just this once?"

"It makes no difference to *me*, Henry. Whatever *you* decide." Mrs. Brant says this like she's doing the both of us a favor. I'm having second thoughts about taking this job, but before I can think of anything to say or do, Dr. Brant offers me his hand, so I climb into the carriage, which bounces and rocks with my added weight. Mrs. Brant presses herself into the corner so she won't catch whatever disease she thinks I must have. She closes her eyes and holds a lacy white handkerchief up to her nose. I try hard not to touch her, but the carriage is small and the pouffy skirt of her fancy silk dress takes up a whole lot of space. Finally, Dr. Brant squeezes into the carriage and the coachman closes the door.

Esther, Miss Holme, and Reverend Macklin stand by the steps and wave. In their eyes, my story has a happy ending. The way I see it, my story's far from over. I look at the people waving goodbye and it feels like I am watching TV. Mattie is probably helping to serve lunch right now, but I wish she had come to say goodbye. That way this scene wouldn't feel like something from out of a movie, it would feel like something real.

The carriage turns the corner and slowly drives past the front of the orphanage. We have had a week of icy rain, and the dirt road is a slushy mess. I steady myself as the carriage rocks and bumps, then look up and find Mrs. Brant's cold blue eyes staring straight at me. I want to stare back so she knows she can't intimidate me, but staring's rude and Mama didn't raise me that way. So I keep my eyes in my lap and hope the ride to their home won't take too long. All of a sudden Mrs. Brant gasps and waves her lacy handkerchief at something outside. "Good heavens, Henry, what does this mean? You said one girl—I won't take *two*."

I turn and look out the window. Mattie is running toward

the road. The hard, crusty snow is halfway to her knees, but she is determined to make her way across the yard. Money is running behind his sister, stepping into the deep holes her feet leave behind. Mattie's face is determined; she won't be slowed down by the snow, even though she has no coat or gloves. I watch her running and I understand how Mattie made it this far—she runs as though her life depended on it. I cannot see the coachman, but the carriage seems to slow down just a bit. The snow-covered dirt road means we can't go that fast anyway. Mattie finally gets close enough to the road to say the words loud enough for me to hear: *Goodbye! Don't forget us, Genna, don't forget!* Then she finally stops running and stands by the front gate, waving and breathing hard.

The carriage starts to pick up speed but I keep on waving until I can't see Mattie anymore. Then I turn around and face Mrs. Brant, who is staring at me from behind her frilly white handkerchief. I stare right back until her hard white face becomes a soft, wet blur. I don't want to cry in front of strangers, but something sharp catches at the back of my throat and a single sob slips out. Dr. Brant pats my knee and silently presses his silk handkerchief into my hand. I thank him and hold it over my wet face to shield myself from his wife's icy blue stare.

9.

This ain't Brooklyn. They keep calling it that, but this just *can't* be Brooklyn. Bushes and trees and hills and fields, and maybe one wooden box of a house here and there. And everything covered in snow, which makes the space between things look bigger somehow. In the Brooklyn I know, there are empty lots here and there, most filled with trash or what's left of a burned-out building. But mostly the blocks are packed tight—stores, schools, brownstones, apartment buildings like the one I used to live in. You hardly ever see open space, except maybe at the park. Brooklyn in 1863 doesn't look like a city, even though that's what they keep calling it. Not a borough, or a part of New York City, but a city in its own right.

When we get downtown, closer to where the Brants live, things start to change. But the houses are still scattered all over the place. Brooklyn is like a mouth that's missing half its teeth. The roads are paved with bricks, and the streets are loud but not because of buses and cars. All I'm seeing are wagons and carriages and a trolley pulled by horses. There are piles of horseshit everywhere, steaming in the soiled, week-old snow. I whisper to the scene outside the window: *this ain't Brooklyn.*

Suddenly I hear Mrs. Brant's voice ricocheting around the carriage and I realize she is talking to me. "I mean it, Henry, I simply *won't* have any nigger talk in my presence. It's uncouth and immoral, and certainly not fit for the ears of my darling boy."

Dr. Brant glances at me and tries to interrupt his wife, but her mouth can't be stopped. "No, Henry, I *must* stand firm on this point. I realize she is ignorant and poor, but if she is to live with us and care for our son, she *must* follow the rules of a Christian household, and it is my duty—my sworn *duty* as a Christian woman—to instruct Jenny in the ways of our Lord. I simply will not have her speaking that way in my presence. Is that clear?"

Mrs. Brant is looking at me, but Dr. Brant nods as though she is also speaking to him. I'm not exactly sure what I said to deserve this little lecture, but this has happened before. In this messed-up world, sometimes the words I think in my head wind up on the outside of my mouth. Did I curse? I decide I'd better look out the window instead of giving Mrs. Brant the cut-eye she deserves. Who's she calling *ignorant* and *poor*? And who's she calling *Jenny*?

Then I feel a hand on my arm and when I pull my eyes back inside the carriage, Dr. Brant is staring at me. "You must answer your mistress when she addresses you, Genna." Mrs. Brant's nose is way up in the air and she is pretending to look out the window, but we both know she is waiting on me. Dr. Brant gently squeezes my arm as if to say, "Trust me, it's easier this way." Dr. Brant seems like a nice enough man, and I feel kind of bad for him being married to such a bitch. So I unstitch my lips and push out a "yes, ma'am," and Mrs. Brant pulls her nose down from the roof of the carriage and smiles like a spoiled child who always gets her way.

I had my doubts before, but now I *know* I'm going to hate this job.

Finally, the carriage pulls up in front of a large, fancy-looking brownstone. It's actually two brownstones joined together, and in the middle is a wide stoop with ornate iron railings running up each side. Patriotic red, white, and blue bunting hangs above the front door. Tasseled red-velvet curtains hang in the tall parlor windows. I take all this in while Adams hops down and opens the carriage door. Dr. Brant climbs out and offers me his hand. Once I'm out of the way, he uses both hands to help get Mrs. Brant and her big pouffy skirt out of the carriage. This is my first time seeing her standing up. With her silk dress, velvet cloak, and glossy ringlet curls, Mrs. Brant looks just like a fancy doll. She's little, too, nowhere near my shoulder and a couple of feet shorter than her husband. I watch Mrs. Brant fuss and complain as Dr. Brant helps her up the front steps. I wonder why he lets her boss him around like that. I'm thinking she better not pull that crap with me.

At the top of the stairs, just inside the doorway, there is an elderly black woman holding a very white child. He is so white, I wonder if he is an albino—his hair, his skin, even his eyelashes are white. The child sits quietly in the black woman's arms, but the minute Mrs. Brant reaches for him, he starts to scream. Everything that was white before turns red (except his hair), and all his little limbs fight against the stiff embrace of Mrs. Brant.

She acts like the kid's upset because he was missing her. "Oh, my poor darling. There, there, darling, Mother's come home and she's brought you something special. Your very own nurse, Henry! Won't you open your eyes and see the wonderful surprise Mother's brought for you?"

After much wheedling from Mrs. Brant and even more whining from the baby, Henry Jr. stops flailing his arms and legs and swivels his head toward me. The kid's face is covered in tears and snot, his skin is pink and splotchy, and his breath is coming out raspy and hard. He's basically a mess right now, but when that little boy looks at me, a piece of glass goes through my heart. For just a moment, I think of Tyjuan and the way his little arms would reach for me when I picked him up from Mrs. Dominguez. For just a moment I see my brown-skinned baby brother, his twinkling black eyes, and the smile he used to save just for me.

Henry puts a pudgy hand up to his eye and peeks at me through his white fingers. I think maybe he's going to start screaming again, but instead the little white hand leaves his red face and reaches out toward me. The piece of glass digs into my heart again, and I almost cry out. But instead, I bite down on my lip and hold out my empty arms. Henry reaches for me again and begins to fight against his mother even harder than before. Mrs. Brant looks flushed and relieved when she finally hands him over to me.

"There," she says as she smoothes down her hair, "that went well. I do hope dinner is ready, Nannie. I'm famished...." Mrs. Brant unties the black ribbon at her throat and lets her heavy velvet cloak drop to the floor. I watch her as she walks into the front parlor and see that the room is full of expensive things—two couches with scrolled arms, a table with carved claw feet, an enormous gold-framed mirror that hangs over the marble mantel, and a sparkling crystal chandelier. A hundred years from now, all those things will be priceless antiques, but I can tell that even right now, they're worth a lot.

Nannie stoops to pick up the fallen cloak but Dr. Brant reaches it first. He folds it neatly and hands it to Nannie, all the while smiling that sad little smile that is like an apology for his wife. Then Dr. Brant turns to me and gently brushes a stale tear from Henry's cheek. "Take Genna into the kitchen, Nannie, and see that she gets something to eat," he says. "We'll dine whenever you're ready."

"Yes, doctor." The old woman curtsies, then smiles and leads me down a dim hallway.

Nannie's kitchen is smaller but just as clean as the kitchen Esther kept back at the orphanage. There are pots boiling and steaming on the enormous cast-iron stove, and judging from the way things smell, Nannie's the better cook. She tells me to sit down at the table while she gets dinner ready. Henry is playfully patting my face just like Tyjuan used to do.

"Soon's I get supper on the table I can show you your room," Nannie says over her shoulder.

"Do you need any help?"

Nannie smiles a funny upside-down smile and shakes her head. "I can manage alright when it's just the two of 'em. You wait 'til they give a party or one o' them society meetin's—then I need all the hands I can get. No, you just rest yourself and get used to li'l Master. I be back." With two steaming silver platters in her hands, Nannie pushes open a swinging door with her hip and disappears into the dining room.

I'm staring at the black dress hanging on a hook on the kitchen wall when Nannie returns. She sees me eyeing it and smiles her twisted smile again. "Glad I left that hem down. Didn't 'spect you'd be so tall. When Missus said they was gettin' a girl from the orphanage, I figgered you'd be a young'un, but you most ways grown. Soon's you get a bite to eat, we can go on upstairs and see if it fit. Henry's 'bout ready for his afternoon nap."

Before Nannie takes the rest of the serving platters out to the dining room, she sets a full plate of food before me. I want to wait until Nannie sits down to eat, too, but that food smells so good and my belly's already rumbling and Henry's putting his finger in the mashed potatoes, so I put a little lump of potato in Henry's mouth and a forkful of chicken in mine. Turns out Nannie doesn't have time to sit down and eat with me. She goes in and out of that swinging door, and each time it's something for Mrs. Brant—hotter gravy, colder water, more salt in this, less pepper in that. Now I *know* that woman's crazy, 'cause I'm eating the same thing she's eating and this is some of the best food I've ever had.

On one of her trips to the kitchen, Nannie sees me scraping my plate clean and her eyes shine the way my *abuela*'s used to back when she cooked for all of us. "You want more? You sure? There's plenty." Nannie peeks over her shoulder to make sure the door to the dining room is shut. "That's one thing I can say 'bout these white folks, they sure do keep the cold box full. You won't go hungry long as you workin' here."

When dinner's over, I try to help Nannie clean up the kitchen, but every time I put Henry down he starts to scream and cry. Nannie just chuckles and tells me to "sit tight." She says Henry is "mighty partic'lar," just like his mother, and if he wants me to hold him then that's what I should do. I look at the baby boy giggling in my arms and hope that Nannie's wrong.

When Henry starts to yawn, Nannie dries her hands and says we'll leave the pots to soak for a while. Then she takes the dress off the hook on the wall and goes over to a staircase at the back of the kitchen. "These stairs here lead up to our quarters. The rooms is small but clean, and there's plenty blankets so you won't catch cold. Later I'll show you how to get up there usin' the front stairs. Missus, she don't like for us servants to use the front stairs, 'less you's carryin' Henry or somethin' valuable that's got to get cleaned. But that's a whole other story. C'mon, I'll show you your room."

Nannie puts her hand on my back and gently pushes me toward the narrow staircase. The light pressure of her fingers lights up the circuits on my back. I jump, and Nannie looks at me. Surprise flickers in her eyes but is soon replaced with silent understanding. "Sorry," she whispers, and I want to tell her it's okay. I want to apologize for my reaction but she is already gone. Nannie is going up the stairs ahead of me, so I just follow her instead.

Nannie was right: the rooms are small. Her room is at the top of the dim, narrow staircase we just climbed. Nannie opens the door so I can see her neatly made bed, which is covered in a colorful handmade quilt. There's a wooden cross on the wall, a Bible and candle on a little nightstand by the bed, a washstand with a pitcher and basin, and that's it. A chipped chamber pot sits in the corner.

"Do you like working here, Nannie?" I ask this as Nannie closes her bedroom door and leads me farther down the hall.

"I like it well enough," she replies. "The doctor's a fine, fine man."

I nod and wonder whether or not I should bite my tongue. "What about Mrs. Brant?"

Nannie laughs, turns, and folds her arms across her chest. "What about her?"

I heft Henry on my hip. His head's on my shoulder and his eyes are starting to close. I try not to say anything too bad about his mama. "Well, she seems like she could be kind of hard to work for. Do the two of you get along?"

"Get along? We ain't exactly friends, if that's what you thinkin'."

"What I mean is—"

Nannie holds up her hand to silence me. "I know what you gettin' at, child. But if you askin' that question, I 'spect you already knows the answer. She ain't easy, but she ain't all that hard, neither. The way to get along with white folks is to know their ways and remember your place. That's the best advice I can give."

I nod, and Nannie opens the door to show me my new bedroom. The room is identical to hers, with a narrow bed, nightstand, washstand, and chamber pot. I walk over to the small window and peer out at the sky. There's a draft coming in through the glass, and I shiver and pull Henry closer to keep me warm.

Nannie walks over to the bed and smoothes down the plain wool blanket. "I got some scraps I been savin'. We could make you a quilt in no time. You know how to sew?" I shake my head and Nannie's mouth makes that funny smile. "I teach you," she says. "It ain't hard."

There is a pause, and I can tell Nannie wants to ask me what I used to do before I came to work for the Brants. I don't have anything to say, so I just wait for Nannie to say something else. "The gal we had before …"

My eyebrows go up, but Nannie doesn't continue.

"Was she fired?" I finally ask.

Nannie looks past me, out the window. She squints against the bright wintry light. "She had some trouble … gettin' along."

"With you?"

Nannie shakes her head quickly.

"With Mrs. Brant?"

Nannie rolls her lips together and just barely nods. Then she looks straight at me. "Dr. Brant's a good man."

I wait for her to say something else, but Nannie just stares at me. Then she reaches out and touches Henry's cheek. He's asleep now, and heavy to hold. "We best put him to bed."

I nod and follow Nannie as she leads me back out into the hall. She pulls the door to my room shut. It creaks noisily. Nannie keeps her hand on the knob and rolls her lips once more. "You have any trouble," she says, then drifts off again. Nannie shoots a quick glance over her shoulder. "You have any trouble up here, you call me. Alright?"

I want to ask Nannie what kind of trouble she's talking about, but it seems like she's too ashamed or too afraid to tell me the truth. I want to tell her, "I'm from Brooklyn. I can handle myself." But this Brooklyn isn't the place I know, so I just nod silently instead and follow her to the nursery.

10.

I want my old life back. Not that this new life is all that bad—working for the Brants, I mean. Nannie was right. They give us plenty to eat, and my room's small, but at least I've got a space all my own. I never had my own room before. Henry's a good kid and real easy to look after. But this life—like this body—just isn't *mine*. I want my old life back.

I want the body that isn't dotted with scars that look like somebody used me to stub out their cigar. I want the back that was smooth and strong, not half numb and covered with bubbly keloid scars. I want my days filled with school and Judah and taking Tyjuan to the garden. I want my plans of going to college and getting out of the 'hood one day. I want the Brooklyn that has subways and black and brown faces everywhere. I want my family to know that I'm alright, and I want to know that they're alright, too. But most of all, I want to take that last wish back.

That must be what landed me here. How else could this be happening? Every night after Henry's put to bed, I come up here to this little room and think long and hard. I know now that this isn't a dream. Too many days and nights have passed. I figure I've been trapped in this world for more than a month now. In the Brooklyn I know, folks will be getting ready to celebrate the Fourth of July. But here we're still stuck in the middle of winter. Mama always said be careful what you wish for. This time, Mama was right.

My first week here, I cried myself to sleep every single night. I'd just curl up, pull the blankets over my head, and cry 'til I fell asleep. In a way, I missed Mattie more than anyone else. Mama and Tyjuan and Judah—I'm missing them all the time, day and night. But they're so far away, it's like a hurt buried deep inside of me—like a splinter you just can't get out, so you walk on it every day until you get used to that kind of pain. Missing Mattie is like losing skin—you scrape your elbow or your knee, and you can see the blood, you can almost *see* the pain 'cause it's right there in front of you. Mattie's just a few miles away in Weeksville, but it feels like there's an ocean between us. And Mattie's the only friend I've got in this world.

I guess the walls are kind of thin up here, 'cause Nannie heard me crying and came into my room late one night. She pulled back the covers, held the candle over the bed, and just looked at me. Nannie's got a nice face—she never really looks happy, even when she smiles, but there's something soft at the back of her eyes. Nannie looked at me that night, and I could just tell she'd already seen the bottom of the hole I'd fallen into. And without asking me a single question, Nannie showed me how to climb back out.

First she set the candle on the dresser and crawled into bed with me. Then Nannie put her arms around me and rocked me like I was a little child. And somehow, being held like that by someone I hardly even know just opened something up inside of me. Before the hurt was just dribbling out. But now it was like Nannie had turned me upside down, and all the pain just poured out of me. "Let 'em go, honey. All the things they done to you don't matter no more, so just let 'em go. Let go the hurt so you can put somethin' good inside. I know you miss your people. Hold onto them instead of the hurt. If you keep 'em inside of you, then they's free, honey. Just like you and me, we's free. You got to let go all that sorrow, 'cause it's too heavy a load to bear."

That's all Nannie said to me that night. She told me to let go, and that's what I did. I cried for Mama and Tyjuan living alone in that crappy little apartment. I cried for Toshi getting thrown out in the street and for Rico getting thrown in jail. I cried for Abuela and Papi, even though they're in Panama. I cried for Mattie and what's left of her family, and for all the other children at the orphanage who don't even have one sibling left to call their own. But most of all I cried for myself—the person I used to be, and the person I have somehow become. I cried over losing Judah, the first boy to notice me and like me for who I was. And I cried for the girl who was tied down and beaten until the skin blistered off her back. If it hurts this much now, it must have hurt even worse then. And I don't care *what* she did—*no one* should be treated that way.

After a long while, the tears stopped coming but Nannie kept rocking me until I fell asleep. When I woke up the next morning, I felt different. Not better, just different. Lighter, maybe. Relieved that I didn't have to go through another day waiting for night to fall so I could let out a little bit more of the pain.

Nannie says that at some point, every heart learns to say *enough*. "When I was just a child, they took my ma'am away from me. The Lord blessed me with four healthy babes, and they took every last one. Two times I tried to run, but they caught me and took me back. They took my sweat, they took my blood. But I decided a long time ago that they wasn't goin' to take my tears. Oh no, I'm keepin' my salt."

Nannie doesn't say much about her life before the Brants, and she doesn't ask me about my life, either. In this world, there's a silent rule among black folks—you can talk about your past if you want to, but no one has the right to *make* you talk. Sometimes the memories are too terrible to share, and sometimes they're all a person has left of something or someone they loved and lost. Memories are sacred—you respect them or you leave them alone.

Since that night I haven't cried much at all. Nannie says you got to keep something for yourself, and to keep it safe, you got to keep it inside. That reminded me of the room inside my heart, the chamber full of green growing things—lilacs and roses and dragonflies. Most days it feels like that room is empty, but sometimes, if I close my eyes real tight, I can remember what the garden was like that day Judah gave his poem to me.

If it weren't for Nannie and Henry, I probably would've left this house and gone back to the orphanage. It's Henry who gives me a reason to smile every single day. And it's Nannie who helps me keep my cool every time Mrs. Brant pisses me off. A hundred times I tell Mrs. Brant my name is Genna, but she doesn't seem to care. She just keeps on calling me Jenny, and I've learned it's better to just accept it than to try and start something with this crazy woman.

One day I decide to ask Nannie about *her* name. "Is Nannie your real name?" I ask all casual like while we're in the kitchen.

Nannie just chuckles and points her sharp eyes at me. "That's what they call me."

For a moment I wonder if this is one of those things I should just leave alone. But suddenly I really want to know Nannie's real name, so I ask her again.

Nannie stops kneading the lump of dough and looks at the slices of fire shining through the black iron grate. "My ma'am named me Elizabeth, but folks back in Virginny called me Lizzy. When I got my free papers, I left that place behind. So don't matter much what folks call me now."

"But why do you let Mrs. Brant call you out your name?" I ask.

Nannie sucks her teeth and doesn't even bother to look up. "That woman don't know me. I been workin' here more than six years, and she don't know a single thing about me. I don't care what she calls me. She calls *herself* a Christian, but that don't mean she is."

I think about that for a minute, then come up with another question for Nannie. "So what should I call you?"

Nannie grunts and presses her knuckles into the thick lump of dough. "You can call me whatever you like so long as you look me in the eye. You look me in the eye, you know I'm a free woman. Got a piece of paper with my true name on it, says I'm free. Don't matter what anybody call me, so long as they know I don't belong to nobody but God."

Sometimes I think about Nannie's babies, the four that were sold away from her while she was still a slave in Virginia. They must be grown now—or dead. I wonder if they ever think about their mother, if they remember her at all. Maybe they're free now and looking for her. Do they know she's in New York? There are so many motherless children in this world—no wonder slaves made up that song. I *am* going to find a way out of here, but even if I don't—even if I get stuck here forever—at least I can say that I knew my mother. She made mistakes sometimes, but I know my mother loves me. And I know she's missing me now. I just hope that wherever Nannie's children are, they know that their mother loves them and misses them, too.

11.

Even though I'm living in a whole other century, whenever I'm around Mrs. Brant, *all* my ghetto comes out. In my mind, I don't even call her Mrs. Brant. I call her "bitch." Or "the bitch," or "that bitch." My mouth says, "Yes, Mrs. Brant" and "Right away, Mrs. Brant." But in my mind I'm thinking, "Do it yourself, *bitch*." But I can't say those things to Mrs. Brant. Because Mrs. Brant's a white lady, she's rich, and she's married to a hotshot doctor. I'm black, I'm poor, and in this world, nobody's got my back. Mrs. Brant's got everybody fooled, everybody except Nannie and me. I know what she's really like, because I see how she lives. I see how she treats Nannie, and I see how she won't give none to Dr. Brant, and I see how she smiles at all those abolition ladies but then screams at Nannie when the bread's a little bit burnt or the sheets aren't folded just so. I see how even her own son can't stand her—she comes near Henry and he starts to wail and fuss and his little face gets all red. She's like Dr. Jekyll and Mr. Hyde—she's a fake. And one of these days, if I get the chance, I'm gonna blow up her spot. In front of everybody, so they can see what kind of person she really is.

One day I'm bringing Henry down from his nap, and I hear Mrs. Brant hollering at Nannie in the kitchen. I know there must be trouble, 'cause Mrs. Brant almost never goes back there. What for? She's got Nannie doing all the cooking and baking and ironing and washing. That woman doesn't lift a finger all day, but right now she's pitching a fit. As I get closer to the door I can hear part of what she's saying—it's something about the cakes for her afternoon tea party. I stand there behind the closed door wondering whether or not to go in. I know Nannie doesn't like it when I interfere, and no one likes to get chewed out in front of someone else.

I decide to take Henry back upstairs to the nursery when all of a sudden I hear a sound that makes my back itch. *Thwap!* Then again—*thwap!* Then the blows start coming too fast for me to count, and before I know what I am doing, I am kicking that door so hard it slams against the wall, and I am setting Henry down too hard on the kitchen floor so that he topples over and starts to cry, and even with her own child crying and me coming 'round that table, Mrs. Brant doesn't let up. That hard, flat wooden spoon in her hand keeps going up and coming down, and Nannie, she's taking the blows like someone who already knows what hurt's about, but Mrs. Brant, she's trying to teach Nannie something new. And then I get around the table and I grab the spoon from out her hand except the bitch won't let go and when I grab it, she holds on tight and spins around like she's going to hit me next, except I don't play that and before Nannie can blurt out NO, I slap that bitch right across the face. That surprises her so bad she lets go of the spoon and I'm about to go upside her head with it when Dr. Brant bursts into the kitchen with a real loud "WHAT THE DEVIL'S GOING ON IN HERE?"

Little Henry's screaming and dragging himself across the floor so he can latch onto my leg. Henry's crying but Nannie's eyes are dry, and Mrs. Brant's face is turning purple. She's so mad she's about to blow up, and if Dr. Brant hadn't grabbed her arm, she'd have tried to crack that iron poker right over my head. She tried to kill me, that bitch, and it's a good thing Dr. Brant got between us, 'cause if that woman ever took a swing at me, it'd be over. Here she is *half* my height, *half* my weight, her ugly face looking worse than ever 'cause it's turning all different shades of red. And she wants to fight *me?*

Dr. Brant finally pries the poker out of her hand and shakes her, saying, "Amelia! Amelia! Get a hold of yourself!" He's saying it over and over like she don't know who she is, like she's somebody else right now and he can call her back just by saying her name. Dr. Brant keeps on shaking his stupid, ugly, evil wife, and after a while her face turns white and her body goes limp and Dr. Brant lays her out on the floor and tells Nannie to go get the smelling salts. I only need one glance from Nannie to know she won't ever thank me for this. I drop the spoon on the table, scoop Henry up in my arms, and walk on out the kitchen.

I go straight upstairs and put Henry back in his crib. But when I turn to leave, Henry starts screaming and my heart tears a bit, and I know I can't just abandon him. So I wrap a blanket around Henry, pick him back up, and then go down the stairs and straight out the front door. I walk out that house swearing I won't ever go back, but after just a few blocks of that cold winter air, I know I have to go back. I have to 'cause I've got Henry in my arms and I can't carry this white child all the way to Canada. And I can't think of anyplace else to go. North or South we're supposed to be free, but the scars on my body tell a different kind of story, and the bruises blooming under Nannie's black dress prove that none of us is truly free yet. Henry stops crying once we reach the park, and suddenly he's smiling and laughing and pointing at birds and wanting to get down so he can run around with the squirrels. I let him down for a little while, then I pick him up and keep walking, trying to leave that scene in the kitchen behind. I'm in the street but my head's still in that moment, and that ugly purple face is still glaring at me, wanting me dead. *I should've killed that bitch,* I keep saying under my breath. Henry smiles and pats my cheek, and I think to myself, *I'd be doing you a favor, kid.*

Then I think about the fact that in half of this country white folks still own us. We aren't people, we're things, and they can do whatever they want to us. And I wonder how many black folks take it and take it and take it until they just can't take it no more. I wonder how many white folks have died the way Mrs. Brant could have lost her life today. Then I think of Nannie and I wonder how it can be so easy to brainwash people. I wonder why she didn't fight back, didn't try to defend herself or at least cry out for help. I think about Lincoln and his worthless proclamation, and as I stand there in the street holding Henry, I realize he's the only thing keeping me safe. If I wasn't standing there holding a white child in my arms, I'd be just a worthless black girl, someone to kick around and knock down and throw away like trash.

I'm holding Henry, and the street beside us is rumbling as horses and carriages go by. I think of myself getting into one of those carriages and driving far away. But I couldn't take Henry. He'd have to stay here. Then I think of him in Mrs. Brant's arms. I think of him crying and fighting and refusing to eat 'cause I'm not around to feed him. Then I remember that time I saw a dog get trampled by a horse, and I think about what horses' hooves would do to a little body like Henry's. *I'd be doing you a favor, kid.*

I think about it just once, and then I shut my eyes tight, and I hold Henry close to me and tell him I'll always keep him safe. Henry's gotten real quiet by now. I know he's hungry 'cause it's getting dark and he never had his snack after waking up from his nap. I know it's time for us to go back, but for a moment I stand there in the dark street, holding Henry close to me to keep him warm. It hurts so much to hold him, and yet I don't ever want to let go. The hole in my heart squeezes out a little bit of blood, and it hurts, but at least I know I'm still alive. I still feel things. I'm still human, and I know this because I love Henry like I love Tyjuan. It doesn't matter that he's white and his mother's a crazy bitch. It doesn't even matter that they pay me to look after him. Henry belongs to me, same as Tyjuan. And that's what love does, it wipes out all the messy parts so you can see the picture clear.

I open up my eyes and the gaslights are burning in the street, and I realize my teeth are chattering, so I hold Henry close and head home. Home. All of a sudden I think about Mama, and I wonder if she's holding Tyjuan the same way I'm holding Henry right now. I wonder if she feels sorry for hitting me that night. I wonder if holding Tyjuan helps her forget just for a minute about losing Rico and Toshi and Papi and me. Can a little baby fill up such a big hole? Henry's sleeping head is heavy against my neck. I turn onto our street and soon I'm standing in front of the house. Lights are blazing in the parlor, and someone has lit the light above the front door.

Nannie must have been watching by the window because the front door opens before I reach the first step. I avoid her anxious eyes and stand in the foyer, ready to hand Henry over and then get my things and leave. I hear Mrs. Brant in the parlor, pleading with Dr. Brant to send for the police. Dr. Brant is ignoring her, but I can tell he is worried, too. He has his gold pocket watch in one hand, and his other fist is pressed into the small of his back.

"Henry, *please*, I'm begging you. Send for a constable *now*, while there's time, before that wretch murders our poor son. She's an animal! You saw the way she attacked me earlier today. And to think you let her walk out of this house with our child, our only child ..."

As Mrs. Brant dissolves into tears, I walk into the parlor and lay Henry in her arms. He wakes up during the exchange and, finding himself in his mother's arms, starts to wail. Mrs. Brant, overcome with joy and relief, begins fussing over Henry, checking him for bruises and scratches and other signs of damage. I glance at Dr. Brant and then head for the kitchen. He catches up with me just as I am going up the back stairs.

"Genna—we ... I—" Dr. Brant falters, then steadies himself by pressing his fingers into the hard surface of the kitchen table. "We won't be pressing charges."

I look at him, and almost without thinking say, "Neither will I."

We stare at each other for a moment, and then the kitchen door swings open and Nannie comes in carrying Henry. She heaves him into my arms and says, "The poor thing must be starvin'. Go upstairs and get him settled. I'll make some hot porridge and milk."

I do as I am told and climb up the stairs without looking back at Dr. Brant.

12.

Later, after Henry has eaten and been put to bed, Nannie comes to my room. Without knocking, she walks in and lays a tray of food on the bed. "Figgered you must be hungry, too," she says.

She's right, and I want to thank her, but I only shrug instead.

Nannie pushes the tray aside so there is room for her to sit down. "I guess you waitin' for me to thank you for what you done today."

I stare at the food cooling on the plate and decide to just let her go on.

"Seems like maybe *you* the one ought to be givin' thanks. Dr. Brant's a good man. He's willin' to let you stay on, and he wouldn't let Missus send for the police. You mighty lucky to be layin' up here 'stead of in the county jail."

Nannie glances at me to see if I show any signs of remorse. I nibble at the biscuit she has brought me so I don't have to reply.

"I don't know where you come from, gal, but you can't act that way 'round here."

I put the biscuit down and try to reason with her, even though I know it's no use. "But you're *free*, Nannie. They can't treat you that way. You shouldn't let *nobody* treat you that way."

Nannie looks at me like she's either real tired or real sick of explaining things to me. "I'm free, but I ain't stupid. You better look in the mirror and remember who you are. A black person raise they hand against a white person in this country—'specially a white *lady*—and your life ain't worth spit. I seen what they can do. Burn you alive, hang you by your thumbs, whip you 'til the bone poke through."

"You're not a slave anymore," I quietly remind her, but Nannie pays me no mind.

"My slave days may be over, but my life ain't. God willin', I got a few more years to live on this earth. Missus ain't perfect, but if you think you can find better, you best start lookin' now. 'Cause I seen the good and I seen the bad, and I ain't going *nowhere*. When Judgment Day come, the Good Shepherd will know I turned the other cheek."

I want to tell Nannie about Martin Luther King and the Civil Rights Movement, and the way black folks refused to fight back even after whites turned their water hoses and their dogs and their rifles on them. I want to tell Nannie they will still be killing black folks a hundred years from now. I want to tell her about Malcolm X and our right to self-defense. But it's 1863, and Nannie's not ready for the way the world will be. I'm amazed that Nannie has lasted this long, but then I look at her and her hard black eyes are speaking to me, they're trying to tell me all the things she has learned in her long life, the necessary things that have kept her alive.

"You young, Genna," Nannie says quietly, but there is still an edge to her voice. "You a big gal, but you think like a child. It's high time you started to act like you was grown." Nannie eases herself off the bed and heads for the door.

Before she leaves I ask her one more question. "Why was she beating you, Nannie?"

Nannie sighs and tells her answer to the door rather than to me. "Missus wanted some special cakes to have with tea this afternoon. She give me a page she tore out a magazine, had a recipe and a picture. I did the best I could, but they didn't turn out like how she wanted."

Nannie's one of the best cooks in Brooklyn—Dr. Brant's always saying so. It's hard to imagine anything she makes not coming out right. "Didn't we have all the ingredients?" I ask.

Nannie doesn't answer right away. Her hand is on the door-knob, and she looks like she can't decide whether to go or stay. Finally, Nannie turns away from the door and looks straight at me. "I don't know. I was goin' by the picture. Recipe ain't no use to me. I can't read."

It takes a minute for Nannie's words to sink in, and she leaves the room before I figure out what to say. But for once I don't feel the need to argue or apologize. Seems someone's always telling me about the things I can't do—because I'm not white, or because I'm a girl. Well, this is something I *can* do. I can teach Nannie how to read.

13.

Mrs. Brant spent the rest of the week in bed. The only time she bothered to lift a finger was to ring the bell for Nannie. It was like that was Mrs. Brant's way of making up for beating on Nannie that day. She couldn't come out and say, "I'm sorry." Instead she made Nannie go up and down those stairs at least a dozen times a day. Mrs. Brant was acting just like Scarlett O'Hara in *Gone With the Wind*. Propped up in bed with a big pout on her face, complaining about the room being too hot or too cold, and Nannie won't you fetch me this, and Nannie won't you make me that, and Nannie won't you sit a while and keep me company. She'd ring that bell and make some special request, and then she'd gush over Nannie and tell her how good and kind and sweet she was. She'd make Nannie sit by her bed and listen while she remembered all the nice things her own mammy used to do for her. Except her mammy wasn't her mother, she was the black woman who took care of Mrs. Brant back in the day, the way I take care of Henry now. I wonder if Henry will tell stories about me someday.

Considering what I did, I guess I got off easy. After our fight in the kitchen, Mrs. Brant decided she didn't have any use for me. For almost a month, I just looked after Henry and kept out of her way, which was just fine by me. Then one Saturday in April, Dr. Brant comes into the kitchen. Henry's upstairs taking a nap, and

I'm helping Nannie with the wash. Dr. Brant comes in looking all serious and says Mrs. Brant wants me to go to church with them tomorrow. He doesn't say why, he just tells me what time to be ready, and then he goes back out.

Nannie, she keeps on stirring the big tub of soapy water with this smirk on her face.

"You going, too?" I ask.

Nannie laughs out loud. "Ain't my soul needs savin'. 'Sides, I don't need to step foot in no church that 'spects me to sit at the back."

I ask her what she's talking about, and Nannie tells me that lots of white churches in Brooklyn make black folks sit at the back, or up in the gallery. "Black folks be tryin' to get closer to God, and white folks keep tellin' 'em to stay back. Watch out for Christians who don't practice what they preach," she warns me. Then Nannie's smirk returns and she says, "I 'spect you be meetin' plenty of 'em tomorrow."

I'm not looking forward to attending church with the Brants, but I can't stop Sunday morning from coming. When it does, Mrs. Brant insists on taking the carriage, even though the church is only a few blocks away. She says people of their standing can't be seen walking down the street. "It's much too common," she says. Of course, it's common. Most people don't have fancy carriages and coachmen to drive them everywhere. But that's not what Mrs. Brant means. She means walking is for low-class people. People like Mattie and Nannie and me.

Mrs. Brant must be feeling mighty Christian today, because she decides to let me ride *inside* the carriage even though little Henry is staying home. I would have preferred to sit up top with Adams, but Mrs. Brant wants to look good in front of her church friends. This is just an act and I know it, but I figure I might as well play along since there's not much else I can do. Before the carriage even starts rolling, Mrs. Brant starts running her mouth.

"Of course, I'm thankful that President Lincoln issued the

Emancipation Proclamation. And I'm ever so grateful that our brave, brave boys are shedding their blood to cleanse this nation of the stain of slavery. But I must confess that I miss the early days of agitation. Hiding slaves in cellars, rescuing fugitives from the jails. I especially miss those mock auctions Reverend Beecher used to perform. Nothing stirred my soul quite so much as seeing a poor wretch up there on the stage beside him, cowering as he took the bids." Mrs. Brant pauses to dab at her eyes with her kerchief. Then she looks right at me, and I can tell she has decided this is something I need to know—*for my edification.* But her face wrinkles with irritation when Dr. Brant joins the conversation.

"Reverend Beecher was known for his vehement opposition to slavery, Genna, especially its effects on unprotected slave women. Once he brought a poor wretch up on stage. He stood in the pulpit and reenacted a slave auction. Members of the congregation 'bid' on the woman, and the money raised paid for her manumission."

Mrs. Brant snatches the story back from her husband. "And he picked the loveliest creature. She stood there beside him, the perfect picture of modesty. Her cheeks burned, and she hung her head so that her hair covered her face—such lovely hair, too, long and wavy, nothing like the wool you see on most colored gals. That girl was quite fair—very nearly white, you know—'octoroons' they're called. And he urged us to think of our own daughters, our own sisters and mothers and wives, to imagine them caught in the clutches of depraved slaveholders, men who care nothing for virtue, who prize gold more than the soul of the enslaved. The brutes breed girls specifically for that foul purpose, you know. They call it the fancy trade—fancy indeed! I believe New Orleans is where most of them are taken. To be sold to Southern gentlemen—hmph—they don't deserve the name!"

I watch Mrs. Brant as she is talking. I have never seen her get so upset over the suffering of someone other than herself. Dr. Brant has a dreamy kind of smile on his face, and he is looking at her like he must have when they first fell in love. Was he fooled then, or now? Mrs. Brant does seem genuinely angry at the way slave women are treated. I wonder if she would feel the same way if the girl up on that stage had looked like me.

Dr. Brant clears his throat as if asking for his wife's permission and tries to squeeze back into the conversation. "Henry Ward Beecher is a very engaging speaker, somewhat more excitable than our own pastor. Reverend Beecher is a renowned reformer and a great friend of your people, Genna. Plymouth Church, where he presides, was called the 'Central Depot' of the Underground Railroad, you know."

"And, of course, his sister is none other than Mrs. Harriet Beecher Stowe. I do adore that novel!" Mrs. Brant exclaims. "I've read it at least three times, and each time I've wept like a babe. It's so moving, and *such* a realistic portrayal of slavery in the South."

Dr. Brant nods in agreement and then takes this opportunity to repair my relationship with his wife. "I'm sure Genna would benefit just as greatly from reading the book, my dear. Perhaps you could lend her your copy of *Uncle Tom's Cabin*, if you're not reading it at the present moment."

Before Mrs. Brant can even consider doing me some kind of favor, I surprise them both by telling them I've read it already. I don't tell them how much I hated it, or how it's an insult in my world to call someone an "Uncle Tom." I'm not surprised Mrs. Brant loved the book so much. All the women in it blush and weep and have porcelain complexions and long silky hair. The black folks who get anywhere are the ones who look, talk, and act white. The rest of the black folks are cooks or mammies or slaves that cut up, turn cartwheels, and speak some hard-core Ebonics. Uncle Tom, of course, is the best slave a master could buy—he's so loyal he refuses to run away, and doesn't fight back when white folks attack him. Instead, he prays and tries to get his masters to be better Christians. I start wondering what kind of white folks are going to be at this church.

It doesn't take long for me to realize that Nannie was right. Before the usher can even show the Brants to their seat, I understand that I will not be sitting with them. Instead, I am directed to a narrow staircase that leads to an upper gallery. Dr. Brant smiles awkwardly at me before following his wife down the carpeted aisle. They slip into a wooden pew packed with other white people, and I climb the stairs to sit with the black folks. The first thing I notice when I get up those stairs is that it's stuffy and hot up here. People are fanning themselves, but it doesn't really help. This space is way too small for all these bodies. I take a quick look at the raggedy benches they got us sitting on and walk right back down those stairs. The Brants are so busy greeting their rich white friends, they've completely forgotten about me. I ask an usher what time the service will end, and then I walk out the church and head down the block.

The neighborhood where I live, and where I am walking now, is—or will be—Brooklyn Heights. A lot of the street names are still the same—Hicks, Montague, Joralemon, Fulton. But like I said before, half the houses that ought to be here haven't been built yet. There's no promenade overlooking the river, and there's no Brooklyn Bridge either—just docks, and a ferry that takes people back and forth to Manhattan.

Since I don't have Henry and that big pram to push around right now, I decide to head down to the river. It's a mild spring day, and the sunshine feels good on my face. I don't think about how I look until I start down the dusty road that leads to the water's edge. Then I notice that people are staring at me, and then I realize that all these people are white. And these white folks aren't the well-to-do kind that I usually see in the Brants' neighborhood. Since it is Sunday morning, most *respectable* people are either at home or in church. These people look a little rough around the edges—and here I am in my Sunday best. All these things are going through my mind, and together they spell DANGER, but I am tired of being locked inside a box. I am tired of being told how to act and what to wear and where to go and what to do. So I hold my head up and just keep on walking down this sloping road that leads to the river.

When I get there, I realize I really have made a mistake. There is nothing worth looking at down here. Just a whole bunch of crates stacked up along the wooden pier, and men—some black, but mostly white—lounging around like they're taking an early lunch break. There are boats docked in the harbor, but they aren't very big. Up ahead I can see the ferry crossing over from Manhattan. I don't have time to take a ferry ride today, but I figure I might as well walk in that direction since some of these dockworkers are starting to pay me the wrong kind of attention.

I keep my eyes locked on that ferry and walk on real casual like, remembering something Toshi told me once: *no matter what, don't never let nobody see you scared.* Mama called that "street sense"—Toshi may not have been good at school, but she knew how to make her way through the 'hood. Though my heart is beating kind of fast, I keep on walking slow, putting one foot in front of the other like I own this part of the dock. Crude words whistle past my ears like bullets, but I don't duck or dodge. Instead, I keep my head held high and scan the barrels, crates, and sacks for a face that looks like mine. That's the other thing Toshi told me: *always make sure somebody's got your back.*

A minute ago the ferry didn't seem so far away. But now the more I walk, the farther away it seems. The dock is filling up with huge wooden crates that are being unloaded from a ship. Rotting cabbage leaves are strewn on the ground, and a pair of horses nibbles at these while dropping a fresh load of shit right there on the dock. I pull out my kerchief and cover my nose and mouth, but the stench is hard to escape. With the dock becoming more and more congested, I veer off to the side, hoping to find a route with fewer obstacles. Instead, I find myself walking through a narrow maze of crates that are stacked so high I can no longer see the river. Before I even hear the first man's voice, I realize I have made another mistake.

"Well, what have we here? A pretty little visitor, eh?"

I stop for just a second and look over my shoulder. Two greasy-looking white men are behind me. One is gripping the neck of a brown bottle, and the other is rubbing the gray stubble on his unshaved face. All Toshi's advice flies right out of my mind. I start to walk so fast I am practically running, and soon the men's laughter fades away as I leave them behind. I slow down to look back once more, and let out a sigh of relief when I see that they have gone. But then I turn around and there they are before me, laughing and leering drunkenly.

"Lost, little lady? Don't worry, we'll help ya find yer way."

The man with the bottle takes another swig while the other man comes toward me, beckoning as if I am a little child or a frightened dog. I back away from the men, and I know I should be thinking about a way to escape, but instead I am thinking *this isn't happening to me, this isn't happening to me.* But this *is* happening to me, and by the time I figure that out, my back is pressed up against one of those giant wooden crates, and the two men are coming straight at me.

"I don't want any trouble." My voice sounds tiny and weak, so I clear my throat and say it again, louder this time. "I don't want any trouble."

The two men move apart from each other so that they are coming at me from different angles. I try to keep my eyes on both men at the same time, but it is hard when they are so far apart. The one with the bottle takes another swig and says, "We don't want no trouble, neither. All we want is a little fun."

Prickles run all over my back, and I remember what Lester and Charlie said that day they found me lying in the dump. I know just what kind of "fun" these men are talking about. That day, Sam Jenkins showed up to save me, but Sam Jenkins isn't here now. Back then I believed this whole world was a dream, but now I know it is real. The scars on my body tell me so. I have been in this world just a few short months, but I have learned a lot in that time. I have learned that I am not helpless. I am free, I am smart, and I am strong. I push my back away from the wooden crates behind me and take a step toward the man with the stubbly gray beard.

"That's it, nice and easy. Won't be no trouble if you come along real quiet like." He says this like he isn't going to hurt me at all, but then he lunges at me and I quickly step to the side. Whatever he has been drinking has slowed this man's reflexes. The older man reaches for me again, but this time I shove him as hard as I can. He stumbles backward, then slips on a rotten piece of cabbage and sprawls out on the ground. Before his friend can help him, I rush forward and kick the man hard between his legs.

He howls in pain, and the younger man glares at me with his mouth open wide. He fills it with another quick swig of liquor, then sets the bottle down and comes at me. I look around and spot a piece of wood lying on the ground. I pick it up and notice there is a nail sticking out of one end. The younger man sees the nail, too, and it slows his advance. The older man is still on the ground between us, holding together what's left of his balls. He is cursing and calling me every filthy name he can think of, and I'm holding that piece of wood up like a bat, thinking maybe I should crack him over the head with it just to shut him up. But right now those dirty words aren't nearly as dangerous as the younger man's eyes. I can tell by the way he moves that he is not as drunk and is steadier on his feet. I can also see just how angry he is, and my body knows already how deadly a white man's anger can be.

"C'mere, you little bitch," he hisses at me.

I pull my arm back even farther so I am ready to take the first swing.

The older man drags himself off to the side so his friend has a clear path to me. "Damn nigger bitch," he mutters, as he props himself up against one of the crates. "Teach 'er a lesson, Mike."

The younger man grunts as if to say that's exactly what he's planning to do. Then he lunges at me, and I swing the piece of wood as hard as I can. He pulls back, but the nail rakes across his arm and he cries out in pain and surprise.

I pull my arm back and swing again, but this time he dodges the blow completely and the nail goes straight into the side of a wooden crate. I tug at the piece of wood with all my might, but the nail is stuck, and this gives my attacker just enough time to reach out and grab hold of me. I am about to scream as loud as I possibly can when another voice thunders over us.

"Murphy! That's enough. Let her go."

Murphy hesitates for a moment, then much to my amazement takes his hand off my arm. "You again," he mutters in disgust. "Always puttin' yer nose in where it don't belong."

By this time the older man has gotten to his feet. He seems somewhat afraid of the stranger, though he slaps a fake grin on his stubbly face. Then he puts an arm around Murphy and begins to pull him away. "We was just 'avin a bit o' fun. No 'arm done."

"Not in your estimation perhaps, but the young lady appears to be of quite a different mind. You owe her an apology, I think."

Even though I am still shaking inside, I take a step closer to see who owns such an important voice. To my surprise, I find it belongs to a boy who looks not much older than me. He is dressed in plain, cheap clothes like the other two men, but something sets him apart. He stands tall with his hands on his hips until the two drunks mumble slurred apologies and move farther down the docks.

I'm trying not to stare, but there is something different about this boy. He comes closer and takes off his hat before introducing himself. I don't even hear his name because I am staring into the brightest blue eyes I have ever seen. And I'm not a hundred percent sure, but I think those blue eyes belong to a black boy. He has what Toshi would call "good hair"—light brown curls that are soft enough for your fingers to pass right through. His skin is honey-colored, and he talks just like a white man, but I'm pretty sure this boy is black like me.

"You haven't told me your name," he says, and this time I actually hear him.

I try to speak, but I can't stop staring at him, and he starts to get concerned. "Are you sure you're alright? Perhaps you'd better sit down." He leads me over to some smaller crates and dusts one off with his cap before offering me a seat.

He waits a moment and then decides to start over again. "I'm Paul Easterly. And you are ..."

"Genna," I say, and try to sneak a quick look at his kitchen to see if there are any naps back there.

His strange blue eyes shine with amusement as though he's used to people staring, trying to figure out "what" he is. "Well, Genna," he says, "you've learned a valuable lesson this morning. It isn't safe for a young lady to come strolling down here alone. Next time you'd better bring your beau!" He winks at me, and I blush even though I'm thinking he means "bow" as in bow and arrow.

"How do you know those men?" I ask.

"Oh, we work together here on the docks."

"*You* work with *them*? You sounded more like their boss."

He laughs at my surprise. "I'm not exactly their boss. They mind me because they know my father owns half the ships in this harbor. If it weren't for that small yet very important fact, they'd have beaten me to a pulp a long time ago." He pauses, and his eyes become serious. "They'd do the same or even worse to you—you really shouldn't be here alone."

I know he means well, but I don't appreciate being told where I can go and what I can do. I'm glad this boy showed up when he did, but I'm no damsel in distress. "I can handle myself," I say coolly.

I can tell he wants to laugh at me, but he keeps a straight face instead. "Where did you learn how to fight like that?"

I have to think about that for a minute. I'm not sure whether I learned those moves in my own world, or if my body learned them here. "I have an older brother, and—I was a slave," I tell him.

"I'll bet your master had a hard time managing you!"

He means it as a joke and I want to take it that way, but instead I suddenly feel the rubbery lumps on my back, and it doesn't seem so funny after all. Paul watches my smile disappear and quickly apologizes. "I'm sorry, that was a stupid thing to say. I can only imagine what you've been through. But you're free now—that's what counts."

Suddenly a distant bell starts to chime, and I realize the church service will be ending soon. I get up off the crate and tell him I have to go.

"Just like Cinderella?"

This boy's full of jokes, but I don't want him to think he can keep making me laugh. So I just roll my eyes and turn to go. Then I realize I have no idea how to find my way out of this maze of crates. Paul lightly touches my arm to indicate that he will show me the way. We walk in silence for a little while, and just when I start to kind of miss his joking around, he starts up again. As we are walking up the dusty road that leads back to Brooklyn Heights, he says, "You do have a beau, don't you, Genna? I only ask because if you don't, a fellow I know of—a decent sort, intelligent, hardworking, not too hard on the eyes—enjoys the company of feisty young women. He might like to take you for a stroll one evening. I'd be happy to arrange it—with your permission, of course."

I can't believe this blue-eyed black boy is flirting with me! If his father really does own half the ships in the harbor, then that means he's rich. And it doesn't matter which world you live in—rich boys don't go for poor black girls like me. Paul seems like a good guy and a part of me wants to believe he's interested in me, but the other part feels like he's making a mistake—a mistake I'll end up paying for. So all I say is, "I'm sorry, but I can't."

Paul nods respectfully. "You're spoken for, then."

I think of Judah but don't dare say his name. Instead, I start feeling kind of flustered inside. I shake my head and try to clear my mind. "It's just that—I'm different."

"In what way?"

"For starters, I'm a nanny—I work for this white family, Dr. and Mrs. Brant. They're real uptight. They made me go to church with them this morning …"

"And yet here you are with me. They can't be that strict if you managed to slip away so easily."

I had to admit he had me there. I tried again. "It's not only that. I live with them because I have no home, no family …"

"So you're a nanny and an orphan. I'm the bastard son of a wealthy white merchant. That sounds like a fair match to me." His eyes are twinkling again, and I find myself smiling even though I know it's not right. What would Judah say if he saw me talking to this boy? Then I think about all those cute girls back in Brooklyn, and I wonder if Judah's already forgotten about me.

When we reach Montague Street, I tell Paul he's walked me far enough. I'll be in trouble if the Brants find out I left the church, but they'll probably fire me on the spot if they find out I spent all that time with a boy.

"Are you sure you won't reconsider my offer? I'm only asking for a little bit of your time—just an hour of your company …"

I shake my head, but this boy is persistent.

"Half an hour then? Fifteen minutes? Surely you have some time to spare. They can't keep you busy all day long."

I am trying not to smile, but my lips just won't stay put. Finally I say, "Listen, Paul, I really appreciate what you did for me today, but I can't go out with you. I'm not going to be here long—"

"Really?" he asks. "Where are you headed? I only ask because I'm not planning to stay here long, either. I've had enough of the city. I'm heading west—to one of the new territories: Kansas,

Oklahoma, maybe even as far as California. The country's opening up, Genna. Of course, not everyone's cut out for frontier living." He pauses and winks at me. "It takes men—and women—of a certain kind of mettle. You have to be strong, and independent, and brave. We'd make a good team, I think."

Team? Kansas? Now I *know* this boy is crazy. I realize there's no point trying to talk to him, so I turn to leave but he grabs my hand. "I have a feeling we're going to meet again, Genna. At least I hope so." He squeezes my hand just a little bit, then tips his cap at me and walks away. I watch him for just a second, then I head back toward the Brants' church. Paul Easterly might be crazy, but I wouldn't mind if we did meet again.

14.

One thing hasn't changed since I came to this world: I still keep extra pennies in my pocket. I figure if it's a wish that got me into this mess, maybe another wish can get me out.

Now that the weather's warming up, every day I take Henry outside for a walk. There are plenty of little parks around here, and a big one not too far from the Brants, in front of City Hall. Each afternoon, once Henry's had his lunch, I put him in his *perambulator* (that's what they call baby carriages) and we go out looking for fountains. Some of the small parks have them, but people look at me funny if I stand there and start throwing money away. I have to remember that even though this is still Brooklyn, it's 1863, and people may expect to see a black girl taking care of a little white boy, but they don't expect to see me doing much of anything else. I don't have all that many pennies to spare, anyhow. And so long as I'm not throwing money away, most white people look at Henry, they don't look at me. It's like I'm invisible—not in the picture at all.

Sometimes I see other nurses pushing babies in prams or chasing after older kids that can run around on their own. I've smiled at a couple of them, but they never smile back. I think it's because I'm black. I've never had a white friend before, but I wouldn't mind having one now, 'cause I got to say, I've been feeling kind of lonely these days. I haven't seen Paul Easterly again, and somehow

I doubt I ever will. Nannie's great to talk to, but she's more like my grandmother. I want to talk to somebody who's my age, someone who can tell me what folks do for fun around here. I only get one afternoon off every other Sunday, but I'd still like a girlfriend to hang out with. Going to the movies or the mall is out of the question, but there must be something young folks can do. I wonder if Coney Island exists yet. I wonder if black people are allowed to go on the rides.

One afternoon I'm sitting in the small park close to where the Brants live when I see a girl who looks like she's about my age. That's the first thing I notice about her, but then I see how the other nurses cut their eyes at her, and that makes me even more interested in this girl. She stares right back at them, proudly tossing her stringy blond hair over her shoulder and even sticking out her tongue at one real snooty nurse. This makes me smile to myself, but my smile disappears as I watch the girl sidle up to the garbage cans and lift up the newspapers to see if any food's lying underneath. Whatever she pulls out of the trash she shoves into her pocket, even though her eyes look like she wants to eat it right there on the spot.

I have an apple and some biscuits in my bag. Nannie always sends me out with food in case Henry or I get hungry and want a snack. I want to give it to this girl, but I'm not sure she will take it from me. Because this hungry, shabby-looking girl is white, and even though I am clean and well-dressed and well-fed, I am black. I clutch the apple inside my bag, not sure what to do.

Eventually the girl makes her way to my corner of the park. There is a trash bin at the end of my bench, and I try not to watch her as she picks through the garbage looking for something to eat. Finding nothing, she wipes her hands on her filthy apron and slowly walks past the bench. Henry gurgles in his buggy, and she peers around the hood to peek at his face.

"Lor', what an angel that one is. Whiter than snow!" she says in wonder.

I decide to take a chance and smile at the girl. "His name's Henry."

The girl wrings her fingers to keep herself from reaching down and touching Henry's milky white skin. "Henry, is it? We got a Henry at home, we do. 'Cept he's bigger 'n this tot and not half as clean. Hello, Henry. I'm Martha."

I listen to Martha as she goes on talking to Henry. Sometimes she pronounces her Hs and sometimes she doesn't. I hear a bit of an accent, and it reminds me of the two jerks who tried to mess with me down by the docks. Ever since that day I haven't been too fond of the Irish, but something about the way this girl is smiling at Henry makes me decide I like her enough to try and make friends. "Does your little brother like apples, Martha?"

She gives me a funny look, then bursts into a wide grin. At least two of her front teeth are missing, and the rest don't look so good. "Lor', Henry'll eat whatever he gets his hands on—which isn't much. Not when there's so many other hands around." Martha looks farther down to the next garbage can. "I better go. Cook'll be wondering where I've gone off to."

I pull the apple from my bag and push it into her hands. "Take this—for your brother," I say. Then I get up from the bench and start pushing the pram away real quick. I don't want to see her throw that apple away just 'cause it came from my black hands. When I reach the gates of the park, I feel a slight tug at my sleeve. It is Martha. She smiles shyly this time, hiding her teeth, and mumbles, "Thank ye, miss."

"Do you come here every day?" I ask, all the while thinking about the bushels of apples down in the cellar and Nannie's fresh rolls and a small hunk of cheese no one would really miss from the cold box.

Martha nods and points down the street. "I work over there in that big yellow house. Missus falls asleep for about an hour every afternoon, and when Cook takes a nip she usually nods off, too. I come here when I know I won't be missed. Can't stay long, but it's nice to get a bit of fresh air. Nice to stand up and give my poor knees a break." I must look confused because Martha stops to explain. "I'm a scrubber, you see. Not a proper maid, or a nanny like you. Just a scullery maid. High-class Yankees won't let the Irish look after their children. They'd rather hire a German or a *nig*—well, they just won't, that's all." Martha blushes and looks down at the apple. Henry sees red and reaches out to grab it, and Martha immediately hands it over to him.

Despite the unforgivable word she *almost* said, I still like this girl. I reach down and take the apple out of Henry's hands and give it back to Martha. "You keep it," I say, as Henry starts to wail. I slip him a biscuit instead and within seconds he stops crying and shoves it into his mouth. Martha blushes again and smiles at me with her messed-up teeth.

"Maybe I'll see you around sometime," I say. I want to tell her to meet me here at the same time tomorrow, but I'm still trying to feel her out. "My name's Genna." I hold out my hand but Martha hesitates, and I wonder if maybe she really does hate black people after all.

Then I realize that Martha's blushing again, her face is pink and her ears are hot and red like the apple. She's wiping her hand over and over on the dirty apron, but her hand's not coming clean. I grab it anyway and smile so she knows it's okay. Martha's hand feels like a piece of steel wool. She's got to be about my age, but her hands look like they're eighty years old.

"Bye, Genna," Martha whispers shyly, as she takes back her hand. I walk away but look back when I'm about halfway down the block. Martha is using the teeth she has left to devour that little apple. I turn back around and decide to ask Nannie for two apples tomorrow in case I see Martha again.

15.

"Genna?"

I jump and the book I was pulling from the shelf falls to the floor. I reach for it, but Dr. Brant is faster than me. He reads the spine before speaking sternly to me. "What are you doing in here? I think I told you, my study is off limits."

I nod and take a quick look at Dr. Brant. His face is serious but not angry. I decide to tell him the truth.

"Nannie asked me to teach her how to read, sir. I was looking for a suitable book."

Dr. Brant's face softens into a smile, but it is a smile that is laughing at me. "A suitable book, eh? Well, I don't think I have any primers in here, Genna. Perhaps something from young Henry's collection would be more appropriate than—" he glances at the book that had fallen to the floor, "Shakespeare's sonnets."

"Nannie's not a child," I say with just a hint of attitude. "And I thought poetry might be a good place to start."

"Do you like poetry, Genna?"

I nod and try to get a bit closer to the door. But Dr. Brant points to the leather chair that faces his desk. I understand his unspoken instruction and sit down. Dr. Brant opens the book, leafs through a few pages, and hands it back to me. "Read that for me, will you?"

Dr. Brant goes around his desk and settles into his own plush leather chair. He sets his elbows on the armrests and presses the tips of his fingers together.

I look down at the poem he has asked me to read. I have never read this sonnet before, so I read it quickly in my head. Then I glance up at Dr. Brant. He is watching me with a small smile on his face, and it is a smile that is laughing at me. It is a smile that expects me to fail. I clear my throat and read in a sure, steady voice. I remember to pause when there is a comma, and to go on when there is not. When I am finished, Dr. Brant keeps on watching me. His smile is gone.

"You read that very well, Genna. Your previous masters obviously took a great deal of interest in your education."

I have nothing to say that will make any sense to him, so I look at my lap and say nothing. I listen for Henry and hope he will start to cry right now. But Henry is fast asleep. I tucked him in an hour ago.

Dr. Brant keeps staring at me until I start to fidget in the chair. He is studying me like there is a magnifying glass between us and I am some kind of interesting insect. I avoid his eyes and look at the weird things he keeps on his desk. When my gaze falls on a small plaster sculpture of a human head, Dr. Brant finally breaks the silence. He picks up the head and turns it around in his hands. I can see that the skull has been removed from half of the head, leaving the brain exposed.

"The human mind has long been a mystery to man. But science has a way of tearing the veil Nature placed before our eyes. Soon we'll understand everything about the body, and that includes the brain. I'd like to know, Genna, what interests you about psychiatry. It seems an unusual choice for someone of your … circumstances."

I lift up my chin so I can look Dr. Brant straight in the eye. "I don't think it's unusual to want to help people deal with their problems. That's what you do, right?"

"Certainly. But I think you would agree that we are two very different individuals in terms of origin and breeding. How does a young woman, and a former slave, learn about something like psychiatry?"

Even though I was born in a time after segregation, I feel like Dr. Brant has just hung a "whites only" sign over the future I want to build for myself. I can feel my cheeks burning, and my tongue starts to feel real slippery inside my mouth. I don't want to go off on my boss, but I also don't want him to think he can talk to me any old way. So I jack my chin up another inch and grip the armrests on my chair. "I learned about psychiatry the same way anyone learns anything—from reading books. It's not my fault I used to be a slave. If it weren't for white folks and slavery, black people would be doing all kinds of things. We just haven't had the same opportunities."

Dr. Brant wants to laugh, but he keeps a straight face so I won't take offense again. "And given the opportunity, Genna, what would *you* do?"

I answer without hesitation so Dr. Brant knows I'm serious. "Go to college, get my degree, and open my own practice."

"You're an ambitious young woman. If you don't mind my asking, how do you intend to pay for your education?"

This time I can't answer right away. Dr. Brant raises his eyebrows and waits to see whether I can come up with a response. I clear my throat and say, "I'm not sure. I could win a scholarship, or I could get a job and work my way through school. I'll find a way to make it happen."

"Alone?"

"What choice do I have?"

"Well, you'll soon discover, Genna, that there are very few things in this world that can be accomplished single-handedly. Wouldn't it be best to ask for assistance? You know, there are many wealthy men and women in this city who would be very interested in helping a bright Negro girl like yourself. I'd be willing to make some inquiries on your behalf—unless you really are determined to proceed on your own."

I don't say anything for a moment. Too many ideas are rushing through my head. Could I really go to college *here*, in this world? Why would Dr. Brant want to help me, and what would he expect in return? My mind goes back to that night when it was real late and Nannie thought she heard somebody coming down the hall. She knocked on my door to make sure I was okay, and for the hundredth time said, "Call me if you have any trouble." Nannie's afraid Dr. Brant might try to take advantage of me. I guess that's what happened to the last girl who quit, but that's *not* going to happen to me. Still, I think maybe all this talk is just a trap and Dr. Brant is using college as some kind of bait. I'm so busy thinking about these things that I almost forget Dr. Brant is still talking to me.

"I'm not certain, however, that psychiatry is the field of medicine best suited to meet the needs of your people. Mental illness is rife among the poor, but it might be best for you to study something more practical—internal medicine, or infectious diseases. As a matter of fact, a considerable amount of time has already been devoted to the study of the Negro mind. And you must, of course, consider your own limits as a person not far removed from the stultifying effects of slavery. Nursing is a respectable profession for a Negro girl, and doctors of any race will always need competent help. I, myself, would have no objections to hiring a Negro as my assistant. Indeed, I feel it is my obligation to uplift those upon whom Nature has bestowed diminished capabilities. It is the duty of every moral, upstanding man to protect and guide those placed within his care, be they women, children, or Negroes."

I blink once, and then I blink again. My lips fall apart and I know I should say or do something, but Dr. Brant keeps right on talking like he hasn't said anything wrong. With my mouth open, I sit frozen in my chair as Dr. Brant tells me in his smiling way just how inferior I am. I watch him as he holds up the sculpture of the human head and points to a section of the brain, but I am so mad I can no longer tell what he is saying. Finally I manage to stammer, "What are you talking about?"

"Hmm? I'm sorry, Genna, you'll have to forgive me. I've been talking to you as if you were one of my peers. Let me see if I can put this in layman's terms. Cranial measurements help us to assess the capacity of the brain for intelligence, reason, and rational thought: the larger the skull, the larger the brain. And obviously those who possess larger brains exhibit greater intelligence."

"And what did you just say about women?"

"Well, research has demonstrated that women, like children, have smaller brains, which explains their intellectual inferiority. Negroes as well have been shown to possess smaller brains—which doesn't mean, of course, that they are incapable of rational thought, rather that there are obvious *limitations* to their intellectual develop-ment." Dr. Brant takes my shocked silence for confusion. He gets up from his desk and pulls a thick leather-bound book from his shelf. He flips to a page with a diagram and sets it in front of me. The diagram shows a white lady with this weird metal instrument wrapped around the top of her head. Below this is another picture of what is supposed to be a black man, except it doesn't look like a black man. It looks more like an ape.

I blink again, but all I'm seeing is red.

I know I should wait until I am dismissed, but if I don't leave *now*, I'm going to hurt this man. "I have to go," I say, getting up from my seat.

Dr. Brant closes the big book and smiles at me like I am a child. "Of course, I didn't mean to keep you up so late. I've enjoyed our conversation, Genna. First thing tomorrow morning I'll contact Dr. Edwards and tell him about the promising young woman I know who would like to become a nurse."

I want to correct Dr. Brant and tell him I plan to become a

doctor, but I am too busy looking at the shape of his head. It doesn't look any bigger than mine.

Dr. Brant comes around his desk and puts his hand on my arm, guiding me toward the door. "In the meantime, Genna, I think you should begin to accompany me on my rounds. You can learn a great deal from reading books, but nothing teaches a student like actual experience. I'll arrange for Nannie to assume your responsibilities while you're with me. Goodnight, Genna."

Somehow I manage to say goodnight to Dr. Brant before leaving the study. Somehow I manage not to slam the door behind me, and somehow I make it up the back stairs and into my little room without smashing anything into pieces along the way. I sit down on the bed and look at my hands in the pale moonlight. They are shaking with rage.

Nannie knocks softly on my door before pushing it open. I had forgotten that she was waiting for me. Even in the dim candlelight I can see that Nannie's face is pulled tight with worry.

"Everythin' alright?"

I look at Nannie and wonder if she knows what Dr. Brant *really* thinks about people like us.

"He didn't try—I mean, the doctor didn't—you alright?"

I nod, but Nannie's eyes dig into me, searching for the truth. I wonder what Nannie would do if Dr. Brant *had* tried to get fresh with me. I wonder what *I* would have done, too.

"Dr. Brant wants me to start going with him on his rounds."

"Why?" Nannie asks, her voice full of suspicion.

"To learn about medicine," I answer. "He said he would help me get into college."

Nannie's eyes are full of doubt. I can tell Nannie doesn't trust Dr. Brant's offer or his intentions. What's worse, she doesn't think I can tell the difference between the two.

Then I remember why I went to Dr. Brant's study in the first place. I tell Nannie that I left the book downstairs.

Nannie just sucks her teeth and turns to go. "You leave them high-tone books alone. Ain't nothin' in there I'm tryin' to read nohow. And from now on, you stay out of the doctor's study. Why, I got the Good Book right here in my room. We might as well start with that." Nannie presses her lips together, then decides she has something more to say. "A man's just a man, Genna. You remember that. White or black, rich or poor. Don't let no man fill your head up with all kinds of crazy notions. The doctor ain't nothin' but a man."

I nod to show Nannie I hear her advice. She goes back to her room to get her Bible, and I try to focus my mind on the best way to teach Nannie how to read.

16.

It's May already. That means spring is here. That also means I have been trapped in this world for almost six months. I still think about my old life every day. But my new life takes up so much of my time, sometimes I forget about finding a way to get back home.

I wonder if this is how slaves felt when they got sold from one place to another—from one owner to another. Nobody owns me here, but I still feel like I got stolen away from my family, my home, everything I used to know. And now I'm here, in this new world, and that splinter's still buried deep inside of me, and I still feel it with every step I take, but I'm still walking around. I'm still living, I'm still breathing, I'm still finding reasons to laugh and smile. The cherry blossoms still look pretty to me, and the sun feels good on my skin. My locks are still growing, and I'm still twisting them each night. I haven't forgotten my roots, but I can feel myself growing farther and farther away.

Right now my life feels pretty full, and I guess I like it that way. When you fill up your days with things to do, you squeeze out all the wide empty spaces where loneliness likes to hide. Each day I get up, wake Henry, bathe him, dress him, feed him, and watch him while he plays. I take him for a walk each afternoon, and usually I get to see Martha in the park three or four times a week. I usually bring something for us to eat, and we sit on a bench laughing while

Martha tells me crazy stories about her seven younger brothers and sisters. I knew people who were struggling just to get by back in Brooklyn—*my* Brooklyn, I mean. But Martha's family is poor—dirt poor. The way Martha tells it, the Irish have it just as bad as black folks here in New York—maybe even worse. White Americans don't like the Irish because even though their skin's the same color, they're foreign, and Catholic, and most of the recent immigrants are poor. Martha's father hasn't had a steady job in months. Her mother works as a hostess in a local pub, but she can't work when she's pregnant, and it seems like Martha's mom is pregnant a lot of the time. So mostly it's up to the older kids to try to earn money any way they can—selling papers, washing dishes, shining shoes, or scrubbing floors for rich white folks in Brooklyn. Times are tough for Martha's family, but that's not all we talk about. Martha tells me about her boyfriend, Willem, and I tell her the things I am finding out about Paul.

Paul Easterly is *not* my boyfriend. That's what I tell Martha, and that's what I keep telling myself. We aren't even dating, really. He's just this guy who comes around once in a while. I don't even know how he figured out where I live. He just showed up at the back door one evening, and Nannie let him in. He finally gave up trying to get me to go for a walk with him, though. We did go one time, but the people we passed on the street thought Paul was a white man, and they weren't exactly thrilled to see him out walking with me. Paul even took his cap off so folks could see his curly hair, but at night, all they saw was his pale skin. Some people just glared at us, but others said some pretty nasty things, and finally a rude constable told us to go back where we belonged. It's not like that everywhere. In Martha's neighborhood, black folks and white folks hang out together all the time. But we don't live in the Five Points, we live in Brooklyn Heights. And folks just don't do that around here.

So instead of taking me for a walk, Paul just shows up at the back door every other night and sits at the kitchen table with us while I give Nannie her reading lesson. To me Paul's just an okay guy, but to Nannie, he's *all that*. He's real polite, he loves Nannie's cooking, and I guess he has a way about him—charming, is what Nannie calls him. She talks about him more than I do, and every night she sets aside a heaping plate of food just in case Paul stops by. At first I thought maybe Nannie was colorstruck—sometimes it looks like she's about to drown in those freaky blue eyes of his. But the more I watch them, the more I realize that Nannie treats Paul just like he's her son. She fusses over him and fixes buttons that are falling off his shirt. And Paul, he doesn't really care one way or the other, but he lets Nannie keep on fussing 'cause he knows it means something to her. Paul has never been a slave. He was born free, and his mother was given her freedom by the last man who owned her—the wealthy white merchant from Maryland who is also Paul's father. Paul doesn't say much about his mother—just that she died when he was a little boy. So in a way, he and Nannie are made for each other—a motherless child and a childless mother.

Paul may have Nannie wrapped around his little finger, but he doesn't have that effect on me. Mostly I just ignore him and pretend I'm too busy helping Nannie learn her ABCs. But sometimes Adams comes in from the carriage house, and he and Paul talk politics. Then I kind of listen with one ear, and if I hear something I disagree with, I join in and give my own opinion. Adams doesn't like that too much—he thinks women should stick to cooking and cleaning. Nannie doesn't exactly agree with that, but she thinks politics should be left up to men. Paul—he just loves picking a fight with me. Sometimes I think he says messed-up things on purpose just so I'll stop what I'm doing and pay attention to him. Then after we've been arguing for fifteen minutes, he'll hold up his hands like he wants to surrender, and he'll wink at me before saying something about how much he admires a woman who knows her own mind. Other times Paul will tell Adams about his plans to go out west, and I'll feel his blue eyes watching me, but I don't ever look up. He can go to Kansas if he wants to. I'm not going anywhere, unless that somewhere is back home.

Nannie calls us sweethearts, but it's not like that at all. I haven't kissed Paul or anything, although I can tell he wants me to. I want to tell Paul about Judah so he'll know that he's wasting his time. But how do I tell him I'm waiting for someone who will probably never arrive? Besides, I get the feeling Paul would just smile and tell me he's willing to wait. It gets on my nerves sometimes how he acts like he's made up his mind about me. But there is a small part of me that feels let down on the evenings when Paul doesn't show up. When that happens, I find myself worrying about him, wondering if something happened down on the docks, or if he met another girl who's lighter, or richer, or who treats him better than me.

Other times I try to make Paul say or do things that will make me like him less. He's kind of touchy about the fact that his father's white, so that's usually where I start.

"Are you white or black?" I ask him after Nannie's gone upstairs and Adams has gone back out to the carriage house.

Paul tries to act like nothing's wrong, but his eyes frost over a bit. "I couldn't very well sit here with you if I were white, now could I?"

"If you were white, you could do whatever you want."

"I couldn't walk down the street with you on my arm."

He's right about that, so I try to come up with another question. "Are you black 'cause you want to be, or just 'cause you can't be white?"

And Paul says, "I'm black because that's what this country tells me I am. There are only two boxes, and one drop of Negro blood locks you inside the 'black' box. So that's where I am, and that's where I'll stay."

"You could pass," I tell him. "You could cut your hair, change your name, and go out west as a white man. No one would know."

"*I'd* know," he fires back.

"So it *does* matter to you, then?" I say this as though it is news to me, even though it's not.

"Apparently it matters to *you*."

Paul thinks the reason I won't call him my "beau" is because he's almost white. He says he knows all about prejudice, but most of what he learned didn't come from whites. Paul told me once that the most hurtful words he's ever heard came out of the mouths of black folks. After his mother died, Paul's father sent him to a private school for black boys somewhere outside of Boston. Paul said he was thankful for such a good education, but living up there with those boys was the worst time of his life. The white teachers favored him because he was smart and light-skinned and spoke proper English. And the other boys hated him because he was the teacher's pet and didn't act or look like them. That reminded me of the problems I used to have at school, with other kids picking on me just 'cause I got As. I told Paul I understood.

"How could you?" he asked. "You've no idea what it's like being one person on the inside and being someone else on the outside."

I wanted to tell Paul that I knew *exactly* how that felt. But instead I said, "I do know what it's like to be judged. I know how much that hurts." I reached over and put my hand on his arm. "But no matter what anyone else says or thinks, I'm proud of who I am. And you should be, too."

"I never said I was ashamed." Paul looked straight at me then, and his blue eyes weren't frosted over anymore, they were warm like a summer sky. My cheeks started to burn, and I had to admit Paul looked pretty good to me even when I was trying to make him look bad. He put his hand over mine before I could it pull it away, and I don't know what would have happened next if Dr. Brant hadn't walked into the kitchen. Paul jumped up and grabbed his hat as if he was just about to leave, but I stayed right where I was. It wasn't like we were doing anything wrong. But Dr. Brant didn't see it that way. He acted like he was my father or something, and told Paul he had to go. I don't think Dr. Brant likes Paul. Or maybe he just doesn't like *me* liking Paul.

Once Paul was gone, Dr. Brant asked me to make him a cup of tea. That's not really part of my job description, but I didn't want to bother Nannie, so I put the kettle on. Instead of going back to his study and waiting for me to bring him his tea, Dr. Brant paced around the kitchen and started giving me a lecture on "chastity." I'd never really heard that word before, but it didn't take long for me to figure out what he meant.

"Above all else, a young woman in your position must keep herself pure. In any profession, a spotless reputation is worth its weight in gold. But if you are to achieve your goals—and if I am to assist you in this endeavor—I must be assured of your willingness to forego the fanciful distractions of youth. There will be time enough for romance after you have completed your schooling. And I daresay you will then meet a young man who is deserving of your affections."

Dr. Brant kept pacing back and forth as he was saying all this, and his face was getting red either from the exercise or embarrassment. He sounded just like Mama when she found out about me and Judah. But Dr. Brant isn't my mother, and I don't believe he's looking out for me. So I didn't fight back or get angry. I just sat there at the kitchen table wishing I had kissed Paul right in front of Dr. Brant. In fact, I made up my mind I *would* kiss Paul the very next time we met. Not just because I wanted to, but because I *could*. Because it was *my* choice to make, not Dr. Brant's.

After a while, the kettle started to boil and I got up to make Dr. Brant his cup of tea. That's when he pulled his handkerchief out and started dabbing at his face. "It's quite a warm night after all. I think a glass of cold water will do."

I wanted to tell Dr. Brant to get it himself, but instead I poured him a glass of water and excused myself before going up the back stairs.

Later on, as I twisted my locks, I thought about Judah and Paul. They're as different as night and day, and I don't mean just the color of their skin. I want to be faithful to Judah, but I also don't want to be alone. It's not fair for Dr. Brant to expect that of me, and I don't think Judah would want that, either. But there's no way for me to know what he's thinking right now, or how he feels about the way I just disappeared. For all I know, people back home might think I'm dead. What would I do if it was Judah who vanished? I'd cry a whole lot, and I'd miss him like crazy. And I guess I might contact the police and try to figure out what happened. And then maybe, after a while, I'd start to notice other boys and I'd try to find somebody who could make me feel the way Judah did.

I don't know if Paul could ever make me feel that special. But he is one of the few people in this world who likes me *because* I'm smart and stubborn and not afraid to speak my mind. The next time Paul asks if he can be my beau, I don't think I'll say yes. But I just might say maybe.

17.

The next morning as I'm bringing Henry downstairs, I see Mrs. Brant storm out of the kitchen. I rush in to figure out what's wrong and find Nannie standing with her hands planted on her hips and her eyes pointed straight at me.

"I'm a Christian woman, so I ain't about to lie. I take a little now and then to support the people at my church. Some of 'em just reached here from down South, and they needs a helpin' hand 'til they gets on they feet. But I ain't been takin' enough to catch nobody's eye. You a big gal, Genna, but I know you can't eat that much—not without help."

I bite my lip and decide to tell her the truth about Martha. Nannie listens to the whole story with her skinny strong arms folded across her chest.

"They Irish, you say?"

I nod. Nannie purses up her lips and asks how many mouths I've been feeding. When I tell her, her lips screw up even more.

"You see this gal every day?"

I nod again, thinking Nannie must be calculating how much food I've been giving away.

"You likely to see her again tomorrow?"

I nod for the third time, and finally Nannie's lips come undone. She whistles soft and low. "That's a lot of mouths to feed. You come back here tomorrow 'fore you take Henry for his walk. I give you somethin' to take over there. But from now on you stay outta my cupboards, understand?"

I say "yes, ma'am" like I mean it, with respect, not like how I say it to Mrs. Brant. The next day when I'm about ready to head to the park, Nannie calls me into the kitchen. There's a package on the table, but I can't tell what it is. It's wrapped up in brown paper like the meat that comes from the butcher.

"You tell that Irish gal to boil these bones with some onions and potatoes. Some hearty beef soup should fill 'em up. If the little ones got tightness in the chest, tell her to put some pepper in theirs—much as she's got and much as they can stand. She know where you live?"

I shake my head and Nannie grunts. "Keep it that way. Now go on."

I take the bundle off the table, then I turn real quick before Nannie can catch me and I plant a kiss on her smooth, worn cheek.

"Get out of my kitchen, you little thief," Nannie says, but I can hear the smile in her voice.

I walk to the park a bit faster than usual. Henry's fussing 'cause he's got to share his pram with the package. It's kind of warm today, and I don't want the meat left on the bones to spoil, so soon as I get to the park I start looking out for Martha. But an hour goes by and Martha doesn't show up. I'm starting to get a bit nervous, and I'm not sure if I should rush back home or walk over to the big yellow house and ask if Martha's there. Finally, just as I'm about to leave, Martha comes flying down the street. She starts telling me some story about the cook, but I cut her off and pull the bundle out of the pram.

"What's that?" she asks.

I tell her, but real casual like so she won't feel a way about it. I'm thinking Martha's going to grin a bit, maybe even hug me or say something funny in Irish. But Martha doesn't say anything. She just stands there blinking at me.

"Don't you want it?" I ask.

Martha blinks again, then wipes her nose with her sleeve and takes the package from my hands. She sniffs kind of loud and nods with her lips rolled in. I wonder if I have done something wrong. I wonder if this is *too much*, too much to give at once. But they're hungry. Her brothers and sisters are starving and sick, so how can anything be *too much*?

"God bless ye, miss" is all Martha can say. We wrap the package up in her shawl, and I watch her as she walks down the street. Before she goes inside the yellow house, Martha turns and looks back at me. I smile and wave from the shadows of the trees. Martha squints in the sunlight until she finds me, then she waves and goes inside.

I walk kind of slow on the way home, thinking about what it means for people like me and Nannie to help people like Martha and her family. Nannie would say a good Christian helps those in need, no matter if they're white or black. For me, it's about being a good friend. And the way I see it, the Irish have it just as bad as black folks in this world. I guess somewhere down the road all that's going to change, but for now, I'm not about to let my friend go hungry just 'cause she happens to be white.

It's a nice, sunny day, and I'm not in any rush to get back home. I'm feeling kind of open inside, like the sun is shining on all the flowers and green things I keep in that special room inside my heart. Up ahead there's some kind of commotion, and I decide to check it out. There is a wagon parked by the curb that is full of furniture, and two white men are loosening the ropes that were used to keep the chairs and dressers from falling off. It looks like a new family is moving into our neighborhood. I stop in front of the fancy brownstone and watch the movers unloading the expensive furniture. A white woman who looks like the housekeeper is standing on the front stoop, fussing and scolding and telling them to watch what they're doing. I laugh a little to myself 'cause this woman reminds me of Nannie. It's funny how some servants act like the stuff that belongs to their bosses actually belongs to them.

I put a hand over my eyes to shield them from the sun and gaze up at the four-story house. A window on the second floor is open, and a white lace curtain is fluttering in the spring breeze. Then the curtains part and so do my lips because a girl about my age appears in the window. Her face is black like mine, but her hair is long and loose. I stare up at her small face framed by this enormous house, and something tells me that she is not a servant. Perhaps it is the fancy dress she is wearing, or the way her hand holds back the lacy curtain. I'm not sure what it is, but somehow I know that she belongs in that window, in that house, in this neighborhood where only the richest white people live—the "best families," as Mrs. Brant would say. I stare up at her and for just a second I wonder why I came back as a runaway. For just a second I wish I was that girl standing in the window looking down at me.

Then something unexpected happens and my heart skips a beat. It's like when you're watching a bird on the ground or in a tree, and suddenly it flies away and you knew it was a bird and had wings and could fly, but still you feel surprised once it's gone. I'm staring up at the black girl in the window, when all of a sudden she raises her hand and waves at me. She waves and smiles just a bit, like she might be kind of shy, and my heart jumps, and then I remember myself and wave back, and I tell Henry to wave, too, and he does. We both wave up at the girl, and she smiles down at us, and then one of the movers says something rude to me and I have to walk away.

But when I look back, she's still in the window, smiling at me.

18.

Dr. Brant has started taking me with him on his rounds. I guess he figures if he fills up my nights along with my days, I won't have time to see Paul anymore. And so far, he's right. I haven't seen Paul in over a week.

What I have seen is just what kind of damage war can do. Here in the North, in a big city like New York, we don't always feel the effects of the war. People talk about it a lot, and we've had to ration certain things. But nobody's trying to blow up our homes or set fire to our crops. And nobody's shooting us full of bullets that have to be cut out with a knife and *no* anesthesia. If half your leg gets blown off by a cannonball, they tie you to the bed, pour some whiskey down your throat, and cut the rest of it off with a saw—for real, like the same kind of saw they'd use to cut wood. I wasn't ready for all that, and Dr. Brant knew it. He's testing me—seeing if I have what it takes to become a doctor. I want to prove that I do, but psychiatry has nothing to do with blood and guts and wounds rotting with gangrene. Psychiatry is about helping people deal with depression or trauma—and some of these soldiers could use a little therapy. They're just about out of their minds. And I guess I would be, too, if I'd seen my friends blown to pieces all around me.

Mostly I assist Dr. Brant in the evenings. He visits the military hospitals during the day, but when Mrs. Brant heard he was taking me away from Henry, she threw a fit and said I could only go with him once Henry was put to bed. So every evening Dr. Brant comes into the kitchen and tells me to get my things. Then Adams drives us out to different people's houses—rich white folks mostly—or else we go back to Weeksville. I don't really like going to the homes of sick white people. They're usually not too happy to see me, and the first thing they do is try to get me to empty their nasty bedpan. Dr. Brant won't allow that, though. He tells them I'm a nurse-in-training, and mostly I just stand back and watch whatever he does. Which is fine with me, 'cause frankly, I'm not trying to catch whatever it is those white folks got. I like it better when we go to Weeksville, 'cause it's all black folks out there, and there's always a chance we'll stop at the orphanage and I'll get to see Mattie again.

Dr. Brant usually treats poor black folks for free—just like he helped me when I first got sent back to this world. But really, even though he means well, there's not always a whole lot Dr. Brant can do. He's got a reputation for being one of the best doctors in Brooklyn—he went to the best medical school, and he's helped a lot of sick people. But this is still 1863, and there's a whole lot about diseases and medicine that people just don't know about yet. Every day I say a prayer of thanks for all those vaccines Mama made me get when I was a kid. Growing up, I never caught anything more than a cold, but what you catch around here could kill you.

Tonight Dr. Brant says we're going to the Bethel Tabernacle A.M.E. Church—not to worship, but to tend to some of the recently arrived men and women who sleep in the church's basement. We're right smack in the middle of the war, although I'm the only person who knows that, of course. I know that the war will end in 1865, and I know the Union army will win. But everyone else is just praying for the day when the fighting and killing will stop.

As things get worse in the war-torn South, more and more blacks try to head north. New York City doesn't really welcome these ex-slaves, and poor whites don't like having to compete with them for housing and jobs. Weeksville's a good place for them to come to, 'cause it's just about the only black part of Brooklyn—here they've got their own land, their own houses, their own school, their own churches. They've got an orphanage and a home for old folks. That doesn't mean black folks in Brooklyn aren't struggling, but at least it proves they got something all their own. I never read about this place in any of my history books, but judging from the names of the streets, I figure Weeksville will one day become Bed-Stuy.

When we pull up in front of the church, Reverend Macklin is waiting for us. He smiles as he shakes Dr. Brant's hand, but I can tell something is wrong. Normally Reverend Macklin would stand around and make small talk for a few minutes. But tonight he practically drags Dr. Brant inside the church's wide wooden doors. He is talking fast and low, and I can't hear most of what he's saying, but two words pry my ears open wide: *typhoid fever.* Reverend Macklin explains that normally, fugitives arrive alone (like I did) or in groups of two or three. But a few days ago, nearly thirty fugitives arrived all at once, having traveled north under the protection of Union troops.

By the time we reach the basement, both Dr. Brant and Reverend Macklin are holding their handkerchiefs over their mouths. Dr. Brant signals for me to do the same, and we edge our way into the room. I try to count all the bodies laid out on the floor. Seems like nearly half the freed slaves are sick. There aren't any beds in this basement. There is just a cold, damp floor and dozens of frightened people huddled together to keep warm. I understand now why Reverend Macklin is nervous—it's real easy to catch a fever from somebody when they're breathing right on top of you. Dr. Brant doesn't waste any time. He starts giving orders to whoever's standing nearby and within minutes things start to change. The really sick people have to be isolated, and everybody else has to get up off the floor. There aren't enough pallets to go around, so most folks are lying on the cold stone with just a blanket or their tattered clothes to keep them warm. Next, Dr. Brant inspects everyone so he can see who has the fever and who doesn't. The ones who show signs are put on one side of the room, and the folks who look healthy are sent upstairs.

This is where things start to get a little hectic, 'cause that means separating families, and folks who just made it out of slavery, who somehow made it out of the South together and alive, aren't about to let their loved ones go now. I try to reassure the anxious mothers that the best thing they can do is go upstairs where it's dry and warm. But it is Miss Holme who really gets through to them. I hear her whispery voice behind me, and when I turn around she is leading a group of frightened women up to the sanctuary. She makes it seem like they're just going upstairs to pray, like God can hear them better from up there. And that singsong voice of hers has just the right effect—mothers stop fussing and fretting, gather up their things, and move right along.

I stay downstairs and help Dr. Brant look after the really sick folks. We lay out pallets close to the big iron stove and then help the people lie down before covering them up with heavy woolen blankets. In 1863, there's not much you can do for a fever besides wait for it to break, but it's a terrible thing watching people suffer that way. The best you can do is hold someone's hand or wipe their face with a cold, wet cloth. Sometimes, if the fever's real bad, they don't even know who or where they are—they're delirious, and you just try to keep them still so they don't hurt themselves or anyone else. We start out with about a dozen really bad cases, but every half hour Miss Holme brings another person back down to the basement who is starting to shake or sweat. I feel a bit dizzy myself, but I figure that's just 'cause I keep bending down and standing up. After a few hours of doing that, I want to stop and take a break, but I know Dr. Brant needs all the help he can get right now. Miss Holme is handling the folks upstairs, and some of the regular church members heard the bad news and came over to

help out. Esther's here, and Sam Jenkins, too, but there isn't time
to talk or catch up 'cause the basement keeps filling up with more
and more sick people.

Dr. Brant gives me a bucket of water and a tin cup and tells
me to make sure everyone gets something to drink. I don't think
that's such a good idea, and I want to say something about spreading
germs, but they don't have paper cups in this world, so I just wipe
the tin cup off as best I can before offering it to somebody else. Since
there are no beds, I have to squat down next to each patient, give
them a drink of water, then get back up and move on. To keep my
knees from locking, I try not to crouch for too long, and Dr. Brant
instructs all of us not to get too close if we can help it.

But I can't help it, really. I keep a kerchief tied over my face and
wipe my hands as often as I can, but these aren't just patients to me.
They're strangers, but they're also my people, and every face I look
into reminds me of someone I know. The boy thrashing beneath
his blankets could be Rico, and the woman moaning with her open
eyes locked on the ceiling looks a little bit like Mama. I can't offer
them a smile because my mouth is covered, and most of them can't
understand anything I say anyway. So I speak to them with my eyes.
My eyes tell them, "Everything's going to be alright," and I try my
best to look like I believe that's true.

It's so unfair—these people have struggled for so long, they've
lived their whole lives as slaves, and then finally they find the door
to freedom only to meet death on the other side. Our first patient
dies just before midnight. When they carry the body out, I have to
fight back my tears. It is an older man, much older than Papi, but
I know he was probably somebody's father or husband. Dr. Brant
gives me one stern glance, and I bite my lip to keep the tears inside.
Upstairs in the sanctuary, a woman starts to wail, and I know others
will be mourning before this night is through. I need to prove to
Dr. Brant that I can handle myself, but I decide to stay strong for
the sake of all those frightened people who are so far from home,

who have sacrificed so much already and yet must pay even more for just a taste of freedom.

"*Genna?*"

The word slips out so softly that I don't even recognize my name at first. I am exhausted. It's nearly three o'clock in the morning, and all night long people have been calling me different names, the fever transforming me into their mother, or their sister, or their daughter, or their wife. When folks got the fever, you don't put much stock in what they say, so I just pour a little water between this young man's cracked lips and wipe his face dry with my towel. Fresh beads of sweat pop up right away, and his weak fingers try to grab hold of my sleeve. I know I need to stand up or else my knees will lock. But I am so tired, and I feel sorry for this runaway, so instead I kneel down beside his pallet. He looks worse than most of the others: his face is bruised, one eye is swollen shut, and his hair is ragged and matted with dried blood. I set the bucket down, wipe his face once more, then take his rough hand in mine and wonder what terrible story he will tell once—*if*—the fever passes. Beneath the heavy woolen blanket his legs move restlessly. Though he is safe now, and free, deep inside he is still running, and his head rolls back and forth as if he is trying to look over his shoulder.

I sit with this young man for two or three minutes, and eventually he starts to calm down. He is almost completely still when Dr. Brant sees me breaking the rules and calls me over to the other side of the room.

"Genna!"

My head snaps back, and I realize I have almost fallen asleep while thinking about this runaway. Something about him reminds me of home, and I don't want to let go of his hand, but I have work to do. I gently ease myself up off the floor but stop when I hear him say my name once more. This time I am looking straight into this runaway's face, and I *know* the name he is calling is mine.

"*Genna!*"

Although his voice is low and weak, his hand suddenly grows strong and grips mine real tight. He is holding onto my hand like he won't ever let go, and I can feel another, invisible hand wrapping itself around my heart. The runaway looks at me with his one good eye, and for just a few seconds the fever disappears and we see one another as we truly are: two lonely, frightened teenagers trapped in a crazy, messed-up world. Then the moment passes and the fever returns. But just as his hand lets go of mine, an electric current sizzles up and down my spine, and I cry out in pain, shock, and disbelief. I snatch the kerchief off my face and will the tears out of my eyes. I need to see clearly, because my heart—my mind, my body—every instinct is suddenly telling me that this is no runaway. The young man dying before me is Judah.

19.

Judah is alive!

For the past six months he has been running, trying to find his way to freedom, trying to find his way back to me.

Judah is *alive*! And nothing—*no one*—is going to take him away from me.

Dr. Brant thinks Judah's my brother. It was an easy lie to tell. I was pretty hysterical once I realized that Judah was here—alive, here in this world, but possibly about to die. I was screaming and crying and holding onto Judah so tight, people thought I'd caught the fever, too. It took two grown men to pull us apart, and Miss Holme actually had to raise her voice to get me to calm down. Then Dr. Brant came and stood in front of me, and he said, "You know this person?" And I could tell by the way he asked that he didn't think much of Judah, and he wouldn't think much of me if I told him Judah and I were in love. I wasn't ashamed, I wanted to tell everyone the truth. But I couldn't stop looking at Judah. He was lying so still on the pallet, and he wasn't sweating anymore, he was just lying there like he'd finally given up, like he didn't have the strength to fight anymore. I looked at Judah for so long that finally Dr. Brant grabbed my chin and made me look at *him*. His face was flushed the way it had been that night when he caught me in the kitchen with Paul. Dr. Brant squinted up his eyes and stared at me like he could make the truth come out of my mouth. So I said whatever I had to say to keep Judah alive: "He's my brother."

I said it one time, and suddenly everyone understood. Miss Holme put her arm around me, and the two men carefully moved Judah's pallet so it was closer to the fire. Dr. Brant let his eyes go soft again, and he promised me he'd do everything he could to make sure Judah lived. I wanted to stay and help Dr. Brant, but Miss Holme insisted that I go upstairs with her. I don't really know what happened after that. I guess after a while I fell asleep or passed out, 'cause when I woke up the next day, I was in my own room and Nannie was standing over me. I tried to talk, to tell Nannie what had happened, but she put her fingers over my mouth.

"Hush now," she said in a quiet voice I'd never heard Nannie use before. "Your brother's doin' just fine. He's restin', and that's what you should do, too. Seems to me you got a touch of the fever yourself, or maybe you just all worked up—you had quite a night."

I tried to nod but my head wouldn't move, and I tried to tell Nannie who Judah really was, but there weren't any words in my mouth. I just looked at Nannie and she looked at me, and our eyes were shining but we saved our tears.

"I'm happy for you, Genna." Nannie managed to smile, but her voice was soft and sad. "You one of the lucky ones," she said. Then Nannie kissed me on the cheek and told me to go back to sleep. I closed my eyes and thought about what she had said. Nannie was right. Thousands of slaves were fleeing the South but in their search for freedom, they often lost loved ones along the way. People who were sold away from their families never saw them again, even after the war ended and slavery was abolished. Judah and I were separated by hundreds of miles and more than a century, but somehow we found each other. Nannie was right. We are the lucky ones.

20.

The fever spared Judah, but a lot of other people weren't so lucky that night. Early the next morning, Reverend Macklin had the local carpenter bring three plain pine coffins to the church, and that carpenter stayed busy for the rest of the month. I was out of commission for a couple of days, but then I went right back to Weeksville and helped Dr. Brant care for the survivors. Judah is a survivor.

Everyone in Weeksville is trying to help out. Folks bring clothes, quilts, and toys for the children, and tents are set up so families can stay together, close to the church. Mattie comes by every day with lunch for me and Dr. Brant, and church ladies make bottomless pots of hot, savory soup. Miss Holme starts a list showing everyone's name and what jobs they can do. When she asks me what job Judah's good at, I tell her he can write poetry.

Miss Holme frowns a bit but makes a note on her list that Judah can read and write. "He's more likely to find work as a day laborer," she warns me, as if a black boy wanting to be a poet is silly, or too dangerous a dream.

"He knows how to play the drum, too," I tell her. Miss Holme looks at me like I'm delirious, then pats my arm and moves on.

Mattie's so excited about Judah, she can hardly contain herself. Really, she's just happy for me, 'cause she's so close to Money and now I've got a brother, too. I don't have time to talk much with

Mattie, so she keeps all her questions to herself for now. And that's just fine with me. I wish I could tell her the truth, but the less I say about Judah, the better, 'cause I'm not sure just how convincing a liar I can be.

I'm grateful to Dr. Brant for everything he did to save Judah's life, and that's why I feel so guilty. But I know I did the right thing. The Brants might be willing to help my long-lost brother, but I don't think they'd feel the same way about Judah if they knew he was really my boyfriend. Dr. Brant says when Judah's fully recovered, he can come stay with us in Brooklyn Heights. The thought of having Judah close by all the time makes me want to laugh *and* cry. I feel giddy every time I think about it, and I do all I can to help Judah get better *fast*.

Within a week, Judah's able to sit up and eat. His face is starting to heal, he can see out both eyes, and he's made friends with some of the other patients. I see him talking and joking with the other men sometimes, but when I go over to join in, Judah shuts down. He seals his lips and just watches me, especially when Dr. Brant gives me instructions. Judah's also just as stubborn as he was back in Brooklyn—*our* Brooklyn, I mean. I keep trying to explain why I told that lie, but Judah doesn't understand. As smart as he is, Judah doesn't understand a lot of things about this world.

Nannie always says, "Sometimes you got to go along to get along," and more and more I'm realizing she's right. But Judah doesn't care what the Brants or any white folks think. Judah says he's not ashamed of who he is or how he feels about me. I'm not ashamed either. I just know how Dr. Brant feels when it comes to me and boys. But when I try to explain this to Judah, he makes it seem like I'm selling him out.

"I'm not saying he's *right*, Judah. I'm just saying it's easier this way. You want us to be able to stay together, don't you?"

"What's the use of staying together if we can't *be* together, Genna?" Judah asks me this a few weeks later, one night after everyone else has gone to bed. We are sitting in the kitchen at the Brants' place, and I am trying to enjoy the time we have alone— together—but Judah won't let me. "You can't always take the easy way out," he says bitterly. "Not when it comes to whites. They *expect* you to do that, Genna—can't you see? They're making us live a lie because they've made you believe in some messed-up idea of 'chastity.' But they don't practice what they preach! I've seen slaves the color of you and me, and I've seen slaves the color of milk— and every shade in between. Why you think that is, Genna? If white men were so damn *chaste*, there wouldn't be so many light-skinned slaves in this world."

I glance at the kitchen door to make sure nobody's coming down the hall. If Dr. Brant heard Judah talking this way, I don't know what he'd do. Nannie wouldn't be too pleased, either. Judah's only been here a couple of days, and already I can tell Nannie doesn't like him the way she likes Paul. Judah can see that his harsh words are making me uncomfortable. He lowers his voice just a little bit and leans closer to me.

"That's what they *do*, Genna. They make you afraid to speak the truth. Then they turn around and call us liars, when they're the biggest liars of all!"

"Judah, *please*. It's only for a little while." I inch my chair closer to his and lay my hand on Judah's arm. I want so much to touch his face, but Judah's eyes are hard and they push me away.

"I'm doing this for your sake, Genna. But I can't live like this for long." Without even kissing me goodnight, Judah gets up and goes out back and I head upstairs alone.

For now Judah is staying in the carriage house with Adams. He's not really working for the Brants, but he helps out by chopping firewood and keeping the stable clean. In return, he gets three square meals a day, a warm place to sleep, and the chance to spend time with me. Most ex-slaves would be grateful to have that much. But not Judah. Nannie thinks Judah's got too much pride, and

Adams doesn't like him much, either. When people look at Judah—whether they're black or white—all they see is trouble. Besides the scars on his face and his hard black eyes, Judah is trying to grow back his locks. But his aren't small and neat like mine, and Judah doesn't cover his head with a scarf or a cap. He's just letting his locks form naturally, which means he's just not combing his hair.

I tried to ask Judah what happened to his locks, but he just shook his head and turned away from me. He has only told me parts of his story—how he was sent back to this Brooklyn, then captured by slavers and sold down South. I know that Judah has been a slave in Virginia, Georgia, and South Carolina, but I don't know how Judah made it back here. I want to know, but he won't tell me, so I just settle for having Judah nearby again. Close enough to look at, but still too far away to touch.

Every time I reach for Judah he pulls back, and he'll only kiss me on the cheek since "that's what brothers and sisters do." I know we've got to be careful, and I know Judah doesn't like playing this game. But six months is a real long time to be apart from someone you love. And I *do* love Judah, I know that now. Maybe I knew it all along, but when I saw Judah lying there in that basement looking like he was about to die, something inside of me woke up. Instead of a whisper, I heard a loud, clear voice and it was saying—shouting—"He can't die! He can't die because I love him. *I love him.*" Losing Judah the first time was bad enough. But I learned to live with the fact that he was in another world, another century, because I believed he was okay. He was far away from me, but he was safe. Losing Judah for a second time would've been more than I could bear, because this time it would have been for good.

So I'm real thankful that he's alive, and that we're here, in Brooklyn, together. But where Judah has been and how he has lived for the past six months is still mostly a mystery. All I know is, he wasn't safe at all. And Judah still isn't okay. We're together now, but in a way it feels like we're still apart. It's like I can see Judah, and he's still the same person to me, despite the cuts on his face and his wild, uncombed hair. But there's also something different about Judah—it's like he's standing behind bulletproof glass, those yellowish sheets of Plexiglas you see at the post office or the Chinese food place. But I'm not trying to hurt Judah, he doesn't need protection from me.

So I just keep waiting for Judah to remember who I am and how we used to be. I keep waiting for Judah to come up behind me and wrap his arms around my waist. I keep waiting for him to steal a kiss when no one's looking, or to maybe sneak up to my room after everybody's gone to bed. It's not easy for us to be alone in this house, but I keep thinking Judah will find a way if he's missed me half as much as I've missed him. But Judah acts like he hasn't missed me at all.

I know talking to Martha about it won't help, because being a teenager in 1863 isn't the same thing as being a teenager in the twenty-first century. Martha and her boyfriend are about the same age as me and Judah, but they're planning to get married just as soon as they save enough money to get a place of their own. And to hear Martha tell it, she and Willem are already doing all the things married people do. I didn't think Catholics were allowed to get down like that, but Martha just laughed and said they'd be married soon enough, and the "bairns" that followed would be her penance. She'll be sorry, alright, if she winds up with as many kids as her mom and no man around the house to help feed them or put clothes on their back.

Martha's kind of funny when it comes to her religion. She says that for Catholics, "Go forth and multiply" is like one of the Ten Commandments. But what's worse is how little she knows about sex. Martha's got funny names for every part of the body, and she can tell all kinds of dirty jokes. But when I ask her about birth control, Martha just shrugs and says, "Willem ain't got no control." And when I talk about sperm or her ovaries, Martha looks at me blankly like I'm speaking French. The only thing she knows about her period is that having it means she's not pregnant, and so she's glad when it arrives each month. That's why she calls it her "monthly friend."

I'm nowhere near as experienced as Martha when it comes to sex, but I sure know a whole lot more about stuff like birth control and STDs. It may be 1863, but folks are still having sex, they're still getting pregnant, and they're still catching nasty diseases from the people they sleep with. They just don't know what to do about it, and folks are either too ignorant, too religious, or too uppity to talk about it in "polite society." AIDS may not exist yet, but Dr. Brant's got a patient with syphilis. I've seen what it can do to a body, and I definitely do *not* want to catch that.

What I really need to know is how to make Judah want me again. We never really went all that far back in Brooklyn—*our* Brooklyn, I mean. But we would've gotten a lot further if this crazy time-travel stuff hadn't happened. We lost half a year together, and I'm not saying we would've been having sex already—I always wanted to wait until I got into college, 'cause I don't need anything unexpected messing up my plans. And Judah never pushed me to go faster or do more than I was comfortable with. But I always knew that he wanted me. Sometimes I would feel him growing hard when we were making out or just standing real close together. And I definitely wanted Judah to be the one—my first. Now I just want to know that Judah hasn't changed his mind about me. I want him to see me not just as the girl I used to be back in Brooklyn, but the young woman I am now—the person I've become. I want him to want *her*, too.

After a week of Judah treating me like I'm his bratty little sister, I get tired of waiting. Late one night, when I hear Nannie snoring softly in her sleep, I take my candle, wrap a shawl around my shoulders, and creep downstairs and out to the carriage house. On the ground floor at the very back, Adams has a private room. Judah sleeps up above in the loft. He hears me open the heavy wooden door, and by the time I reach the ladder Judah is peering over the edge of the loft, looking dangerous and scared.

"Oh, it's you." He says it with relief, but not like he's happy to see me. I grab the hem of my long nightgown and slowly climb up the ladder. Judah helps me up onto the loft, and for a moment we just stand there looking at each other. Judah is wearing only his pants. I see him glance at a shirt lying on the floor, but Judah can't decide if he should reach for it and put it on. Instead he stands awkwardly in front of me, his long body leaner and more muscular from the months he has spent working as a field slave.

Even though I have carefully planned out just what it is I want to say, right now I can't think of anything but the smell of Judah's bare skin. So instead of spitting out a week's worth of angry words, I just lean in real quick and kiss Judah on the lips. For just a second, his mouth remains hard against mine, but then his lips soften and Judah's hands go around my waist and he pulls my body close to his. I kiss Judah the way I have kissed him in my dreams, stronger and for longer than I have ever kissed anyone before. With his lips still on mine, Judah gently leads me over to the corner where his pallet is. We are about to lie down together when we remember I am still holding the candle in my hand. We both laugh a little and pull apart so I can find a safe place to set it down. I take a moment to carefully brush away some loose stalks of straw, but when I turn back and reach for Judah, he moves away from me. Judah backs himself up close to the wall and starts rubbing his palms on the front of his pants like there's a stain on his hands that just won't come off.

Judah doesn't look me in the eye, but I can tell he still wants to touch me. I pull the scarf off my head so Judah can see my locks. Then I step toward him and undo the top button of my nightgown.

"Genna, don't—"

"I'm not your sister, Judah. We don't have to pretend anymore."

When the last button is undone, I let the gown slide off my shoulders and onto the straw-covered floor.

Judah takes one long look at me before turning his face toward the wall. "Get dressed, Genna. Please."

I hear him but stand there just as I am. My body is warm, but the heat does not come from shame. It comes from something stronger, something deep inside of me that I have never felt before. I want Judah to want me. Even with my scars and the rubbery lumps on my back. I want Judah to look at me, but he is looking at the floor.

"Cover yourself up, Genna!" he barks at me.

"Why?"

Judah finally looks me in the eye, then his gaze slides over my body and back down to the ground. "I can't—we can't. Not like this. Not until—"

"Until what, Judah?" I take a step toward him, but Judah turns away. Suddenly the air between us grows cold, and I realize that Judah doesn't want me the way I want him. Feeling foolish, I shiver and step back into my nightgown. I can tell Judah is watching me now, but I can't look at him. I do up the buttons on the front of my gown, then I reach for the candle and move back over to the ladder that is propped against the edge of the loft.

"Genna, wait—"

I don't have to turn around to know that Judah is reaching for me. But I leave his outstretched hand hanging in the air and grab hold of the ladder.

"I killed a man." Judah tosses the words at my feet the way men in the street throw dice. I want to look down so I can find my way. I don't want to step on those words and fall into the dark below. But instead I fix my eyes on the small piece of mirror that is hanging on the wall. In the candlelight I can see Judah's flickering reflection. I watch him as he says it again.

"Genna, I killed a man." Judah says it softly, like a confession, like it is something fragile he needs me to hold. I turn to face him, and now Judah's eyes tighten as he looks at me to see if I am afraid of him, or ashamed. I look at the hard line of his mouth. There is no apology there.

I whisper, "A white man?"

Judah nods silently, then sinks down to the floor and curls up tight in a knot. I step back from the ladder and once again find a safe place to set the candle down. I kneel next to Judah and touch his bare arm. Then it is like a vacuum sucks all the air out of the loft; there is no space between me and Judah—the bulletproof glass has disappeared. There is just Judah shaking inside my arms. He is squeezing me tight, and his tears are falling warm on my neck. Tears are streaming from his eyes and words are pouring out of his mouth, and I can't stop his tears from flowing though I try to kiss them away. So I just hold Judah tight, tight, tight as he lets go of the six months of pain he has been holding inside.

After a while, the words stop coming and Judah's tears grow cool on my neck. He's still holding me tight, like I am the only thing solid in a wide, angry sea. I am holding onto Judah, too, but my embrace is loose enough for my hands to roam all over his broad, bare back, the space where his locks used to be. My fingertips slide over the thick, raised lumps, the scars that the whip left behind. Judah's back is like a strange subway map, with each welt leading off in its own direction, each track starting and ending in pain. I silently hope that the man he killed is the same one who took the skin off of Judah's beautiful back.

While my fingers slowly travel over the swollen tracks, Judah begins to relax. Instead of gripping me tight, he opens his hands and starts to really *feel* me. He pulls back, though, when his palms settle on the mounds of skin left behind after the beating. I want Judah to keep on touching me, but I am also afraid he will find the button that sets off the pain in my spine. So I turn around, undo only the top buttons on my nightgown, and slide it down to my waist. I hold

my breath and wait to feel Judah's fingertips on my back, but nothing touches me besides the night air. I wait a bit longer, then slide
the gown over my shoulders and button it up once more.

When I turn to look at Judah, the first thing I notice are his fists.
His hands are balled up like two hard, black stones. Even though
I am dressed and facing him once more, Judah continues to look
through me, as if he can still see the scars on my back.

"Who ... ?" It is the only word Judah can push through his
clenched teeth. I am glad I have no name to give, because right now
Judah looks like he's ready to kill again.

"I don't remember who or how—I don't even know what happened, or why. It was like that when I woke up. When I got here—
got sent back."

Judah sinks to the floor, his granite fists pressed against the sides
of his head. I go over and sit next to Judah. I wrap my shawl around
us both, and we sit without talking for a while.

I want to ask Judah about the white man he killed. I want to
know whether he used a knife or a gun or his bare hands. I'm a
little bit excited, even though I know that's wrong. But I can't be
like Nannie and always turn the other cheek. And I know Judah
wouldn't hurt anyone unless he had no choice. It must have been
self-defense, which is more than I can say for *them*. I want to tell
Judah about the terrible things that happened to Mattie and Nannie,
and all the times I have wanted to hurt Mrs. Brant. But Judah
already knows these things. He has been a slave in the deep South.
He has seen more than I have heard. Judah has seen too much.

21.

Even though the fever's gone and he's officially free, Judah's legs haven't stopped running. We've just found each other and already Judah's ready to move on.

After that night in the loft, I thought for sure things between us would change. But since that night, I've seen Judah even less than before. One afternoon when it's too rainy to take Henry to the park, I go out back to give Judah some gingerbread Nannie just baked. But when I get to the carriage house, Judah isn't there. Adams is brushing down the horses by himself, and he's got an attitude. "Hmph. He ain't been here half the days this week," Adams tells me. "Nights, neither." Adams gives me a long, hard look to make sure I get the point. Then he tells me I can leave the plate of gingerbread with Judah's things, up in the loft.

Except I'm not really thinking about gingerbread anymore. I know what Adams is trying to say—that Judah is seeing some other girl, and that he knows we aren't brother and sister after all. I know I should be worried about Adams telling the Brants the truth, but instead I'm thinking about Judah chatting up some other girl. Is that why he doesn't want me? But Judah *does* want me. I can tell. He just thinks we ought to wait. Or maybe he just thinks *I* should wait while he keeps running around.

All I'm seeing is red right now, but I climb the ladder anyway and go over to Judah's corner of the loft. There isn't much to look at—just a blanket, some clothes, and a couple of stacked crates. I set the plate on top of the crates so the mice won't eat the gingerbread. I'm about to turn around and leave when a pamphlet lying in the straw catches my eye. I can read it from where I am standing: *African Civilization Society*. Below those words is a picture of two black men. One is holding a Bible, and he is wearing a fancy suit and a ruffly white shirt. The other black man is kneeling before him, and he's practically naked. He is reaching out as if he wants the Bible the other man is holding. I pick up the pamphlet, take a quick look at the other side, then shove it in my pocket and climb back downstairs.

Later that evening, when Dr. Brant comes out to the kitchen to get me, I'm not there. Nannie tells him I'm having "female trouble" and won't be able to assist him on his rounds tonight. I hide quietly in the back stairwell, watching Dr. Brant's expression through the crack in the door. To my surprise, he looks more disappointed than angry. Dr. Brant tells Nannie to make me some chamomile tea, then he leaves and Nannie signals for me to come out.

"It ain't right, lyin' to the doctor like that. You don't want to help him no more, you should just say so—'stead of gettin' me all mixed up in it." Nannie's frowning like she's real upset, but we both know that Dr. Brant trusts her word more than he trusts mine. I have told Nannie the truth about Judah, and in return, Nannie has told me what she knows about the African Civilization Society. She says they are a group of people—white and black—who feel freed blacks ought to go back to Africa to "civilize the Dark Continent." Rich people have even donated money and supplies to help free blacks from the United States set up a country of their own in Africa. It's called Liberia. Nannie knows about it because her church donated Bibles to be given to the "heathens" over there. This doesn't sound like something Judah would want to be a part of, but I'm glad I know at least this much before I confront him about where he's been.

I take the pamphlet out of my pocket now and head out to the carriage house. Adams is driving Dr. Brant on his rounds, so it's real quiet out back. I don't have a candle but it is still light outside, and the carriage house is lit by stripes of dusty orange sunlight. I sit down on the bottom rung of the hayloft ladder and wait for Judah to come.

After more than an hour has passed, I hear the wooden door to the carriage house squeaking on its hinges. Judah's lean body slips in like a shadow and disappears in the dark interior. The sun has set, and the quarter moon is too weak to light the carriage house.

"Where you been, Judah?" I speak out of the darkness, startling him, but Judah quickly regains his composure.

"Excuse me?"

"I said, *where you been*? Folks been needing you around here."

Judah steps into the dim moonlight coming through one of the small windows. "Oh yeah? For what? Dr. Brant need his shoes shined?"

I want to say something about gratitude, about how the food Judah's been eating, the clothes he's been wearing, and the roof he's been sleeping under belong to Dr. Brant. About how Judah might not be alive today if it weren't for Dr. Brant. But that will only make things worse, so I say, "What about *me*, Judah? What about when *I* need you and you're not here?"

Judah's face looks cold and sullen in the pale moonlight. "What you need me for, Genna? You got your precious little white baby to take care of, you got your little white girlfriend to gossip with. You got your high and mighty white doctor taking you out every night. And there's that blue-eyed half-breed keeps coming 'round here asking for you. So what you need me for, huh?"

Right now I am glad that Judah cannot see my face. I had no idea he knew about Martha or Paul, and I didn't know that Paul was still coming around. When Judah turned up, I told Nannie to tell Paul I couldn't see him right now because of a family emergency. But maybe he didn't believe her, since I told him when we first met that I had no family. I am having a hard time keeping my lies straight these days, but I am only lying to keep people from getting hurt. I can tell by looking at Judah, though, that he feels hurt anyway.

There are a thousand words swirling around in my head, so I take a few more seconds to pick out the ones I need to say right now. "That's not fair, Judah. Yes, I have friends, and yes, I have a job. What did you expect—that after six months I'd just be standing on a corner somewhere, waiting for you to come along and rescue me? I couldn't just wait for things to go back to the way they used to be. You weren't here, Judah. And I didn't know if I was ever going to see you, or my family, or the real Brooklyn ever again!"

I am standing up now, the gray light from the window spilling over me. Judah tightens his eyes to see me better, to see if I am telling the truth. Then he sucks his teeth and looks away.

"So you took a job working for some rich white folks and made yourself right at home, huh?"

Judah has a right to be mad, 'cause I haven't been totally honest with him, but he can't talk to me like this. He's making it sound like I took the easy way out. But what else was I supposed to do? "Right now, yes, this *is* my home, Judah—and it's the only one I've got. Do you have any idea what it's *like* being a black girl in this world, *alone*? Do you know how many men have tried to mess with me? That's how I met Paul—he helped me out when I was in trouble, and afterward we became friends. *Friends*, Judah, nothing more."

"I'm the one who's supposed to protect you." Judah says this softly, like he's sorry that he couldn't be there for me, but also angry that Paul was.

I take a step closer to Judah and reach out to him. Judah turns his face away, but he doesn't shake my hand off his arm. "But Judah, *you weren't here*. And I don't blame you for that—you couldn't help it. But neither could I. Don't blame me for doing what I had to do to get by, just to survive. I'm *safe* here. And it's not much, but I actually get paid for what I do. I'm not a slave, Judah, and neither are you. You don't have to fight anymore."

Judah laughs bitterly and turns his hard eyes on me. "'*Emancipate yourself from mental slavery,*' Genna. You may not be in chains, but they've still got your mind locked down. You're acting like you're grateful for what you've got—what they've *allowed* you to have. So they give you a few pennies for taking care of their little brat, so what? You think *that* makes you free? You think that white doctor's ever going to let *you* become a doctor—become his *equal*? You can't do anything in this country without asking some white person for permission first. And you and I both know that that's not going to change, Genna. Black people will never be free in this country."

Judah says this solemnly, like it is a truth written in stone somewhere deep inside his heart.

I plead with him, even though I know my words won't change his mind. "But freedom's coming, Judah. In a couple more years the war will end …"

Judah's eyes darken as a cloud passes over the moon. "I know how the story ends, Genna. A hundred years from now black people will *still* be asking to be treated like human beings. They'll be marching and protesting and sitting in. And they'll still be no better off than they were before. These people—they're not human, Genna. And they won't be satisfied until they've taken that away from us, too, made us just as ugly and evil and cruel as them." Judah pauses and looks at me to make sure I don't miss his meaning. "I can't stay here, Genna. If I do, I'll kill them all or die trying."

Judah is not saying this to frighten me. He is telling me how he truly feels. Suddenly I remember the pamphlet I have been clutching in my hand. I uncrumple it now and hand it to Judah. "Is that what this is about?"

Judah takes it from me and calmly smoothes away the wrinkles. "We've got to get out of here, Genna. These people—they'll send us to Africa. We can build a life there together—we can get married, start a family."

"I thought you wanted to wait." I try, but it's hard to say this without attitude.

"I do, at least until we're in Africa. I want my children—our children—to be free, Gen, totally and completely free. And that won't happen in the United States. Not now, not when the war ends, not ever."

I back away from Judah and sit back down on the last rung of the ladder. Part of me is thrilled to hear Judah saying these words—*marriage, children, family*. But another part of me is frightened of the price we'd have to pay. And we're still so young ... so much could happen in the next few years. But then I remember that those years have happened already, and Judah's right—we both know how the story of slavery ends.

"You're willing to move to Africa? To leave everything behind—our families, Brooklyn, the world we know ..."

Judah comes over and kneels in front of me. He puts his hands on my shoulders and looks straight into my eyes. "They're gone already, Genna. We're never going to find a way back—it's a miracle I even found my way back to you. I don't know how this happened, or why, but I know the destiny of black people is to go back to Africa. Marcus Garvey said so, Bob Marley—all the great prophets knew that someday we would rise above our downpressors—it even says so in the Bible: '*And Ethiopia shall stretch forth her hands ...*'"

As soon as he mentions his countrymen, Judah's accent returns. It has the same effect on me that it used to have back in Brooklyn. Suddenly I feel like I am on the outside, like there is a border between us. It's easy for Judah to talk about leaving the United States because this isn't where he's from. But America is my country, it's the place where I was born. And I know it's not perfect, but I'm not so sure any place is—especially in 1863. I point to the pamphlet in Judah's hand. "And is that what your prophets had in mind? You think they wanted us to go back to Africa and 'civilize the savages'?"

Judah looks down at the pamphlet and folds it in half so the image of the two black men disappears. "I'm not saying this plan is perfect, Genna. But the Society is willing to *pay our way*. They need people to go over to Africa—black people—so we can prove that all those lies aren't true. This is our chance to show the world that we're *not* inferior, we're *not* children, and we don't need *them* to tell us what to do."

"So you're saying we should become missionaries in order to prove to white folks that we're just as good as them."

Judah squeezes my shoulders harder like that will help me understand. "If we really became missionaries, we'd be just as *bad* as them. But that's not what I'm asking you to do. It's only for a little while, Genna. Once we get to Liberia, if we don't like what they're doing there, we'll go someplace else—Ethiopia! It's the only country never colonized by whites. Africa's a continent, Gen. It's more than just one country. Anything's possible over there."

I want to ask Judah how what he's suggesting is any different from me asking him to stay here and act like he's my brother. Instead I try to get Judah to think about some of the negative possibilities. "What if we get there and they don't want us?"

"Who?"

"The Africans, Judah. What if we get there and they're not happy to see us? What if they try to hurt us, or send us back—sell us into slavery all over again?"

Judah lets go of my shoulders and stands up. "That's not going to happen," he says bluntly.

"How do you know, Judah? What makes you think we can just sail over to Africa and live happily ever after? We don't speak any of their languages, we dress differently, we don't eat the same food—"

"That doesn't matter."

"*Of course*, it matters, Judah! Just because we look like them doesn't mean we'll be able to fit in—"

Judah raises his voice over mine. "We don't have to be *like* them, Genna. We *are* them! We're *African*."

The words are dangling on the tip of my tongue, but I'm afraid to let them fall. I'm afraid that if I say these words, Judah will leave me behind. But I can't go to Africa pretending to be something I'm not. So I take a deep breath and say, "I'm American, too, Judah."

"I'm not" is his simple reply.

We just look at each other for a moment. Then Judah presses the pamphlet back into my hand. He steps back, and the bulletproof glass slides between us once again. "Think about it, Genna. Think about what this might mean—*for us*. I care about you, Gen, you know I do. You're the only reason I've lasted so long in this world. But I can't stay in this country." Judah pushes the air through his teeth so that it sounds just like the ocean. "*Babylon* ..."

Just then we hear the sound of the carriage rolling up the gravel drive. Judah speaks quickly. "There's another meeting next Friday." His voice turns sarcastic and sharp. "If you're not too busy, maybe you could come."

Judah unlatches the doors and opens them wide so Adams can bring the horses in. I silently slip the pamphlet in my pocket and head back to the house.

22.

All week long I think about what Judah has asked me to do. I think about Mama and Tyjuan and the rest of my family, and how I'll never see them again if I go with Judah to Africa. I look at Nannie and little Henry—even Dr. and Mrs. Brant—and I wonder if the next home I live in will be as safe as the one I have here.

Liberia. I wish there was some way of knowing what it would be like before we went over there. I wish there was some way of knowing for sure that we won't ever find our way back to twenty-first-century Brooklyn. That's what makes this decision so hard. There are so many "what ifs" and so few answers that we can really count on. I've never been an immigrant, unless you consider time travel a form of emigration. But Papi was an immigrant, and after a few years living in the United States, he went right back to Panama. I know from what Martha's told me that folks aren't always glad to see you when you move to their country. And it doesn't matter if you look just like they do. You can't just walk up in somebody's house and expect them to welcome you. You have to be invited first. Judah says the African Civilization Society is inviting us to go to Liberia. But it seems to me it should be the Africans sending out the invites, not a bunch of folks from over here.

I haven't made up my mind yet, but I have been feeling other people out. Adams says he'd never leave the United States; he says his people worked this land for two hundred years, and they got a right to call this place home. "Paid for it with their blood, they did, and it don't matter one bit if white folks think we be better off someplace else. We be better off *here* if they just leave us alone, let us work and pray and vote like any other man." Nannie thinks it's the duty of all good Christians to "spread the good news." But Judah and I aren't really Christians. At least I know I'm not.

I'd like to ask Paul how he feels about it, but Paul hasn't come around these past few weeks. I wonder if maybe he ran into Judah—if they had words or got into a fight. But that doesn't seem too likely, 'cause Judah hasn't been around that much, either.

One evening there's a knock on the back door. Nannie pushes back the curtain to see who's there, and I can tell by the way her face lights up that it's Paul. She opens the door and throws her arms around him, and my heart beats kind of fast as I wait for Paul to come in. But he just talks quietly to Nannie for about a minute, then she turns and tells me to go outside.

It is early July so the days are much longer now. The sun hasn't fully set yet, and the sky is the same color as the heart of a rose. I step outside and pull the door shut behind me so we can have some privacy. Paul is standing at the bottom of the steps, a canvas bag slung over his shoulder.

"I'm leaving, Genna. I just came to say goodbye."

I can feel my heart inching up my throat so I swallow hard to push it back down. Then I take a deep breath and go down the three steps so I am standing next to Paul. His cap is pulled down so low I can barely see his blue eyes. I reach up to push it back off his face, but Paul flinches and grabs my hand.

"Don't."

Despite the cap and the dim evening light, I can see the purple bruises on Paul's face. My first thought is of Judah. "He didn't—"

Paul glares at me for a moment, his lips pulled in a tight, thin line. "He who? Your *brother*?" I look at the ground as my cheeks burn hot like the sky. Paul's voice isn't as hard when he speaks again. "I can fight one man at a time, but I can't fight twenty. There was trouble on the docks. The longshoremen are on strike, so we brought in Negro workers to take their place. But the damned Irish, they came down there with knives, clubs, bottles—anything they could use to 'beat the niggers off the docks'..."

The bruises on Paul's face tell me this is true, but somehow I still can't believe anyone would dare treat him this way. "But your father—can't he fire them, punish them in some way?"

Paul only shakes his head bitterly. "Even if he did let them go, there'd just be another lot to take their place. But let a Negro on the job, and the whites refuse to work. Or they come down to the docks in broad daylight, drunk and bloodthirsty, ready to drive the black workers into the river. And all they want is a chance to work, to earn wages and support their families, the same as any man."

"But your father's *white* ..."

"It makes no difference, Genna. I've got more than one drop of black blood in me, whether it shows or not. I'm a Negro, and they know it. And they hate me for it—would kill me for it, even."

"Then I'm glad you're leaving." I say this almost without thinking, not realizing how it might sound, and Paul takes it the wrong way.

"I'm sure you are. You don't need me around now that your brother's back from the dead."

My gaze slides over to the carriage house. I want to give Paul the explanation I know he deserves. But there is no way for me to explain to him how Judah and I have traveled back through time. So instead I say, "I want you to leave so nothing bad happens to you. I don't want you to get hurt."

"It's a little late for that, don't you think?" Paul says it lightly, as a joke, but I can see the disappointment in his eyes.

"Are you heading west?"

Paul shakes his head and looks off as though the frontier is

somewhere beyond the end of our block. "Not yet. Not ever, perhaps. I'm heading north."

"To Canada?"

"To Boston."

"Boston? What's up there?"

"The Fifty-fourth and Fifty-fifth Regiments. Here in New York
they're desperate for soldiers to fight this war, but the Irish hate the
draft, and they won't let colored men enlist. At least in Massachusetts,
a colored man's got a fighting chance—and a chance to fight. Not
just dig trenches or mop a deck. I hear the Fifty-fourth's headed to
South Carolina right now, but I've got some friends in Boston. I'll
go there first and see what I can find out."

Part of me feels proud of Paul—proud that he wants to fight,
and with a regiment of black soldiers. But another part of me
wonders what's up with guys, why they always have to be fighting
each other, tearing someone else down just to build themselves up.
Judah and Paul are alike in this one way. I wish Paul could feel like
a man without risking his life or taking the life of somebody else.
I wish Judah could feel like a man without going three thousand
miles away.

Guys always feel like they have to prove something to somebody. Then I think about the way I act around Dr. Brant, how I
never want him to know when I'm scared, or to think I'm not
smart enough to become a doctor. Even Martha wants the other
servants on the block to know she's just as good as them. I guess
nobody wants to be told that they're inferior, or that they don't
belong, or can't have or do things like other people. But in this
country, at least in 1863, it seems like somebody's always telling us
what we can and cannot do—just because we're black or poor or
female or young—or all those things at once. But I don't want to
believe that that's never going to change. And I don't want to lose
my life trying to *make* it change. I wonder if that makes me a bad
person, wanting my life so much. After all, Paul's willing to make

the ultimate sacrifice, and Judah was willing to risk his own life by killing the man who tried to take his freedom away.

Paul's eyes are avoiding mine, but I look up into his face anyway. "Paul, I'm sorry about Judah. I didn't know what to tell you—I didn't know if I'd ever see him again."

"You don't have to apologize, Genna. You made no promises to me." Paul sets the bag down heavily, like it is more of a burden than he can bear right now. He kicks it lightly then looks at me. "Once the war is over and slavery is abolished, hopefully there will be more stories that end like yours."

"Except my story isn't over yet."

"No. I guess in a way, it's just beginning. Have you two made any plans?"

I look down at the bag resting on the ground and wonder if I could really pack up my life and simply walk away. "Judah wants me to go with him to Africa."

Paul presses his lips together and looks at me with a serious face. "What do *you* want?"

I shrug and look up at the early stars. They glitter like tiny diamonds in the purply blue sky. For once I am able to tell Paul the truth. "I don't know."

Paul looks at the ground for a few seconds, then picks up his bag and hefts it over his shoulder. "There's no telling what the future holds, Genna. If I go to war, I may not come back. And if I do survive, there's no guarantee I'd come back to this city." Paul adjusts his cap and absently fingers the bruises on his face. "The way I feel right now, I wouldn't care if I never saw Brooklyn again. But I'll miss you, Genna. I hope you'll always remember me as a friend. And if you're still here when I get back …"

This doesn't seem real, this kind of final goodbye. I can't think of anything to say and I can hardly see through the tears in my eyes, so I just put my arms around Paul and hold him close to me for a moment. Then I let him go and Paul walks out of the yard, quickly and without looking back. When I can no longer hear his feet crunching along the gravel driveway, I turn to go back inside but a quick movement in the carriage house window catches my eye. For just a second I see the candlelit outline of Judah's dark, unsmiling face. Then it vanishes and the window is empty and black once more.

23.

Something is happening in the city—or about to happen. I'm glad Paul left before things got any worse. The longshoremen's strike is over, but I read in the papers just what it took to get them back to work. The white workers got what they wanted—a fifty-cent raise and black men kept off the docks. Adams says this has been going on for years, that more and more blacks have been leaving the city as more and more employers give in to the pressure to hire whites only. Any decent job—any honorable trade that pays "a white man's wage"—is closed to blacks. Which leaves only the dirtiest and most demeaning jobs for black men and women. I can hardly believe that one day New York City will be home to millions of black people, working all kinds of different jobs. Judah would say that in 2001 black people are still being forced into the jobs white folks don't want, but that's not entirely true. There are black lawyers and doctors and teachers and politicians. There are black athletes and entertainers who are not only celebrities but millionaires. Trouble is, we're not there yet, we're here, and I got a feeling something big's about to jump off in this city. And I'm not the only one.

Nannie's been jumpy all week, and even Adams looks a little worried these days. On Friday night, I got ready to go to that African Civilization Society meeting, but when I went out to the carriage house, Judah said he didn't think we should go.

"They drew the first names for the draft today," he tells me as he buttons up his shirt. "I think maybe we'd better lie low for a while."

I found Judah lounging on his pallet up in the loft, reading the day's news in one of Dr. Brant's newspapers. Judah can't stand working for the man, but he doesn't seem to have a problem helping himself to whatever belongs to Dr. Brant.

"So?" I ask, a bit angry that I took so much time getting ready when Judah didn't even bother to get dressed. "What's that got to do with us?"

Judah looks at me like I just said something funny. "You really don't get it, do you? You sit up there in that fancy house without a clue about what's going on in the rest of the city—the rest of the country." Judah shakes his head and motions for me to climb back down the ladder. He climbs down after me, then pushes open the carriage house door so he can walk me back to the house.

"In case you haven't noticed, Judah, there's no TV in this world, no Internet, no radio. How am I supposed to know what's going on all over the country? I read Dr. Brant's newspapers whenever I get the chance, but I *do* have a job, you know. I can't spend my days hanging out on the corner, keeping up with the latest news."

"You don't need to be out on the street to know what's going on, Gen. You just need to keep your ears and eyes open. You notice the good doctor been acting funny lately? Or his missus?"

"I told you already, Mrs. Brant's crazy—she's always acting funny." Then I stop and think if what Judah's saying might be true. Dr. Brant has seemed a bit preoccupied lately, but he's a busy man—he gets that way sometimes. I tell Judah I haven't noticed anything out of the ordinary.

"Then you must not be paying attention. I'll bet the good doctor's feeling a little nervous today—some poor Paddy's heading off to war because he didn't have the guts to go himself."

"What are you talking about? Dr. Brant's exempt from serving in the war because he's a doctor—he's needed here at home."

Judah looks at me with contempt, like I am a gullible child. "Your doctor *bought* his way out of the war, Genna. He paid three hundred dollars for somebody to take his place. You think they don't need doctors on the battlefield? You think those Paddies don't got jobs?"

I am so shocked by what Judah has said about Dr. Brant that I can barely think of what to say. "You shouldn't call them that," I finally mumble halfheartedly.

"Why not? Want to hear what they call me?" Judah sighs impatiently. "It's not the Paddies—*the Irish*—I'm worried about right now. They drew the first names today, and that means all the poor suckers who couldn't buy their way out of the draft are now on their way to war—*for us*, Genna. At least that's how they see it. They think they been sold for a lousy three hundred bucks—less than what a slave goes for on the auction block."

"So what's that got to do with us? We didn't start slavery or this war."

"No, but once it's over—once they win the war *for us,* the Irish figure all the freed slaves will head north—steal their jobs, their homes, their women …" Judah sucks his teeth with disgust. "They're angry, Genna, that's all I'm trying to say. They're angry at us, the antislavery Republicans who started the war, and all the rich bastards who bought their way out—like your precious doctor. If you ask me, he ain't nothing but a coward."

I have heard enough. "That coward saved your life, Judah. Dr. Brant goes all kinds of places and does all kinds of things that most white doctors wouldn't do. He takes care of our people and he doesn't get paid for it—not one red cent. So you better think twice before you start pointing fingers. I don't see *you* rushing off to war."

Judah just shrugs at me. "They don't take colored soldiers in New York City. This war—like all the jobs around here—is for 'whites only.'" Judah watches me and slowly smirks, like he can read my mind. "Guess you think I should follow your *friend* to Boston—enlist there, if they'll take me."

"They *should* take you. You'd make a good spy."

Judah laughs out loud and grabs my arm before I can head up the stairs and let the kitchen door slam in his face. "How you think I stayed alive so long in this messed-up world, Gen? A slave's got to have all his senses turned on, all the time."

"You're not a slave anymore, Judah. And I don't appreciate being spied on like that."

Judah winks at me and offers a corny excuse instead of an apology. "I just wanted to make sure he didn't convince you to run away with him."

"Why? So you can convince me to run away with *you* instead?"

Judah takes my hand and pulls me close to him. He puts his lips next to my ear and runs his fingers over the locks sprouting beneath my head wrap. "I just want us to be together, Gen, to be free. What's wrong with that?"

I like standing close to Judah like this, but I am very aware of the fact that we are standing in the middle of the yard where anyone can see us. I take a small step back, but Judah doesn't let go of my hand. Instead, he cups my face in his palm and kisses me on the lips.

I fall back another step and take a deep breath. Judah looks so good to me right now, I just want to say yes yes yes to whatever he suggests. But this is serious, this decision will change our lives forever. So instead, I tell him the truth. "I don't know if I'm ready, Judah. To go to Africa. To get married. To give up on our real lives, the world we came from."

Judah sits on the steps and pulls me down beside him. "I'm sorry we had to miss the meeting this evening. I wanted you to meet some of the people who've already been to Liberia. And I wanted the Society people to meet you." Judah holds my hand between both of his and tangles his fingers up with mine. "We don't have to get married, Gen—we can wait until you're ready. The Society people like it when husbands and wives sign up together, but we can tell them we're brother and sister. Or we can sign up separately. Whatever you're comfortable with."

"Do you want us to get married?"

Judah nods and squeezes my hand. "Eventually. I think we're meant to be together, Gen. I mean, I done some things for girls before, but I never went through *nothing* like this. It's hard to think about being with somebody else. You and me—we go back—*way* back." Judah looks at me, and we laugh together. "No one else could understand me the way you do."

I look down and trace Judah's calloused palm with my fingertips. "Sometimes I feel like I don't know you anymore," I confess quietly.

"I know. I'm different—I've changed—we both have. But I still care about you, Genna. You'll always be special to me. Do you remember that haiku I wrote for you last summer?"

I nod and say the words out loud so Judah knows how much they still mean to me.

Judah smiles shyly and presses another scrap of paper into my palm the same way he did in the garden all those months ago. "Read this when you're alone. And keep your ears and eyes open from now on, Gen. I got a feeling things are about to get hectic around here."

Judah kisses me quickly this time, then pushes himself off the steps and walks down the gravel driveway and into the street. I know I should try to stop him, or at least ask him where he's going—if I can come along. But there's no point. Judah is going to his sources, the men and women who keep their dark fingers on the racing pulse of the city. What he learns from them Judah will share with me—when he's ready.

I uncurl the piece of paper Judah left in my palm. It is another haiku:

freedom is more than
a bright star in the night sky
it's our destiny

24.

New York City is burning.

Plumes of black smoke drift toward Brooklyn, and we're all worried the rage-fueled fires will spread across the river, too. People are fleeing Manhattan in anything that floats—black people mostly, but they're not the only ones. Even rich white folks have had to leave their homes—or what's left of them—and flee for their lives. Because a mob doesn't know anything about mercy. It doesn't care if you're male or female, white or black, an adult or a little kid. A mob is like a ferocious pit bull—the kind that's fed pepper and trained only to attack—once it gets hold of you, its jaws clamp down and won't let go until you're dead. The people getting off the ferry in Brooklyn look like they've been mauled—like someone pulled them from the pit bull's jaws just in time and told them to RUN! And that's what they did. They remind me of the people I saw on TV coming out of that building that was bombed in Oklahoma—they're smeared with soot and dust and blood, their clothes are in shreds or missing altogether, and they have this look of shock and terror stamped on their faces—like they have seen something so horrible it just won't go away, it's there before them, playing over and over again.

Pit bulls aren't born vicious. When they're young, they can be gentle and playful just like any other puppy. And regular people aren't vicious either. But if you're cruel to a pit bull, it grows into a monster on a chain. And if you put a whole lot of poor, angry people together in the city during a heat wave, during a war, during an unpopular draft, suddenly you've got a mob—a seven-headed monster *without* a chain.

Monday is when the riots begin. When the first ferry full of refugees arrives in Brooklyn, Dr. Brant takes me down there with him to see what we can do. It's pretty chaotic, because nobody saw this coming, and no one is prepared to handle a situation like this—not the politicians, not the preachers, not even the police. Dr. Brant—he takes one look at the white ladies weeping into their handkerchiefs and he sends me right back home. I want to stay and help, but Dr. Brant insists it isn't safe for me to be out in public right now. I want to say, if it isn't safe for me, then what about all these refugees? But Dr. Brant assures me he'll make sure they all have a safe place to stay. Then he puts me in a cab and sends me home. I know the real reason, though. He's worried that if a mob attacked rich white women in Manhattan, they might try the same thing here in Brooklyn. And he and I both know Mrs. Brant starts to panic the moment anything goes wrong.

Sure enough, soon as Dr. Brant gets back home, Mrs. Brant flies off the handle.

"Henry, what is Adams doing?"

"I instructed him to take down the bunting—just for now, my dear—Amelia!"

But it is too late. Mrs. Brant storms out the front door, nearly knocking down the ladder Adams is standing on.

"Come down from there at once, Adams! Those cowards— they wouldn't dare assault the flag. And *if* they dare, let them *try!*"

Mrs. Brant's eyes are blazing, and her cheeks are flushed as well. I look at her and part of me thinks, this crazy bitch is going to get us all killed. But then I look at her again and a part of me actually respects this woman—for the very first time. I can tell by the way Dr. Brant is watching his wife that he feels the way I do. Kind of sorry that she doesn't have more sense, but proud that she has enough guts to stand up to a mob.

While Adams hangs the red, white, and blue bunting back up over the doorway, Mrs. Brant flounces back inside. She catches a glimpse of herself in the tall mirror and stands before it to smooth her hair and dress. "They'd find us anyway. We're known supporters of the abolitionist cause and defenders of the Union. I won't hide from them, Henry. So don't even *think* of bundling me off to stay with Aunt Grace in Long Island. Leave if you must, you have your duty to fulfill. But I have *my* duty, Henry, and it is to stay here and safeguard our child and our home. Nannie will be with me, and Genna—I daresay she can fend off an attack single-handedly." Mrs. Brant flicks her eyes at me, and I almost laugh when I remember that day she and I fought in the kitchen. Then I realize that Mrs. Brant just called me by my proper name—for the very first time.

"I'll leave Adams with you as well, and he'll be armed. It isn't safe for him to be seen in the streets anyway."

"Even with a white gentleman?" Mrs. Brant asks.

"Especially with a white gentleman, I'm afraid." Dr. Brant turns to me and Nannie. "All of you had best stay close to home—inside, unless it absolutely can't be helped. So far the riots have stayed on the island, but you never know what rabble might become roused here in Brooklyn. Many of the wealthy Republicans they so despise reside here, in our neighborhood. So we had better take all the necessary precautions. I'll have Adams put the shutters up, and keep watch at the door. The rest of you should just make yourselves comfortable and settle in. I'll return as soon as I can."

Dr. Brant comes over to where I am standing with little Henry in my arms. He gently kisses his son's blond head. Then he looks straight into my eyes. "I know I can count on you to help your mistress, Genna." Dr. Brant lowers his voice and leans closer to me so

Mrs. Brant won't overhear. "Please come to my study before I leave."

I nod silently and Dr. Brant goes over to say goodbye to Mrs. Brant. Knowing this will take a while, I go upstairs, lay Henry down, and take the back stairs down to the kitchen. I peek out back real quick to see if Judah's around, but there's no sign of him. I head to Dr. Brant's study, knock on the open door, and close it behind me once he tells me to come in.

"You're a bright girl, Genna, and by now I've seen enough of your work habits to know you have a steady head and a steady hand. Have you ever fired a gun?"

I am so used to acting cool around Dr. Brant that I don't even show my surprise. You might think that a black girl from the 'hood knows all about guns, but I've never even touched a gun before, and I'd like to keep it that way. I do know something about riots, though. I was just six years old when the Crown Heights riots took place—almost the same age as the little black boy who was run down by that Jewish driver. But I remember how loud and angry people were, and how frightened Mama looked when she came home from work that night. She kept all of us inside the apartment for days, and we sat all together on the couch, watching reports on TV of people from our neighborhood setting cars on fire and smashing storefront windows. One group of black men stabbed a Jewish student to death, and he didn't even have anything to do with killing that little boy. Folks were just angry and upset, Mama said, and they took it out on whatever or whoever happened to be nearby. The same thing happened the next year in Los Angeles— people exploded because they were sick and tired of getting beat down and shot down and run down by cops who got off just 'cause they were white.

The riots in Crown Heights took place ten years ago, but I'm not so sure blacks and Jews like each other any better now. We all live together in the same community, but it's like they live in one world and we live in a world of our own. Sometimes I wish it didn't have to be that way, but when I think back on the riots, I think maybe that's how it's got to be so nobody else gets hurt.

Now, even though I don't really like guns, I step closer to the desk and look at the old-fashioned pistol Dr. Brant is holding in his hand. It looks like a toy, or something out of an old cowboy movie, but then I realize that this is how all guns look in 1863. Not sleek and compact like the guns dealers on my block used to carry in the pockets or waistbands of their baggy jeans. This gun is almost pretty—it has a creamy pearl handle and a long silver barrel that's so shiny the gun must be brand-new. But when Dr. Brant hands it to me, I find out the pistol is heavy and awkward to hold, and I'm not so sure I can do any damage with this—unless it's to myself.

Dr. Brant shows me three or four times how to pull back the hammer and tug on the trigger. He warns me that the gun might "kick"—knock me back a few steps—once I fire it. "But I'm hoping it won't come to that, Genna," Dr. Brant says solemnly. "Frankly, just the sight of a gun might be enough to scare an attacker away. That's what I'm hoping, at least."

I'm hoping the same thing myself, 'cause I don't know if I have what it takes to kill someone. I guess if it was self-defense, then I'd have no choice—you either shoot or end up dead yourself. And if anyone tried to hurt Nannie or little Henry or even Mrs. Brant, I'd do whatever I could to stop them. If anyone hurt Judah, I don't know *what* I'd do. But like Dr. Brant, I'm hoping I won't find out—not now, not ever.

Dr. Brant takes the gun back from me and places it inside its red velvet case. Then he closes the box and leaves it on top of his desk. "I don't want Mrs. Brant to know about this. We'll leave it here, and you come get it if there's an emergency. But only if it's an emergency, Genna. In these types of situations, cooler heads always prevail."

"I still think I should go with you," I say. "Black folks who have just been attacked by whites might feel better seeing my face alongside of yours."

"I understand, Genna, and I wish you could come—we could certainly use the extra help. But right now I need you to stay here—for your own sake, and for mine. Amelia … she doesn't do well in these types of situations." Dr. Brant smiles that tiny smile that's more like an apology.

I try to smile back, to let him know I understand, but I'm not thrilled about the fact that I can't go help my people because Scarlett O'Hara doesn't know how to act right. Before Dr. Brant leaves, I find the courage to ask him about Judah. "Dr. Brant—you haven't seen my brother, have you?"

Dr. Brant looks at me strangely, as though he is sorry that I still feel the need to lie after he has put his trust in me. "No, I haven't seen him. But I'm sure he's fine, Genna, wherever he is. Surely he has enough sense to avoid the city right now. Perhaps he's already back in Weeksville, preparing a place for the refugees."

I want to believe this is true, but I know that Judah just might be crazy enough to go *into* the city when everyone else is trying to get out. "If you see him—"

Dr. Brant nods sympathetically and gives my arm a reassuring squeeze. Then he heads out into the street and walks briskly down the block, searching for a cab.

Things still look normal in Brooklyn, although by now every-one must know about the riots across the river. I watch the street anxiously, hoping to see Judah's tall, dark form moving toward me, coming home. Instead, I see a drunken white girl weaving her way down our block. More than once she staggers into the gutter, then catches herself and climbs back over the curb. Her dirty hands grip the black iron spokes of the fences that run along the front yards of the row houses across the street. Slowly she pulls herself along, her dress torn and trailing on the ground. I have never seen a beggar in our neighborhood, at least not one as filthy as this. I wonder if she is hungry, knowing that Nannie has food in the pantry she could spare. I am about to go to the kitchen when the girl stops dragging herself along the fence. She looks across the street, into the window of Dr. Brant's study, and straight into my eyes. I gasp and rush outside just in time to catch Martha before she sinks to the ground.

25.

"And who might this be?" Mrs. Brant flashes her indignant blue eyes at me and waits, hands on hips, for an answer.

I push Martha a bit behind me and take a deep, quiet breath to steady myself. I don't want another fight with this woman, but I'm also not about to back down. "This is my friend, Martha. She just escaped the riots in Manhattan." I pause and try to think of a way to appeal to Mrs. Brant, but what more can I say? Martha is an Irish scullery maid, and I am her Negro friend. We are poor and desperate, and we have nowhere else to go. "She needs someplace to stay," I say with as much humility as I can muster.

Mrs. Brant taps her toe nervously on the floor. I can tell she wants to be hard, but Martha looks so pitiful right now, even Mrs. Brant is moved. She puts up a front, though, so I won't think she's gone soft. "Escaped? So they were after her, too, hey? No doubt because of the company she keeps." Mrs. Brant bites down on her lip to keep herself from spitting out another insult. "Well, where do you intend to put her? This isn't a hotel, you know. And I certainly won't have Irish waifs sleeping in my guest room."

"She can stay in my room for now." I make this suggestion quickly, before Mrs. Brant has time to harden her heart once more.

"Well, then you'd better take her up there. Clean her up first, if you can, and see that she gets something to eat. She looks like she's about to faint."

Mrs. Brant turns and sweeps out of the kitchen, and I let out a sigh of relief. I'm glad she decided to let Martha stay, 'cause if she put my friend out in the street, she'd have had to put me out, too. And I'm not trying to be out in the street in the middle of a race riot.

I sit Martha down at the kitchen table and wet a cloth so I can wipe the blood off her face. Martha still hasn't said anything, and Nannie's heating up some soup but watching her out of the corner of one eye. "Somethin' ain't right 'bout that gal. She say anythin' yet?"

I shake my head and gently wipe the smears of soot and blood off Martha's cheek. She just stares straight ahead while I wash her face, turning her head when I ask her to as though she has been hypnotized.

Nannie brings over the bowl of soup and sets it in front of Martha. "You gon' feed her, too? Don't look like nothin's wrong with her, she ought to be able to feed herself."

I can tell Nannie's not too happy about having Martha stay with us. I can't blame her, really, not when there are thousands of Irish women and men hunting black people like animals in Manhattan. I try to reassure Nannie that Martha won't bring trouble our way. "I'll take care of her, Nannie."

"How? You already got one baby to mind in this house."

I decide I'd better just ignore Nannie right now and focus instead on getting Martha to eat. I hold the spoon of hot broth up to her lips, but Martha just stares straight ahead like she's seeing something we can't see. "C'mon, Martha, open your mouth."

Again, like a child, Martha obeys. She eats nearly the whole bowl of soup, which seems to satisfy Nannie somewhat. Next I take Martha upstairs and help her get out of her clothes. They are torn and stained with blood, so I set them aside, knowing Nannie will likely burn them instead of trying to scrub the blood out. I slip one of my nightgowns over Martha's slender body; it is much too big for her and makes her look even more like a child. Then I help her crawl into my narrow bed and turn to go back downstairs.

"Don't leave me!" Martha cries out, grabbing hold of my skirt.

I'm so glad to hear Martha speak finally that I smile and sit back down on the bed. Martha pulls herself onto my lap and buries her face in my dress.

"Oh God, Gen, I'm so sorry! I'm so sorry, I didn't know—I swear I didn't know it'd come to this!" Martha weeps and clings to me, and I rock her back and forth the way Nannie once rocked me.

"Shhh, it's not your fault, Martha. You don't have to apologize."

"But, Gen, I was there, I was there! It was just like a game at first. Like a holiday, a day off work. Folks was drinkin' 'n singin' 'n makin' all kinds of noise, but nobody was gettin' hurt."

I stroke Martha's hair as she holds onto me, sniffling against my sleeve. I'm not sure I'm ready to hear her confession, but I can't stop Martha from talking now any more than I could stop her from being silent a moment ago.

"It was the draft they was on about, not the coloreds. Tommy said it was just about the draft."

I remember that Tommy is Martha's oldest brother, the one she said belonged to some kind of gang.

"They burned the office where the draft was held—but the boys was gonna put the fire out, the engine was right there, but then they smashed it ..." Martha pauses and I can feel her grip tighten on my arm. "I don't know what happened, Gen, all of a sudden it weren't a game no more. Folks was yellin' 'n shootin' 'n smashin' all the store windows, and they was pullin' people outta their houses—white people—'n settin' everythin' on fire! They hadn't seen no coloreds yet. But then somebody said, 'Let's get the niggers, let's burn all the little niggers!' and next thing I knew they was runnin' down Fifth Avenue toward the Colored Orphan Asylum. And I tried to stop 'em, Gen, I swear I did. But there was too many, there musta been thousands by then. All shoutin' 'n cursin' 'n callin' for blood like they was animals and not men. But there was women there, too, Gen—I couldn't believe my eyes, the things I seen women do. Women who looked like me Ma, and men who looked and talked just like me Da—just like Tommy and all the boys on our block ..."

Words are quickly spilling out of Martha's mouth, and my heart is beating just as fast. "What happened to the orphans—where were the police?"

"There weren't no police, there weren't nobody there that could help 'em. But somehow they musta found a way out, 'cause the place was empty when the mob got there. But they burned it anyway—threw everythin' out the windows and set the whole place afire."

"But they're children—they haven't done anything!" I cry.

"It's the draft, Tommy told me, it's the draft they're on about—"

I know that the rioters are upset about the draft, but I can only think of the orphans—homeless and innocent and helpless and black—in a city that has turned against them. I think of Mattie and the children at the orphanage in Weeksville and pray the fury and flames won't reach that far. "If it's the draft they're angry about, why go after children? For God's sake, Martha—"

"Because they're COLORED, Genna, they're COLORED, just like him ..." Martha dissolves into tears once again, and I do what I can to comfort her but she is becoming more and more hysterical.

"They killed him, Genna, they killed my Willem!"

"Willem? I don't understand. Why would they go after him?"

Martha stops crying for just a moment and looks up at me with bleary red eyes. She wipes her nose with the back of her hand and blinks at me. "'Cause he's colored, Gen. Willem's a Negro."

My lips fall apart in surprise, and suddenly everything Martha has been saying makes sense to me. I see all too clearly now why the mob would turn on a young black man who dared to fall in love with a white girl. Yet all this time, in the months that I've known her, Martha never once mentioned that Willem was black. And I never thought to ask—why would I? He was her boyfriend and I just assumed Willem was white and Irish, too. But he wasn't and now he's dead—murdered by a mob because he loved one of their own.

Martha's eyes glaze over again and she collapses against me, speaking through her sobs. "He was so beautiful, so gentle, 'n lookit what they done! We was tryin' to get away, we just wanted to leave. After they burned the orphanage, Tommy took me back to our ward. He knew there was gonna be trouble, not just for Willem but also for me. He told us to go, to get off the island, he said he had friends who could find us a boat. But they saw us, and Willem said, 'Martha, let go my hand,' but I didn't want to leave him, I thought he'd be safe with me. After all, I'm not colored, and they knew us, *they knew us*—we wasn't rich folks or Yankees, we was one o' them. We lived with them, they knew us, but oh God, they killed him anyway … draggin' 'im through the street, kickin' 'n punchin' 'n stabbin' at 'im. Me 'n Tommy, we tried to get to 'im but the mob was too thick, 'n they woulda killed me, too, only Tommy got me away. 'The nigger's filthy whore,' that's what they called me. 'N you could see it in their eyes, how they wanted my blood. 'Twasn't enough, what they done to Willem … what they done to my poor Willem … God damn 'em to hell! They want *all* the jobs and *all* the women, too—for their own lousy selves! I hope they burn in hell for what they done—all o' them!"

Martha's sobs shake us both and make the iron bed frame rattle against the wall. I try my best to quiet her down so Mrs. Brant doesn't hear. But right now I am feeling sick to my stomach and furious myself. In my own time I had heard about blacks being lynched in this country. I knew that mobs of white men and women once burned black people alive, hanged them from trees, and shot them full of bullets. But I always thought lynching was something that took place in the South, in "good ol' Dixie," in the days before Civil Rights. That sort of thing didn't happen up here, not in the North. Not in New York City.

Suddenly I hear Nannie's voice hissing over my shoulder. I turn and Nannie is there in the doorway, scowling fiercely and pointing at Martha.

"I heard her, she was there—she's one o' them! We ought to turn her over to the police."

I speak to Nannie as harshly as I dare. "She's *not* one of them—they nearly killed her, too! Because she loved a black boy, Nannie, because she loved one of us!"

"Sure, she loved him, and what good did it do, hey? Her 'love' is the reason that boy's probably swingin' from a lamppost right now."

"Oh God, Jesus God! Leave 'im be, leave 'im be!"

Martha starts to shriek again, and even Nannie realizes we must do something to calm her down. Nannie disappears but returns seconds later with a tiny glass of brandy. "Here, give her this."

I hold the glass to Martha's lips, and she swallows it all in one quick gulp.

Nannie snorts and takes back the empty glass. "Hmph. She's Irish, alright."

I glare at Nannie and she looks away, ashamed. I feel Martha's grip loosening, and soon she's slumped in my arms, fast asleep. I settle her under the covers, then follow Nannie out into the hall.

Before Nannie can lead the way back downstairs, I reach for her shoulder. She turns and shines the candle in my face. "What is it? What's wrong now?"

"Nannie—" I hesitate, unsure whether I should say anything. But Nannie's sharp eyes pierce into me, and I find myself confiding in her anyway. "I don't know where Judah is."

"What?"

"Judah—he isn't here. I haven't seen him since the riots began."

Nannie snorts again and turns back toward the stairs. "Hmph. Maybe he left for Africa without you."

"Judah wouldn't do that."

"What you know 'bout what that boy would or wouldn't do?"

Nannie's words cut me because they are cruel, but also because they are true. I bite my lip to keep from crying, and try to push past her so I can go out back and check the carriage house one more time. But Nannie grabs me and presses her face close to mine. "You're not going out there, Genna. Not 'til this mess settles down. That boy's got a way of findin' trouble, but he's no fool, least not as far as I can tell. If he made it here all the way from the rice fields of Carolina, then he'll know how to lie low 'til this trouble's passed. You stay inside, you hear me? *You hear me?*"

Nannie grabs hold of my wrist as though she can somehow tether me to the house. I nod silently and for a moment we look at each other, seeing all the terrible things Martha has just described. People—our people—are dying, being tortured and beaten and hunted and hanged. And there is nothing we can do about it. Nothing but stay here and hide.

Once Nannie's sure she's gotten through to me, she lets go of my wrist, then turns and calmly leads the way back downstairs.

26.

None of us sleeps well that night. Yet except for the clanging bells of a fire engine that races past our house around midnight, trouble doesn't knock on our door. Dr. Brant comes home at three o'clock in the morning, sleeps for a couple of hours, then goes back out to Weeksville where most of the black refugees have been taken. I've never seen him look this way before—tired, but not just from working so late at night. Dr. Brant looks like he is tired of seeing so much suffering—tired of healing bodies that people of his own race keep trying to destroy.

By six a.m. on Tuesday, Dr. Brant is gone, though he promises this time to be home before supper. The rest of us are left inside the house, trying to keep cool and keep ourselves busy so we don't think about what is happening across the river—and what still might happen here. Even little Henry seems to sense that something is wrong. He's hot and cranky, and I can't take him outside for a walk, though I long to walk the streets and search for Judah. Instead, it is Martha who finds all kinds of ways to keep Henry quiet. She doesn't say much to anyone else, but she stays real close to Henry and Mrs. Brant doesn't seem to mind. Instead of giving orders like she normally does, Mrs. Brant mostly stays upstairs in her room, standing by the shuttered windows, peering out into the street.

By evening time, all of us are feeling restless. The summer heat is unbearable, and we've got all our windows shut tight. What's worse, Dr. Brant hasn't returned yet. Despite Nannie's warning, I slip outside after supper and check the carriage house once more. But there is still no sign of Judah. I sink down on the last rung of the ladder and let out all the tears I have been holding inside. I cry for the orphans in Manhattan, and Martha's Willem, but mostly for Judah, who might already have shared Willem's horrible fate. When the tears stop falling, I wipe my face and take a deep breath to steady myself so I can go back inside and face Nannie. I have just about pulled myself back together when I hear somebody sniffle behind me.

"Who's there?"

For a moment I hear nothing but the rustling sound of mice scurrying through the straw. Then a frightened voice pleads with me, "Please, miss. Don't tell. Don't tell anyone."

It is hard to see in the dark interior of the carriage house, but the setting sun sends a few shafts of orange light through the small windows. I step around the ladder and peer into the shadows. There, crouched in a corner near Adams's room, is a black woman with three small children. "Please, miss. We just need someplace to stay. We won't make no trouble, I promise."

"Come out here in the light where I can see you. Don't be afraid—I'm not going to hurt you."

Slowly, the woman gets up and leads her children over to the window. I can tell they are frightened, hungry, and weary, though they seem to have spent the night in the carriage house. The three children look up at me with grim, sad eyes, and I wonder what unspeakable things they have seen over the past twenty-four hours. But they are alive, they have made it to Brooklyn, and somehow they have made their way here.

For a long moment we simply stare at one another, then at last I think of something to say. "Do you need anything—I could bring you some food, some blankets ..."

"We won't trouble you none, miss. We just needed someplace to go, and we saw the Union colors over your doorway ... We hoped you might be—friends."

I smile and nod at her, and the woman relaxes somewhat. "How did you get here, away from the city?" As soon as I ask this question, I wish I had kept my mouth shut. The woman's body stiffens again, and her eyes drop to the ground.

"My husband—he paid a man to row us across. We gave him everything, every cent we had. They burned our home. They burned our house, our furniture, and everything we owned ..." She says this with awe, as though it is something she still can't believe. Her eyes, when she looks at me, tell me the rest of the story: *they tried to burn us, too.*

I have sense enough not to ask what happened to her husband. Instead, I look outside; it will be dark soon. I'm not sure if I should leave them out here or bring them into the house. Nannie wouldn't object, I'm sure of that, but Mrs. Brant ... she agreed to help Martha, but Martha's white.

"Come with me." I open the carriage house door and motion for them to follow me. But the woman backs up instead, clearly terrified of showing her black face outside.

"No, Miss, we'll stay here. We won't make no trouble."

"But you can't stay out here," I reason with her. "If you do, I'll have to go back and forth with food and water, and people will know that someone's out here. Come inside—you can clean up, and the children can have something to eat. It's better this way. Come on." The children look up at their mother, waiting to see what they should do. "Adams, our coachman, he's inside standing guard. He's armed," I add. This last point seems to convince her. She takes the hand of each of her smallest children, and I take the hand of the eldest child. I peek through the door to make sure no one's around, then we slip outside and rush across the yard.

Before I can reach for the knob, the door swings open and

Nannie hisses at me, "Have you lost your mind?"

"Nannie, let us in!"

"Haven't you brought enough trouble into this house?"

I simply stare at Nannie, shocked that she would close the door against her own people. But Nannie's resolve falters when her eyes fall on the three frightened children.

Their mother surprises us both when she says, "I realize we are putting you in danger. But please, at least take the children. I can find somewhere else to stay."

"Mama! No!" All three children cling to their mother, making any kind of separation impossible.

Nannie's ferocity vanishes completely, replaced now with sympathy. "Sweet Jesus, forgive me. Get inside, all of you, quick." Nannie pulls us inside, then closes the door and arranges the kitchen curtains so no one can see inside.

"Where should we put them?" I ask quietly. I'm not sure what to do next. Even though this was my idea, I'm secretly hoping that Nannie will take charge.

"They could stay in my room, 'cept it's hot as an oven up there." Nannie goes over and opens the cellar door. "It ain't much, but it's the coolest place in the house."

I light a candle and hand it to the woman. "Don't let it go out," Nannie warns her, "'cause it's black as pitch down there. The mice'll keep away so long as you got that light." Then Nannie turns to the children. "Don't be afraid. There's plenty of apples and pears down there—you just go on and help yourselves. I'll come down with some hot food soon as it's ready."

"God bless you—God bless you both," the woman tells us with shining eyes.

Nannie and I watch them inch down the steep cellar stairs. I am just about to close the door behind them when Mrs. Brant catches us by surprise.

"What's going on?"

Nannie and I spin around. Mrs. Brant is standing on the other side of the kitchen holding Henry. And for once, he is content—even relieved—to be in his mother's arms.

Before Nannie or I can think of what to say, Mrs. Brant surprises us again. "How many are there?"

"Four," Nannie tells her. "One woman and three little ones."

"Will they be alright down there?" Mrs. Brant asks all her questions as though she is merely curious, not angry or upset.

"For now. It's nice and cool in the cellar, the children will probably fall asleep 'fore too long. I'm gon' make 'em somethin' to eat right now."

Mrs. Brant nods wordlessly and turns to go. I want to say something to this woman, to show her that I appreciate what she's doing for Martha and these refugees. "Dr. Brant's okay," I blurt out, before I even know what I am saying. Mrs. Brant looks at me, her pale face drawn tight with worry. "He's probably still over in Weeksville," I say, "helping folks get settled over there. He's okay."

"How do you know?" Mrs. Brant asks quietly.

Truth is, I *don't* know what's happened to Dr. Brant. He wouldn't stay away from his wife and child at a time like this—not if he could help it. But I can't say that to Mrs. Brant, so instead I say, "I just do. You know what he's like—he wouldn't take chances with his own safety, or ours." I say this with complete confidence, as though I am the mistress of the house and Mrs. Brant is the servant girl.

Mrs. Brant nods slightly, then nods more certainly as if my words now make sense to her. "Yes, you're right, Genna." Again Mrs. Brant turns to go, but she stops before pushing open the kitchen door. "Your brother—"

This time it's harder to put up a front. I don't know what's more dangerous right now—to be a rich white man or a poor black man in this city. I press my lips together and look away so Mrs. Brant won't see the tears filling my eyes.

"He's probably with my husband," she says in the same strong voice I used to convince her a moment ago. "They're probably both in Weeksville."

I force myself to look at Mrs. Brant. I cannot smile, but I nod to show her that I still have hope, too. Mrs. Brant holds Henry close to her breast and disappears through the swinging door.

"Why don't you get some rest," Nannie suggests. "I can manage down here."

I don't feel sleepy, but I decide to go upstairs and see what Martha's doing. When I don't find her in my bedroom, I go up the narrow flight of stairs that leads to the roof. Sure enough, the door is propped open and Martha is standing out there alone, watching the fires burn across the river.

I pull my feet across the sticky tar rooftop and stand next to Martha. She is quiet, but her face is wet with tears, so I put my arm around her and pull her close to me. "I'm so sorry, Martha" is all that I can say. And I truly am—sorry that a mob killed Willem simply because the color of his skin didn't match the skin color of the person he loved.

Martha begins to weep openly now, and as we stand there on the roof watching the city burn, I begin to understand why Judah is so desperate to leave this place. I don't know what kind of challenges we'd face in Liberia, but it couldn't be any worse than this. Across the river, just a couple of miles away, black people are being beaten, dragged through the streets, driven from their homes, and terrorized by whites. *Whites*—and they have the nerve to call Africans "savages." I want to feel angry, to feel a rage inside of me equal to the fury that's driving that mob to destroy everything in sight. But all I can feel as I look out over the smoldering skyline is a deep, overwhelming sense of loss. I feel as though I am watching a funeral. With the black sky all around me, I feel like a mourner, except I have no tears to shed. It is an empty, hollow grief that nothing—not even time—can fill.

Unlike Martha, I know that in time the riots will end, the fires will be put out, and the city will be rebuilt. And even though black people are leaving the city now—with good reason—someday they'll come back. Someday there will be millions of us living and working and going to school in New York City—there will even be a black mayor one day. And Brooklyn won't be its own city, it will be one of the five boroughs, and the bridge will cross the river, bringing the city together. All these things will happen someday. But someday isn't going to come anytime soon, and it can't come soon enough for me. As I stand on the rooftop, with the burning lights swimming before my eyes, I silently vow that I will go with Judah—to Liberia, Jamaica, Canada—wherever he wants to go. Anyplace but here.

The sudden sound of glass shattering somewhere below pulls our attention away from the burning city. I rush to the edge of the house and peer down into the street. A group of about twenty white men is gathered in front of our house. Martha only needs one glance from me to know that the mob has found her once again. Together we rush across the sticky tar roof and race back downstairs.

Adams, from his position behind the tall, shuttered parlor window, is warning the group of men to get away from the house. They laugh and in response hurl bricks and paving stones, breaking the glass and the shutters and forcing Adams to step back. "C'mon out, nigger. We got somethin' for ya!"

Adams glances at us, four women huddled together at the foot of the stairway. "I'm ready to fire, missus. You just say the word."

Mrs. Brant is wringing her hands and pacing back and forth. "This can't be happening. This simply can't be happening. They wouldn't dare assault us here. They wouldn't dare—I'm a white woman!"

I want to tell Mrs. Brant this *is* happening, and men as drunk and angry as the ones outside would dare to do just about anything.

I want to say, "Martha's white, too, and they still attacked her." I want Mrs. Brant to know about the white ladies who got off the ferry yesterday with nothing left but their lives. But I know it's pointless trying to talk sense to Mrs. Brant right now. Instead, I remember the gun in Dr. Brant's office and race down the hallway to get it. By the time I get back just a few seconds later, Nannie is alone in the wide foyer.

"Where is she?"

Nannie tries to speak, but the best she can do is nod at the front door, which is standing open. I groan and feel my stomach sinking inside of me. Mrs. Brant has done the unspeakable—she has gone outside to face the mob.

I'm about to rush after her with the gun in my hand, but Nannie grabs me and pulls me back inside. "Don't you show your face out there! They see one black face, and next thing you know they be coming in here after all of us—all of us!" Nannie nods her head toward the floor, and I remember the woman and children hiding in our cellar. All we can do is stand in the shadows of the foyer, listening and praying as Mrs. Brant starts to speak.

"Good evening." She stops, unable to force herself to address them as "gentlemen."

Several of the men take off their hats and bow mockingly as though facing a queen. These men look as though they have just stumbled out of a bar. Their faces are flushed, and they lounge against the iron rails of the fence as though they're only stopping to rest before heading on to yet another rum shop. Those that were singing before stop now to listen to this bold white woman.

Mrs. Brant clears her throat and grabs hold of the iron banister to help steady her nerves. "This is a respectable home and a respectable community. We've never had any trouble before, and we don't want any trouble with you now. I'll have to ask you to leave immediately …"

The men look at one another, more amused than amazed by her request. One stocky man with thick black hair and an unshaven face moves to the front of the mob. "Sorry, missus, but we can't do that. Ya see, we're here on official business."

Mrs. Brant hesitates, as though she actually believes this might be true. "Well, what is it you want?"

"We come to see the doctor."

"Yeah, we ain't feelin' so good tonight!"

Mrs. Brant frowns at the men's impertinence and responds icily, "He isn't in. You'll have to go someplace else—" Mrs. Brant turns to come back inside the house, but the mob will not be so easily dismissed.

The black-haired man hollers after her, "Don't go nowhere, missus. If the doctor's not in, you'll do." Then several of his friends take up the conversation.

"Did he pay you, too, lady?"

"Yeah, did he pay three hundred dollars so's you'd stand out here and be his substitute?"

"The good doctor's that much of a coward, hey?"

"He's probably hidin' under 'er skirts."

"Let's search 'em and find out!"

Mrs. Brant's cheeks burn with indignation as she spins around to face the mob again. "Don't you dare come through that gate! I've told you already, my husband isn't in, and moreover he is any-thing *but* a coward. At this very moment he is tending to those wounded by ruffians like yourselves. *You* would not come to this house alone, to speak with my husband man to man—no! *You* wait until darkness has fallen, then suck your courage out of a bottle and come here as a mob to harass a lone white woman. Shame on you—all of you!"

For a moment the men stand awkwardly on the sidewalk, look-ing at one another instead of at Mrs. Brant. Sensing that he might lose the support of his friends, the ringleader speaks up again.

"You ain't alone. We heard your nigger threatenin' us just a min-ute ago. Send him out here and we'll be on our way, right lads?" The men cheer with approval and tighten the knot of bodies they have formed around our gate.

"I'll do no such thing. The Negroes in this household are under my protection." Mrs. Brant pauses and I hold my breath, waiting to hear what she will say next. It's clear to me that Mrs. Brant is feel-ing herself now—she knows that morally she has the upper hand, and she honestly believes she can shame these men into acting right. I want to believe that, too, but I'm not so sure the creatures outside *are* men, so why should we expect anything but danger from them?

Mrs. Brant points up at the bunting wilting in the humid night air before continuing with her speech. "And we are all under the protection of the glorious Union, which our brave soldiers are fighting to preserve. Why not turn your fighting spirit against the true enemy and enlist! Fight with honor, fight for a just cause—"

Some of the men actually seem moved by Mrs. Brant's passion-ate performance, but others grow restless and rowdy.

"Aw! Shut 'er up already!"

"It ain't *our* cause, lady, and it ain't *our* war!"

"Why should we die to set the niggers free?"

And again, it is the black-haired ringleader who speaks above all the other voices. "Here, missus. You give each of us what your husband paid to skip out on the draft, and we'll leave you to your niggers and your 'glorious' flag." The men roar in agreement and try to untangle themselves so they can come up to the house to receive their pay.

Mrs. Brant falls back against the doorframe, amazed that her plea has had no effect on the mob. "Certainly not! Now get away from my home—all of you, this instant!" Mrs. Brant's voice is becoming more and more shrill, and the men in response only laugh louder and jostle one another as they fight to get through the narrow gate.

Suddenly a shot rings out, and the mob collectively ducks as a bullet whistles overhead.

"You lot! Get away from that residence. I'm warning you—turn back or I'll fire." All heads turn to see where the voice and the warning shot came from. It is Mr. Wharton, our next-door neighbor. He is standing on his stoop, his rifle aimed at the mob.

But when the men see Mr. Wharton's white hair and palsied hands, they only laugh and hurl more bottles and bricks at his house, forcing him back inside. Shots ring out again, however, and this time it is Adams, firing through the shattered parlor window. For a moment there is complete chaos—those struck by the bullets cry out in pain, others go to their aid, while still others turn their anger on us. Nannie rushes out, grabs Mrs. Brant, and hauls her inside the house just as a member of the mob lunges up the front stairs and tears at the bunting hanging over our door. Others follow, and despite Adams's steady barrage, attempt to force their way into the house.

Nannie's hands are full—she is restraining and holding up Mrs. Brant, who looks like she's either about to faint or else charge back outside. I look down at my own hands and know that the time has come. I take a step toward the front door, raise the revolver with both hands, and fire at the body pounding angrily on the frosted glass. The man cries out, then slumps against the door, his wounded arm leaving a pinkish smear on the window as he slides down to the stoop. I cock the gun and fire again, this time shattering the pane of glass completely, so that I can clearly see what's going on outside. A man with yellowish eyes glares at me before heaving his fallen friend up and lumbering back down the stairs and into the street. From where I am standing, I can hear him telling the others that a "nigger wench" fired at him. This news enflames the others, and they are about to come back for me when more shots ring out from across the street.

This time it is Mr. Reilly and his son—a young veteran who

went to war willingly, and sacrificed one of his legs. He still has both his arms, though, and right now I'm thankful for that. What's more, the Reillys are Irish. Mrs. Brant never liked them much because of that fact, but now it is those same "Pope-loving foreigners" who are driving back the mob.

"Back to the wharves, you rats! Get back, I say! You're a disgrace to Ireland and a disgrace to your race—attacking women and coloreds who have done you no harm! Get back!" Mr. Reilly's son punctuates his father's statements by shooting into the mob. He has expert aim, and several more men go down. The mob takes this new threat seriously and backs away from our house. I cautiously approach the front door and peer through the shattered window. What I see stops my heart completely—Judah is coming down the street. Judah is coming home.

27.

"No, no, no—"

The word bubbles up from somewhere deep inside of me, growing louder with each step Judah takes toward the mob. With the pistol still in my hand, I throw open the front door and rush down the stairs.

"NO, NO, NO!"

I push my way through the few men who are either too bold or too stupid to get out of the line of fire. They are so stunned to see a black girl running *toward* them that for a moment they just stand and watch in disbelief.

"What the devil … ?"

"She must be mad!"

Behind me I can hear Nannie and Martha screaming for me to come back. But ahead of me is Judah, and I have to reach him, tell him to turn back before the mob gets sight of its prey. To avoid hitting me, Mr. Reilly and his son hold their fire, but this gives the mob an opportunity to advance once again. I am almost as far as the corner of the block when a hand grabs me by the arm and spins me around. Without even thinking, I smash the pearl handle of the pistol into his white face as hard as I can. Stunned, the man releases my arm and holds his broken nose instead. Blood gushes through his dirty fingers and drips onto the paving stones. I hold my skirt up with one hand and clutch the pistol in the other. And I run like I have never run before.

"There she goes—get 'er!"

The cry goes up behind me, but all I can think of right now is Judah. I hear more shots ringing out as Adams and the Reillys start firing again, then the thunder of men's feet as they begin the chase.

By now Judah has seen me. I am panting and trying to shout at him, "Run, Judah! RUN!" But Judah is running *toward* me, he is running straight into the mob. I stop in my tracks and try to ward him off by waving my arms. "No—NO! Turn around, *turn around!*"

But Judah keeps on coming and I race on to stop him and within seconds we collide in the middle of the street. Judah takes one swift glance at the pursuing mob, then grabs my arm and pulls me down a side street. He sees the gun and reaches for it, and I gladly give it to him. I try not to think about the man I shot, or what the others will do to me in revenge. There is no time to think right now. Judah and I are running for our lives.

As we sprint down the dark street, the cries of the mob echo behind us. Every house along the street has turned down its lights and fastened its shutters. It is as though all of Brooklyn has turned against us. I feel my legs starting to tire, but we run on, turning down one street, then another, until the mob loses sight of us for the moment. Judah pulls me into a doorway that is darkened by the shadows of a nearby tree. Though I know it is pointless, I make the desperate suggestion anyway. "Maybe we should knock on one of these doors and ask for help. Or go to a church—they'd help us, wouldn't they?"

But Judah only shakes his head while checking the gun to see how many bullets are left. "I never thought I'd say this, but our only hope is the police."

But the precinct house on Middagh is far behind us now, and we can't turn back. Judah and I stand in the shadows, our chests heaving, our hands still clasped together. "We've got to get to City Hall." Judah looks steadily at me. "Think we can make it?"

I nod quickly, and we are off, Judah tugging at my hand, urging me to run as fast as I can. We stay as close to the shadows as we can, but the trees in Brooklyn are still young—it will take another hundred years before their canopies offer much shade. This leaves us no choice but to run in the wide, empty, gaslit street, our feet pounding loudly against the paving stones. Still, we make it two full blocks before the mob gets sight of us again.

"There they are!"

We freeze and look over to the next block. The mob is one street over, on Montague, but now it splits in two, with one group of men rushing on to cut us off and the other coming up Henry Street toward us. Judah pushes me behind him and fires at a man holding a flaming torch. He topples to the ground, and two of his friends crowd around him, while others pick up the torch and run straight at us.

"The nigger's got a gun!"

"He's shootin' white men!"

"Get that black bastard!"

We race on, determined to get ahead of the other half of the mob that is trying to reach Clinton Street in order to circle back around and trap us on Remsen. Stones fly over our heads and skid along the dark street. Judah turns and fires a second shot but the mob surges on, seemingly unstoppable and bigger now than when it first formed outside the Brants' home. We make it past Clinton before the other half of the mob can block our way, but they simply merge with the men behind us, forming an angry sea of white faces.

One block more and we will reach City Hall. Though there is no guarantee that we will find safety there, Judah and I run on, exhausted but desperate to stay ahead of the vicious mob. When we reach Court Street, Judah and I stop short, amazed by what we see.

The triangular plaza is lit with blazing gas lamps, and at the foot of the steps of City Hall is a line of uniformed policemen. Behind them, crouching on the steps themselves, are dozens of black people. Judah and I race toward the line of policemen, which opens to let us pass through.

From the safety of the steps, we can now face the mob. It has grown, and clusters of men walk brazenly up the streets that lead to City Hall. Although there appear to be close to a hundred men, the twenty police officers before us show no sign of fear. Instead, they stand at attention, waiting for their chief to give the command. The police chief is a tall, pale man with a thick mustache and a long, crinkly beard that reaches all the way to his broad chest. He slowly paces in front of his men, calmly surveying the mob, measuring its determination and strength. The mob, in turn, draws closer to City Hall, but the men are noticeably quieter than before.

A young white man who looks like some kind of clerk hurries up the steps and motions for us to follow him. "C'mon, all of you, inside! Chief's orders. You'll be safe there—no one's ever broken into or out of that jail." The other blacks, mostly frightened women and children, take the young man's advice, but Judah stops me from going along.

"But we'll be safe in there," I tell him.

Judah just shakes his head and pulls me farther up the steps. We crouch behind one of the enormous stone pillars, Judah still clutching the pistol. "Once you're inside a building, you're trapped. The mob in Manhattan torched most of the precincts—they might try to do the same thing here. Better to stay outside, in case we need to run again."

The thought of having to run for my life a second time tonight makes me want to break down and cry, but instead I hold onto Judah and wait to see what will happen next.

The police chief has decided it is time to address the mob. In a deep, thundering voice he says, "You have brought chaos to the streets of Brooklyn. But there shall be ORDER in this city! Turn back or bear the consequences—this is your last warning."

The chief then gives a tiny nod, and all at once the officers begin beating their wooden nightsticks upon the ground. The steady tapping of twenty batons echoes through the plaza, sounding more like a marching army of a thousand men. I have seen riot police on television do the same thing—except in our century, the batons are metal and are beaten against bulletproof shields. Just seeing that on TV used to give me goose bumps, and now, through my sweat-soaked dress, I feel a chill run up my spine. Judging from the looks on the faces of the rioters, many of them are afraid, too. A few turn around and head back down the streets Judah and I were chased through a moment ago.

Suddenly, the stocky, black-haired ringleader emerges from the sea of men. He approaches the police chief, his face ugly, flushed, and defiant. "There you go, always protectin' the niggers! Well, what about *our* rights? Hey? Who looks out for *us*?" He turns to the mob, and the men roar angrily. The black-haired man then lifts up his arm and signals for them to follow him. Like a wave, the mob surges toward City Hall.

The police chief raises his own baton, his officers do the same, and then the entire line moves forward like some kind of chopping machine. But it's not trees or weeds that are falling, it's the rioters instead, their skulls cracking loudly each time an officer brings his nightstick down. Now the real chaos begins, with the officers showing no mercy and some of the rioters showing no sense—instead of getting out of the way, men rush at the police with knives or clubs of their own. But the mob is desperate and unorganized, and the officers are efficient and well-trained. Within minutes they divide the mob and push the rioters out of the plaza, leaving dozens of bodies strewn on the ground.

Judah and I watch the terrible scene from the steps of City Hall. It takes all of my strength to keep him next to me—Judah is ready to fight, to help the officers beat back the mob. But I have learned this evening what a mob will do to a black person who dares to fight back. When Judah shot at them before—or when I shot that man trying to break into the Brants' home—the mob went wild, as if they could not believe a black person would dare to defend herself. It's as if they expect us to just give up without a fight, to *let* them kill us, as if this is their right.

When the worst seems to be over, Judah and I make our way down the steps and onto the littered plaza. Some of the men are unconscious, others moan pitifully as their blood spills onto the ground. Judah stares at them coldly, kicking at the limbs that happen to be in his way. I look at the wounded rioters and cannot help but feel sorry for them—perhaps it is my training as a nurse, or perhaps it is because these whimpering men no longer resemble the howling beasts that chased us through the streets earlier on. Judah holds my hand tightly in his, and together we weave our way through the bodies toward the fountain at the end of the plaza.

Despite everything that we have been through this evening, I reach into my pocket and pull out the few coins I usually carry in case I pass a fountain during my day. Judah looks down into my palm and smiles sadly. "What would you wish for tonight, Gen?"

I wrap my fingers around the pennies and wrap my arms around Judah, holding him close. For a moment I can't even speak, I am so thankful that he is alive. Then I remember the promise I made up on the roof. "Judah, when this is over—when the riots are over—I'll go with you to Liberia. I'm ready to go now. I just want to be with you …"

I am looking straight into Judah's eyes, and I can see the love and happiness and relief there. I know he is thankful we survived this night, and from now on we will work together to build a future outside of this country. But before Judah can say anything, someone presses the button that lights up the circuits in my back. An electric fire shoots straight up my spine, and I scream before sinking to my knees and slumping over the edge of the fountain. The pennies I had been clutching slip through my fingers and slowly sink to the bottom.

"Thought you could best us, did ya? Thought you could shoot white men and get away with it, did ya? Damned niggers—"

Judah pulls back the hammer and fires at the black-haired man, stopping only when there are no bullets left in his gun. Stunned to see that Judah is still armed and still so defiant, the man lifts his arm and the blade of his knife flashes in the moonlight. But Judah's bullets have found their mark. The knife drops from the man's hand, and he topples forward on his face.

Judah hurls his empty gun at the dead man and then kneels down and tries to turn me over. "Genna! Gen, are you alright?" Before I can even answer, Judah sees the blood spreading across the back of my dress. "Oh, God. Hang on, Gen, just hang on. I'll find a doctor, or—we'll get you to a hospital, there's got to be a hospital somewhere around here. Just hold on, Gen, please. Don't die—not now, not here …"

I am trying to focus on what Judah is saying to me, but there are so many voices whispering in my ear … *I can't stay here … I may not come back … they killed him … I didn't know it'd come to this … at least take the children … fight for a just cause … RUN!*

Judah's face is hovering above me, and his shadow falls over my body like a dark woolen blanket. I reach up to touch his missing locks, but my fingers find only the warm night air. My eyelids begin to feel heavy, so I close my eyes …

"Gen?" Judah shakes my shoulder and tips my chin up so he can look in my face. "Gen, you got to stay with me, okay?" Judah quickly presses his lips against mine, then stands and searches frantically for an officer. "Help us! Please—she's hurt. SOMEBODY HELP US!"

"I wish …"

Judah drops to his knees once more and brings his face close to mine. "Shhh, Gen, don't try to talk. Just try to stay with me. Don't go, Gen, please don't go."

"I wish ..." My last words slip out along with my last conscious breath.

"NOOOOOOO!" Judah roars like a wounded lion and buries his wet face against my neck. Then the darkness swallows me up completely, and I am gone.

PART III

I am alive.

My senses come back slowly. I open my eyes but there is only darkness at first, then gradually I see a thin line of light. It is close to me, but I cannot move my hand to open the door that is shutting it out. I can taste the salty, sticky blend of blood and tears that covers my face. I can smell the strong scent of pine and feel the prickle of needles beneath my palms. For a long while I lie silent on the ground, not wanting to turn my head and find out that I am alone, not wanting to call his name and find out that Judah isn't here.

But even without looking, I know. Judah is still *there*. Once again, I got sent back alone.

After a long time spent weeping quietly on the ground, I push myself up on my knees and look around. I am under some kind of living canopy—a tree. I search my memory and find there an image of the weeping hemlock at the Botanic Garden—an ancient tree that grows close to the ground, its boughs forming a skirt beneath which animals—and humans—can hide. I lift one of the boughs now and shield my eyes as warm sunlight strikes my face. I am back in the garden again. I am back in Brooklyn.

I crawl out from under the weeping hemlock and try to stand, but my legs are weak and I fall back to the ground just as a cart rolls up with two security guards. I have the impulse but not the energy to run, so I stay as I am and wait to see what they will do.

"Genna? Is that you? What you doing here?"

I squint at the guard climbing out of the cart and realize it is Judah's cousin, Samuel. He seems embarrassed to find me here and turns to his partner. "I got this, man, you go on ahead." The other guard stares at me for a moment, but drives off, leaving us alone.

Samuel helps me stand up and leads me over to a nearby bench. Next to it is a drinking fountain. I swallow several mouthfuls of water, then splash some on my face to loosen the dried blood. Then I sit down on the hard stone bench and take a look around. As my eyes drink in the familiar sights of the garden, I slowly realize that I am home. *Home.*

Samuel is staring at me. I look down at my body and find that I am wearing the same jeans and T-shirt I had on the day I disappeared. My clothes are grimy but intact, and for the first time I can feel the sun shining on my locks. It is a beautiful day, but the garden is empty. Yet even if it were full of people, I would still feel alone. Because Judah isn't with me. He's still *there.*

"Damn, girl. What happened to you?"

There is nothing I can say that will make any sense to Samuel, so I say nothing at first. Then I realize Samuel might know something about Judah. Perhaps he got here first, or "landed" someplace else. "Have you seen Judah?" I ask anxiously.

Samuel looks at me like maybe somebody knocked me upside the head. "What?"

"Judah—where is he?"

"How should I know? That cat disappeared about the same time as you—didn't leave no note, nothing. We all figured you was together somewhere. You don't know where he's at? You two wasn't together after all?"

I shake my head silently, knowing there are no words to explain how Judah and I lost each other, then found each other, then lost each other again. "What day is it?"

"It's Monday—that's what I been trying to tell you. The garden's closed—you can't be in here. You better go home and see about your moms, let her know you're okay." Samuel stops and looks at me. "*Are* you okay?"

"What month is it—what year?"

"What year?" Samuel laughs and shakes his head. "This is some Rip Van Winkle shit right here—you sleeping under that tree, then waking up and not knowing what year it is."

I know all of this must seem bizarre, but I don't have time for jokes right now. "Just tell me the date, Samuel—the full date—day, month, year."

"A'ight, a'ight, chill. It's Monday, September 10, 2001. Ain't nothing special 'bout this day. You just in the wrong place at the wrong time. Now come on, I'll walk you out. You can come back tomorrow."

Samuel helps me stand up and slowly we walk toward the exit. On the other side of the garden gate are Mama, Tyjuan, and our building—the life I left behind. I want to search the garden, go back to the fountain and wish for Judah. But the heavy rock that's sitting where my heart used to be tells me there's no use.

Samuel puts his hand on my shoulder and gently pushes me toward the street. "Go on, girl. Go home and let your moms know you're okay."

I'm not okay, I want to tell him, but these are more words to be kept inside. There is no one in this world I can talk to, no one who will understand. I take a deep breath, walk through the gates, and step out onto the street. Alone.

Sounds rush over me like a tidal wave—the blare of sirens and car horns, the wheeze and groan of a passing bus, the laughter of children, the pulsing bass from a stereo high above the street. I rock back on my heels, then regain my balance and slowly head home.

I should have known it would happen this way—that I would get sent back alone. But I didn't know how to bring him with me.

It doesn't seem real, and yet I know this is not a dream. I am here. But Judah is still *there*.

It is strangely quiet on our block. There is no one hanging out in front of our building, and I have no key. I stare at the intercom for a full minute, trying to remember our number. Finally, I find it and press the button.

"Who is it?" Mama's voice crackles through the mesh speaker.

"It's Genna," I reply.

"What? I said, *who is it*. Don't be playing games with me."

I swallow hard and try to speak more clearly this time so Mama will recognize my voice. "It's not a game, Mama. It's me—Genna." I wait to hear the buzz and click that lets me know the door has been opened from inside. But there is only silence, so I try again. "Please open the door, Mama. It's *me*." I look through the scratched-up glass to see if anyone inside can let me in, and then I see Mama—thinner than she was before—walking cautiously toward the front door.

I step back and wait for my mother to cross the wide foyer, knowing that once she lets me in, things will never be the same. I can't go back. Much as I want to, I can't go back.

Mama presses her face up to the glass and simply stares at me. I know I look a mess right now, but she has to know that it's me. I have changed, but I'm still her daughter. "It's me, Mama." These are the only words I can find the strength to say.

Finally, I hear the buzz and click, and Mama opens the door for me. Her face, like mine, is wet with tears. "Genna? Oh my God, my baby's home ..."

As I step into my old building and into my mother's embrace, I tell myself this is only the beginning of the story, not the end.

He found me the first time, and I know he will find me again. Judah will find his way back to me.

The End

A WISH
AFTER MIDNIGHT

STUDY GUIDE

Discussion Topics

- What is speculative fiction? How can an author create a convincing narrative by "bending" the facts and/or "stretching" the truth?

- How does reading historical fiction differ from reading facts in a history textbook?

- The novel begins with Genna telling the reader about the wishes she makes in the fountain at the botanic garden. Why are wishes so important in this story?

- Is Genna someone you can relate to? If you could change something in your life simply by making a wish, what would it be?

- Genna uses the garden as a sanctuary, a place she can go to in order to feel safe. Where do you go to find sanctuary?

- Genna feels as though her family is crumbling around her. What could each member of the Colon family do to improve their relationships with one another?

- At the garden, Genna meets Mr. Christiansen and Hannah, who are both white. How do Genna's ideas about race differ from her mother's? Does Genna have a better relationship with white people in 2001 or in 1863?

- Why does Genna compare her Panamanian father to Timothy McVeigh? How do you feel about the "melting pot" theory? Should immigrants forget their heritage and just try to "fit in"?

- Explain these two sayings: "opposites attract" and "like attracts like." What is it that draws Genna and Judah together? Do you think their relationship is likely to last?

- Genna has a hard time connecting with her siblings Toshi and Rico. Predict where Toshi and Rico will be in five years.

- Consider Genna's description of her community. Is this "the real Brooklyn"? Who is responsible for the problems in Genna's community, and what could be done to improve conditions in her building?

- Is Genna naïve to believe she can escape "the ghetto" by attending an Ivy League school? Do you think she will one day realize her dream of becoming a psychiatrist? Do your plans for the future include leaving your community? If so, is that "selling out"?

- What makes Judah different from other teenagers at his school? Is he someone you would be likely to befriend? Why or why not? Why does he want Genna to lock her hair?

- What does "sankofa" mean? Find the adinkra symbols that represent sankofa and explain how they relate to the novel.

- A major turning point in the novel occurs when Genna defies her mother and is slapped. What would you have done in that situation? Genna says, "I realize I am no longer a child." How did this encounter force her to mature? Is Genna now an adult?

• When Genna flees into the garden, she makes a fateful wish that opens a portal leading to another time. What do you think Genna wished for?

• What is significant about the city of Brooklyn in 1863? Why do you think Genna arrived at that particular moment in time?

• Sam Jenkins plays dumb in order to fool the police captain into giving him custody of Genna. Later, Genna also plays dumb in order to avoid answering Reverend Macklin's questions. Why was playing dumb a useful strategy for blacks in the past? Is it still useful today, or does it reinforce stereotypes about blacks being less intelligent?

• Mattie is one of the first friends Genna makes in the other Brooklyn. Why do you think Mattie is drawn to Genna? What twenty-first-century knowledge does Genna possess that can help Mattie?

• Why is Mattie ashamed of her African heritage? Do young people today know (or care) about their origins?

• Do you agree with the advice Mattie's mother gave her about not looking back at the past? How might this advice help fugitive slaves? Is it helpful to free people living in the twenty-first century?

• Why does Genna feel the need to impress Dr. Brant? Which member of the Weeksville community do you respect most? Why?

- Mrs. Brant's behavior in the carriage suggests she will not be a good employer. Have you ever had a difficult boss? How can Genna, as a new employee, make sure Mrs. Brant respects her?

- Nannie and Mrs. Brant seem like total opposites. How have their respective histories made them into the women Genna meets in 1863?

- Nannie seems to respect Dr. Brant, yet there is something about him she cannot admit to Genna. What do you think happened to the servant girl that Genna replaced?

- At first, Genna desperately misses her family, but over time she learns to adjust to life without them. How would you react if you were suddenly pulled away from the only world you'd ever known? Does Nannie's ability to live with the loss of her children prove that human beings are resilient, or not as attached to others as they'd like to believe?

- The Brants are ardent abolitionists who support the Union cause. Do you think they believe that blacks and whites are equal? What role will freed slaves have in the Brants' world once slavery ends?

- If you were in Genna's position, would you have befriended Martha? What, if anything, do they have in common?

- Does Martha's poverty make her a more sympathetic character? What does Martha's life teach us about race relations in New York City circa 1863? Are two teens from different races likely to become friends today? Is it still risky to date someone of another race? Why?

- Another pivotal moment in the novel occurs when Genna strikes

Mrs. Brant. Do you feel Genna's action was justified? How would you have reacted in that situation? Would you have returned to the Brant household? What other options did Genna have?

• Why didn't Nannie defend herself? What is the connection between literacy, self-esteem, and power? Would Nannie have reacted differently if she could read?

• What is a pseudo-scientific theory? Why does Dr. Brant think Genna should be a nurse rather than a doctor? What would you have said to him?

• How do you think Judah reached the other Brooklyn? Write a brief scene describing his journey back in time.

• How does Genna's reunion with Judah change her attitude about living in the past? What do you think would have happened with Paul if Judah had never appeared? If you were in Genna's position, would you choose to build a future with Judah or Paul?

• Why can't Judah envision a future for himself in the United States? How does his religion shape his sense of destiny?

• Where is Genna most likely to find freedom: In Brooklyn circa 1863? In Brooklyn circa 2001? Or in Liberia circa 1863?

• Why does Judah refuse to have sex with Genna? Have they grown closer or further apart since being thrown into the past?

• What is a "mob mentality"? Are members of a mob responsible for their actions? What prompted the New York City Draft Riots of 1863?

- Martha witnesses the murder of her black boyfriend, Willem. Where will she go once the riots end? Does Martha have a future in the Irish community?

- Mrs. Brant seems to become a different person during the riots. Did your opinion of her change after hearing her speech to the mob?

- Do you think Judah will try to follow Genna back to the future, or will he pursue his plan to sail to Africa?

- Why do you think Genna returns to New York City the day before 9/11? What has she learned in the past that might help her cope with the terrorist attack on the World Trade Center?

- When the novel ended, which character did you care about most? Which characters would you like to "meet again" in the sequel?

- What did you learn about African American history that you did not know before? Has it changed the way you think about Brooklyn?

- Would you recommend this book to a friend? Who would benefit most from reading this book?

Activities and Research

Imagine that you are a reporter. Your assignment is to write an article for your newspaper on one of the following topics:
- Timothy McVeigh's execution
- The opening of the Weeksville Heritage Center
- Henry Ward Beecher, Plymouth Church, and the Underground Railroad
- The New York City Draft Riots and their impact on Brooklyn
- Marcus Garvey, Rastafarianism, and the "back to Africa" movement
- Life for Irish immigrants in New York City in the nineteenth century
- The role of black soldiers in the Union Army

Watch Kiri Davis's Web film *A Girl Like Me:*
video.google.com/videoplay?docid=1091431409617440489

Write a review of this film and connect it to Genna's insecurities about the way she looks. What impact do music videos have on the self-esteem of teenage girls? What messages do these videos send to teenage boys? What can teens do to improve their self-esteem?

Research the Emancipation Proclamation. Who was actually freed by it? How did President Abraham Lincoln really feel about African Americans? Was he an abolitionist? Did he believe in racial equality? Did he believe the future of black people lay in the United States or abroad?

What are "blackbirders"? Research the Fugitive Slave Law and find out what life was like for fugitive slaves hiding from their masters in New York City. What actions did black and white abolitionists take to help these fugitives?

Research the American Colonization Society and the African Civilization Society. What were the major differences between them? Describe conditions in Liberia in the early nineteenth century. If you were an African American living in the nineteenth century, would you stay in the United States, or emigrate to Liberia, Mexico, or Jamaica?

Write a two-minute script between the following characters:
• Genna's mother and Hannah
• Mr. Christiansen and Rico
• Toshi and Judah
• Mattie and Martha
• Paul and Judah

The haiku is a Japanese poem that traditionally captures an image of the natural world. Judah uses haiku to express his feelings to Genna. Write ten haiku that serve as "snapshots" of various moments from the novel.

Write ten questions and then "interview" one of the characters in *A Wish After Midnight*.

According to Judah, sankofa means "return to your source." Write a personal narrative that explains your family's origins. In what ways do you honor your cultural heritage?

Watch the film *Sankofa* by Haile Gerima. Write a review of the film and include a definition of "neo-slave narrative." What's "new" about Gerima's representation of slavery? If you made a film version of *A Wish After Midnight*, which actors would you cast in the lead roles?

Research the term "reparations." Write an argument in favor of or in opposition to reparations for descendants of slaves in the United States.

Find an image of The Door of No Return. Write a letter to one of the millions of enslaved Africans who passed through that door, survived the Middle Passage, and arrived in the Americas as a slave. What advice could you offer to help them endure the hardships of slavery? What would you want that enslaved person to know about your life in the twenty-first century? Describe the progress you feel the United States has made in terms of race relations.

Acknowledgments

I once met an author whom I admired; when I asked if she was working on something new, she admitted that she found writing novels "excruciating." I don't think I would write if I found it painful in any way, and writing *A Wish After Midnight* was an absolute joy for me. Of course, writers require a great deal of support even though a book might seem like a solitary achievement. I would like to express my gratitude to all those individuals who helped to make the writing of this novel such a deeply satisfying experience. I finished *A Wish After Midnight* while living with my father in Crown Heights; he died of cancer a few months later, and I suspect his deteriorating condition led me to write with a sense of urgency I might not otherwise have possessed. I thank my mother for her thoughtful remarks about my novel, and for keeping me afloat financially when I was starting to sink. Members of my extended family in Canada have supported my writing from the start, and their pride and faith in me sustained me when publisher after publisher (on both sides of the border) closed door after door. I thank my friends who always made me feel prolific, even when I felt like I wasn't making any progress at all. I thank my Rastafarian friends, Tre and Sayida, who provided me with the preliminary information I needed to create

Judah; I am also deeply indebted to Sonia Gilkes for catching two errors I nonetheless made about Rastafarian culture.

My experiment in self-publishing would have failed miserably were it not for the support of some remarkable women. I thank Shadra Strickland for designing the first edition's beautiful cover, and for her constant encouragement and free technical advice. I thank Rosamond King for introducing me to Create Space, and for providing her artist management services for free. Brooklyn educators Tricia Hazlewood, Myrdis Kelley, and Patrice Pinder are outstanding literacy coaches and were the first to share *Wish* with their students and peers; Yana Rodgers, Roni Natov, and Jessica Siegel were the first professors to invite me into their classrooms as an artist and not an academic. Doret Canton, Edi Campbell, and LaTonya Baldwin were the first bloggers to embrace my book, and I can't thank them enough for their tireless efforts to promote *Wish*; I thank everyone online for their thoughtful reviews, especially Colleen Mondor and Lyn Miller-Lachmann who granted my novel the legitimacy so often denied self-published books. Alison Hendon and Megan Honig acquired *Wish* for the Brooklyn Public Library and New York Public Library, and I thank them for making my novel available to patrons across the city. And of course, I am grateful to all the book lovers out there who gave my book a chance, and by doing so gave this struggling writer the confidence I needed to persevere.

Last but not least, I thank my editor, Alex Carr, who found depth and merit in my writing and exceeded all my expectations of what a professional partner could be. The entire AmazonEncore team has treated me like an equal, valued my expertise, and listened patiently to my concerns. I am extremely grateful for the opportunity to work with a publisher who realizes that innovation should be embraced, rather than feared, and I am honored to be part of this exciting new endeavor.

About the Author

Born and raised in Canada, Zetta Elliott moved to Brooklyn in 1994 and earned her Ph.D. in American Studies from NYU. Her poetry has been published in the Cave Canem anthology, *The Ringing Ear: Black Poets Lean South*, *Check the Rhyme: An Anthology of Female Poets and Emcees*, and *Coloring Book: An Eclectic Anthology of Fiction and Poetry by Multicultural Writers*. Her novella, *Plastique*, was excerpted in *T Dot Griots: An Anthology of Toronto's Black Storytellers*, and her essays have appeared in *The Black Arts Quarterly*, *thirdspace*, *WarpLand*, and *Rain and Thunder*. Her award-winning picture book, *Bird*, was published in October 2008. Her first play, *Nothing but a Woman*, was a finalist in the Chicago Dramatists' Many Voices Project (2006). Her fourth full-length play, *Connor's Boy*, was staged in January 2008 as part of two new play festivals: in Cleveland, Ohio, as part of Karamu House's R. Joyce Whitley Festival of New Plays ARENAFEST, and in New York City as part of Maieutic Theatre Works' Newborn Festival. Her one-act play, *girl/power*, was staged as part of New Perspectives Theater's festival of women's work, GIRLPOWER, in August 2008. She currently lives in Brooklyn.